THE MAN ON THE
MIDDLE FLOOR

A book about disconnection

THE
MAN
ON THE
MIDDLE
FLOOR

ELIZABETH S MOORE

RedDoor

Published by RedDoor
www.reddoorpublishing.com

ISBN 978-1-910453-54-4

Cover designer: Patrick Knowles
www.patrickknowlesdesign.com

Illustrator: Tommy Moore

Typesetting: WatchWord Editorial Services
www.watchwordeditorial.co.uk

Printed and bound by Nørhaven, Denmark

To my family:
Gerald, Philippa, Cassie, Olivia and Tommy.
Thank you for loving me. I love you more.

'*Life is not a problem to be solved,
but a reality to be experienced*'

— Søren Kierkegaard

Prologue

'He melts, I think. He goes like a drop of froth.
You look at him, and there he is. You look at him
again, and there he isn't.'

— Charles Dickens, *Barnaby Rudge*

Tomorrow, my laundry will come. I know that because it always comes, every week, on a Tuesday. Hanging on the door, no creases. No metal hangers, only wooden. In my cupboard I have seven pairs of beige trousers and I have seven white T-shirts, four white buttoned shirts, ten pairs of socks and ten pairs of underpants. Every week I wear them and then they are all put in the laundry basket and I leave it outside my door to be taken away when the clean ones come back, but my jacket and my coat stay here because they are dark and only go over clean clothes so they only get washed every two weeks, but I have a spare for each of those too. My shoes are in the cupboard. My mother told me you should never wash shoes. I keep them here safe. I once heard some people on a bus laughing because one of them had a husband who got drunk and urinated into her shoes. In a cupboard. People are disgusting. I get new ones if mine get smelly. I don't want smelly shoes and even if you have three showers your feet have to be on the ground for you to go anywhere and there is nothing you can do about it. The ground is covered with dirt and germs and spit. I shiver right up my back when I think about the stuff on the pavement.

On the back of my door, stuck with Blu Tack right in the middle facing me, I have a list. It's a list of all the things people do if they are functioning normally. I have made it myself by watching other people and by getting advice from my mother and some instructions from my grandpa. I read it before I go out and try to stick to it and if it goes wrong I just get into bed and wait for the next day to come and I make a new start. I used a new pad and very neat writing, all capitals. From the top it says:

WHEN SOMEONE GIVES ME SOMETHING, SAY THANK YOU AND SMILE.

WHEN SOMEONE SAYS HELLO TO ME OR ASKS ME A QUESTION, REPLY POLITELY AND TRY TO MAKE EYE CONTACT OR JUST LOOK NEAR TO WHERE THEY ARE.

WASH OFTEN. BE CLEAN, SMELL NICE. WASH MY HANDS AND FEET AND PRIVATE PARTS MOST.

MAKE MY BED NEATLY AFTER BREAKFAST.

TAKE SHOES OFF OUTSIDE FLAT AND CARRY THEM INSIDE.

SPEND NO LONGER THAN TWO HOURS ON THE COMPUTER IN ONE SESSION (OR NO MORE THAN FOUR HOURS IN ONE DAY).

EXERCISE WITH MY DUMBBELLS. A HEALTHY BODY MAKES A HEALTHY MIND.

LAY THE TABLE BEFORE I EAT, TO PRACTISE MY TABLE MANNERS.

There are a lot of rules if you want to look like a functioning adult and I need to concentrate on that all the time. It's a BIG responsibility living by yourself and if I want to be independent this is the way I can do that. I hate living in shared accommodation and I can't live with my mother any more, with her watching me, looking worried, and everything dirty and untidy. I like to be alone, and I like to decide what I should do with my days. I will follow all the rules if it makes sure I can live here.

I can communicate on my computer without actually having to meet anyone. I hate meetings, people looking at me, staring at me. It makes me uncomfortable and I feel their eyes turn towards me, and my body reacting in all kinds of ways, sweating or getting excited. I know how I look to other people, and I don't like it one bit. I am white. *Pasty*, my mother calls it, but she likes to be outside. *Pasty* means you don't go in the sun enough. I should put that on my list: GO OUTSIDE. I sit down too much and my grandpa says I am three-quarters legs: from my head to my hips I am a dwarf and once he made me stand still and he measured that with his hands, putting germs all over me. When he remembers that day it always makes him laugh. At least I'm not fat. I watched a programme about the fattest man in the world, and I couldn't eat my dinner. *Watch your weight. Keep yourself to yourself.* Those are some of my grandpa's wise words.

Breakfast time, I hate crumbs and crunchy food that can scratch your mouth, so I have the toaster on thirty-five and that is out of a hundred which must make completely black toast which can also give you cancer which I don't want to get. My toast has to be soft and just a little bit pale brown – don't give me hard burnt toast. When I was at home I had hard butter and hard toast and I got thinner and thinner from not putting it in my mouth. I don't have enough spit to make it soft quick enough. Tidy up the crumbs, wipe the side, don't make the toaster crooked and put the plate on the mat. All done. I sit with my soft butter in front of me, and my glass of water for hydration, eight glasses a day, no drips. Breakfast.

Today is Monday, so tomorrow is Tuesday and the day after that is Wednesday. Wednesday is visit day and my grandpa is coming. He always comes on Wednesdays even when I ask my mother to tell him not to. At least my clothes will be clean and my flat will be tidy so he shouldn't be cross, and I might not have to be corrected. I hate being corrected and even though Grandpa said I should be used to it by now, I'm not, and that is why we have to have it as a secret or I will have to go back and live with my mother for my own good, and Grandpa is trying to help me stay independent. Now that I have my lists and put out my rubbish and have a routine I must nearly not need correcting, but there is always something I need to add, because life is very complicated. *If you don't want to be corrected, then plan ahead*, he says to me, so I always make a plan and today I will go for a long walk, which might make him think I have learned everything now. I think again about adding GO OUTSIDE to the list, but it isn't a list thing. I might just go out and never come in again, or forget how often, or where to go. I like definite things on that list. It could go on my other list, which is stuck with Blu Tack by my bed, but I already have a walk in for today.

I look at it to check.

MONDAY: GO TO GET FRESH MILK AND SHOPPING AND THROW AWAY ALL FOOD OVER ITS SELL-BY DATE. GO TO BANK IN TOTTENHAM COURT ROAD AND COLLECT ALLOWANCE FOR THE WEEK.

TUESDAY MORNING: PUT OUT DIRTY CLOTHES AND TAKE IN CLEAN CLOTHES.

TUESDAY AFTERNOON: GO FOR A WALK IN THE PARK.

WEDNESDAY MORNING: SEE GRANDPA AND MAKE PLANS.

WEDNESDAY AFTERNOON: DE-STRESS AND DO EXERCISES AND HAVE AN EARLY NIGHT.

THURSDAY: CLEAN THE FLAT, PHONE MY MOTHER BEFORE SIX PM.

FRIDAY BUT NOT EVERY FRIDAY: SEE MOTHER.

I start to feel panicky going through my whole week. I like to do my week a day at a time. Today I am going to the bank, because it is Monday. I will make a new plan, but not now.

Making conversation is also very important; Grandpa says that you never know when you will need to be ready to answer things, or when things are *spiralling out of control*. Grandpa says they are spiralling more and more in the modern world, which is worrying for him, so that is another reason that he has to correct me, for my own good. What Grandpa does to teach me how to be tough and strong hurts quite a lot, and the things he is trying to prepare me for might never happen so I would rather he just waited and I could just learn the lessons if I ever need to, not every single visit day on Wednesday just in case, but I can't seem to make him understand and I don't want to be in trouble.

I itch. I rub my arms with each other, as I hate the idea of skin under my nails and I hate the feel of clothes on my skin. It isn't just pasty, it's covered in little red bumps and they make me feel a bit sick; they catch on material and the more I try and rub them off in the shower the more bumpy they get. I should go outside. The fresh air will help... my mother says it will help and it will stop me thinking about Grandpa's visit; I will just go now. City air is not very clean, it has pollution, and the tube is dirty, but I am going to the park tomorrow which will clean my lungs with fresh air.

Grandpa says that a cat would help too, not with the bumpy skin, but I would look responsible, and have company, and all the things that my family talk to me about. Even when I am happy they see a problem to be fixed. I want to be by myself and I can't really see what a cat is going to do to help anything, but Grandpa says you have to try these things to look more in control and I think that if I agree then he might not have to visit any more, I'm not sure but it must be worth getting one just for that. I don't know why people worry but if you want to be independent you have to take everyone's feelings into consideration. That's what my grandpa says.

Three weeks later …

1 | Tam

'Better a sparrow, living or dead, than no bird-song at all.'

— Catullus

Monday morning, early autumn

As Tam exited the Tube and walked towards the building, his past washed over him in a rush. It rose up from the broken pavement beneath his feet, from the faint smell of bins and urine, and the perpetual rubbish kicking around wet and sorry for itself with no future except getting caught by the wind and forever wrapped around an overlooked bush in a long-untended piece of scrub that had once been a garden.

This had been his beat when he was a newly minted plod, and his hopeful steps must have contributed to the worn-out condition of the place. He certainly didn't remember improving it much, or ever finding an inspiring way to better the lot of the sad grey population around him, although he was sure that had once been the intention.

This was the inner city at its most dystopian. Broken window blinds greeted him as he came round the corner and walked up the track leading to his office. It was hardly recognisable these days as a path, but there was a hint in the cracked paving, and the banks of grass that bordered it. In the twenty-three years since he had arrived for his first day at work, the benches and soft expansive grassed areas on either side had been grubbed up, trees cut down and the whole lot replaced with a concrete car park, which stretched away to where the least important members of Her Majesty's Constabulary parked. 'General Parking', it had been named, officially, in a ceremony. Tam smiled to himself when he remembered the amount of research that had gone into choosing that piece of politically correct branding. Closer to the impressive doorway with its tinted glass and view of the arboretum beyond, the parking spaces were demarcated, with plaques proclaiming 'Commissioner', 'Deputy Commissioner', 'Assistant Commissioner', 'Deputy Assistant Commissioner', and 'Commander'. In General Parking it was each man for himself, much like life, and Tam approved.

He collected his thoughts, scratched his buttock, stretched and yawned. He hadn't become a policeman to pay lip service to a bunch of upwardly mobile public servants intent on congratulating themselves. He had wanted to do something real, something *important*. He couldn't quite remember what it had been, but he was certain of it: he had dreamt of a significant life.

OK, it hadn't panned out. The world seemed to be propelling itself in a direction where celebrity pervaded every profession, even the police force. The BBC had even screened a series called *Britain's Bravest Cops* recently and he had fallen foul of the powers that be when he hadn't wanted to take part, let alone appear. No one could understand it. Then there was the Pride of Britain awards, with the commissioner giving out prizes to have-a-go heroes. A joke, all of it – he could probably have solved a couple of murders single-handed, or come up with some decent ideas on how the Met should be run, while his colleagues were spending hours on breakfast TV or *The Graham Norton Show*. Victor Meldrew and Tam seemed to be sharing a lot of common ground these days – though who even knew who Victor Meldrew was any more? Even his points of reference were off point. He reckoned he wasn't the only one who thought like this though, whatever the *Guardian* might say. One more dinner handing out gongs and slapping backs, one more commendation, one more piece of paperwork which would be filed and forgotten and he might thump someone. What any of it had to do with solving crime was beyond Tam.

And he had had a lot of time to think about it. Since he had taken a bullet to the leg one afternoon in Peckham ten months ago, he'd done a lot of lying around and had come to a few conclusions. Now, finally he had a chance to talk to the boss, the big boss.

Tam took a deep breath and pressed the silver buzzer for his guv'nor's office. It wasn't his voice that answered, of course; it wasn't the traditional pretty secretary either. It was his male assistant, who had a title that Tam couldn't remember, although he knew it was some acronym. He did remember that the young man in question was unusually well groomed and fragrant – and very close friends with those in positions of power. What the fuck was his name? He couldn't summon it from the depths of his coffee-deprived brain, so he did that drinks party nightmare thing of: 'Hi, Tam here.'

'Hi, Tam, it's Lucas, I'll buzz you up.'

Lucas, that was it. Emphasis on the second syllable. He was Portuguese, so in the new hierarchy of the Met he had two things going for him: his sexual orientation which he wore like a weapon, and his nationality. You were in big trouble if you were a born-and-bred heterosexual, white, vaguely middle-class guy on the force these days. No chance of promotion – not that Tam wanted it, there was enough paperwork and glad-handing already. Fuck that.

He walked up the stairs, hoping it would ease the pain in his hip from too many hours in front of the television while he'd been on leave. It didn't. The traditional lino had gone, and the stairs were carpeted tastefully below clean pale grey painted walls with the ubiquitous camera on every floor. God forbid that an accident might take place during the long walk up five floors and no one could see it on a screen. Strange times, when policemen couldn't be trusted not to trip over their own feet. Tam was disorientated by the endless monotone walls. Elephant's Breath – he remembered the bizarre name of the paint from a nightmarish in-house drinks party when the design for the new building had been 'run up the flagpole', and Tam had laughed out loud when the interior designer had announced it. That hadn't gone down well. Everyone else had stood in reverent silence while he guffawed, the only man drinking a beer in a room full of Pinot Grigio and prosecco.

He reached the fifth floor and leant against the wall for a minute to make sure he didn't look out of breath when he finally reached his destination. Although the building

14

went no higher, there was a plaque announcing that this was indeed the fifth floor in front of him and yet another discreet silver buzzer.

'Hi … Lucas, it's Tam.'

'Did you walk up?'

The guy sounded amused and Tam was immediately angry. His appointment was at 11 a.m. and it was only 10.55; he prided himself on not being late.

'Yes, I walked—'

He was halfway through the reply when the door buzzer cut him off. He managed to push it open just in time and landed like Alice in Wonderland in the hallway, flustered and disorientated. Swearing under his breath, he smoothed down his hair, checked the front of his shirt for crumbs from the Cornish pasty he had eaten on the Tube, and looked for the right door. It had to be three years since he'd been up here, and the individual offices now led off a central reception; the old wood panelling on the walls was gone, and in a nod to universal equality it was hard to tell where the commissioner's office was. Everyone passing him seemed to be heading somewhere very important, faces down, or on mobile phones; some with headphones in their ears were talking out loud into the air.

Suddenly, there was Lucas, all smiles and solicitousness and soft handshake. 'How are you Tam? We're all so happy to see you – have you recovered completely now? No pain?'

He talked as quickly as he walked, and Tam found himself breathless outside an anonymous door. A quick knock and they were in, and it became clear what had happened to most of the original offices and the corridor: they were now incorporated into the single biggest workspace that Tam had ever been in, with banks of mahogany joinery, shelving, a desk that looked as if it had been designed by a woodcutter from Africa, and more huge hardback books on shelves than Tam had ever seen outside of a library.

It was a bit like a bad Hollywood film set of an imagined London. Tam stood for a moment, apparently alone, as Lucas scuttled out, until the leather swivel armchair in front of him swung around and away from the huge picture window that had been installed on an entire side of the office. Echoes of James Bond. Tam tried not to laugh.

The commissioner stood up. His uniform gave more than a nod to the Swiss Guard, or the ceremonial, brass-buttoned craziness of Trooping the Colour. Thinking about it, the longer Tam stayed in the police force, the more the top guys resembled the more decorative, less effective armies of the world. Tam tore his eyes from the yards of white and gold braid and put out his hand.

'Morning, sir.'

'No need for any of that, Tam, we're old mates. Great to see you. Sorry about the kit, we've got a mounted event later on the Mall.'

Tam was swept up in an awkward bear hug which involved back-patting, until the commissioner took control and nonchalantly perched himself down on the side of his polished desk, adopting the air of an avuncular uncle, head at a sympathetic angle.

'So, Tam, how are things?'

'Well, I feel much better, I've had a hell of a lot of physio, and I think my leg is stronger than before the shooting. The tendons have all reattached and I'm ready to go to work. I really feel I can offer something important. "Authentic police work", I think they called it in the last seminar you sent me on.'

The commissioner laughed, kindly, then reframed his serious but concerned face and continued. 'That's great news, Tam, but how *are* you? *In here?*' He tapped the side of his head and looked at Tam quizzically, as if he was trying to work out the answer to a very complicated problem. It was not a good sign.

'Sir, I'm fine. Honestly. Keen to get back out there.'

The commissioner used an intake of breath to get up from his casually relaxed position on the desk and go round to the other side and sit back in his capacious armchair. Tam began to seriously consider whether he was on *Candid Camera*.

'Take a seat, mate.'

Tam took a breath and began. 'Sir, I really don't want to take up too much of your time. I don't want a promotion or a pay rise, I just want to get on with doing what I joined the force to do. I want to make the streets safer and society better for all. You put me where you think I'll do the most good and I'll give you a hundred per cent.'

Tam had rehearsed this several times in his head and was disappointed when his boss's reaction was a pained expression of regret and a shake of the head.

'That's the thing, I suppose, Tam – times have changed. You and I came up together and I have a lot of respect for your not wanting to play the game like everyone else. You're your own man and that's a brave path to follow. The problem is, these days, who are you or I to say what society should be? Who are we to claim we know better than anyone else what works? That's the question.'

Tam thought he'd finished and took another breath ready to speak, grasping for a sensible answer to an incomprehensible statement, but, before he could, the commissioner was off again.

'Tam, our model of copper is outmoded; our time has gone. Do you know how often each week I have representatives in here from every dark corner of the urban sprawl? Last week I had a meeting with an imam from Tooting who was defending the imposition of Sharia law in parts of south London, and I had to listen politely to his request for four more senior Muslim police officers in the area who would look at female abuse through Muslim eyes. Then there was the paedophile rights lawyer who came in with a young man who had yearnings for adolescent blond boys and I was supposed to engage in conversation and be impressed that he didn't act on them. He just wanted "understanding", apparently, and to be "a mouthpiece for his community". It's a fuck-up out there and you just don't fit.'

For a moment Tam thought he had said '*we* just don't fit', and then it sank in. He didn't fit. This wasn't going well at all.

'Sir,' he tried, 'we are the Metropolitan Police Force, the line in the sand between good and bad, the defenders of the weak if you like, and if we're not sure of our position then who's going to fill our role? Are you seriously telling me we're giving up? Chucking in the towel? I don't fucking believe it. There are people in all these new developing areas of our society who need help and regular police assistance, surely. Our legal system hasn't changed. Under our statutes you can't tie your daughter to a bed because she isn't dressed modestly. Surely we can't be in the business of pleasing all the people all the time?'

'Of course we aren't giving up. We're adapting, and you're a valuable tool in that process, Tam. While none of us wants you out there on the street risking your life on a daily basis, we do want you in the plan going forward, part of the solution rather than the problem. We all want that. I want you by my side as a liaison co-ordinator. Outreach, with all your years of experience. I want you talking to the kids in schools whose brains are being poisoned; I want you gathering intelligence, bringing a bit of sanity to the situation.'

'You want me in a *desk job*?'

'We want you where you will be most valuable, most visible to us and to society. This way you're not just another bobby on the beat, you're the guy with the intelligence, literally. Someone I can use as a confidant, a wing man—'

Tam's feet propelled him to the big door and he struggled to open it before he realised it was on some sort of security buzzer. He nearly kicked it, but squashed his inner adolescent back down, then turned round to look at the man behind the desk whom he'd known since they were both eighteen and full of ideals. He was still talking about the New Society, and didn't seem to have realised that Tam had moved until he looked up. Surprise and confusion mixed on his face and his speech slowed, until finally he understood the look on Tam's face and fell silent.

'Mate, come on, be reasonable.'

Tam stared at him and smiled thinly. He knew he looked furious; he'd never been able to hide his feelings. There was nothing more to say, and he watched as the commissioner reached down and released the door lock using an invisible button somewhere under the desk. Their eyes met and Tam thought he saw regret, and a bit of a mental shrug on the huge frame of this man whom he had once thought of as a brother in arms. The last image of him, mouth hanging slack and open, buttons taking some strain and the braid that wound round his shoulders puckering, was like a snapshot. Who was it who said we don't remember days, we remember moments? There was nothing for him here.

'Sir, my resignation will be in the post.'

Tam realised as he said it that no one posted anything these days and that it had probably been noted as another anachronism, but he couldn't be fucked. He needed a drink.

He brushed past Lucas and had another embarrassing encounter with a locked door. As it was buzzed open by a now silent receptionist, he was aware that the anger was flowing off him like mist off a mountain. He tried to slam the door behind him but it didn't slam; it was on a soft-close hinge. Fuck this world and the people who lived in it.

The pavement was drizzled on, just damp enough to make navigating it treacherous, and the Tube station seemed further away now that he was deflated and emotionally drained. What the fuck was he going to do with himself now? His principles were fast evaporating into a panicked vision of standing outside a dodgy nightclub doing security. He probably couldn't even get employed to do that, come to think of it. He'd seen the guys outside his local pub and he was pretty sure he was twenty years too old and three feet too narrow for the job.

Why did he never think things through? They were probably really chuffed to get rid of him. He hadn't negotiated a redundancy payment, he'd insulted his boss, and generally made an exit which must have satisfyingly confirmed their opinion of him.

Tam's head dipped forward as he concentrated on avoiding patches of wet horse-chestnut leaves, always the first hint that autumn was on its way, when suddenly his forward momentum was stopped dead. The pavement in front of him was taken up by a tall man, travelling in the same direction as he was, who was blocking his path with a combination of physical presence and flailing arms. Still staring down, all Tam could see in his path were feet, feet which appeared to be dancing across the fucking local authority paving stones deliberately to disrupt his journey home. It was all he needed. He tried to walk around the guy, but he jumped into his path, on tiptoe. He tried the other side and the bloke did the same thing. It was like some weird rehearsal for a modern ballet, and it wasn't improving Tam's mood.

'What the fuck are you doing, mate? I'm trying to get home. Can you get out of my way?'

He got no response, and looked up to try and make sense of what was happening. A young man in his twenties, in a neatly done-up coat, belt tied round his middle, combed and parted hair and a nerdish air, was apparently jumping the cracks in the pavement. His feet were moving surprisingly quickly, but as they had to cover a lot of horizontals he wasn't making speedy progress. Tam looked left to see if he could step into the road and get round him that way. Buses and taxis, messenger bikes and cyclists sped along inches from the pavement. He was either going to have to knock the idiot over, or pace himself behind him.

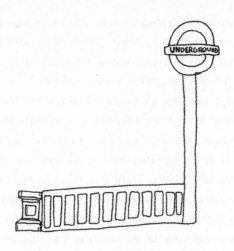

The issues with the locked doors, the weather and the general misery of the day had knocked the stuffing out of Tam, and he decided he didn't have the energy for a quickstep which would probably culminate in the death of a drunk or a care-in-the-community citizen, or more likely his own demise under the wheels of a bus. He slowed down. It wasn't as if anything was waiting for him at home. What should have taken three minutes took ten, and the stairs down into Tottenham Court Road Tube station looked perilously steep for a tiptoeing line-avoider. Inwardly shrugging, Tam took the parallel staircase, looking round once to see the guy placing two feet on to each step carefully, brushing down the front of his coat at each descent and carrying on to the next one. Mild fascination was washed away by the thought of a single malt and an episode of *Inspector Morse*, although it might be a bit masochistic to watch period detective drama tonight. It might have to be porn and a curry.

Despite his laboured methods of descending a staircase, the bloke from the pavement arrived five minutes later on the same platform, and stood waiting for a train, alone, by a pillar. When they got on to the train Tam could see him in the next carriage through the glass dividing window, sitting balanced on the edge of a seat with his hands in his lap, then reaching into his pocket for a small clear bottle and applying what looked like sanitising lotion to his fingers, one by one. Tam reminded himself he was no longer a detective, closed his eyes, and mentally counted the stops until he reached Waterloo, changed on to the Jubilee line and dozed all the way to Kilburn. When he emerged from under London's busy crust, the sun was low in the sky and the drizzle had stopped. Although it was only early afternoon, Tam could feel that the warmth in the sun was fading. He knew he should probably pick up some groceries, but he couldn't summon the energy. He walked up the path to his flat, tiredness wrapped round him now, along with an overwhelming sense of anti-climax. The bins on his right were in a straight line and he tried to remember which day the bin men came now; it seemed to change every couple of months.

He opened the door of the house and crossed the hall to pick up his post. As usual the letters for the three people who lived in the flats under this Victorian roof had been meticulously put into piles, biggest letters at the bottom, magazines and catalogues below those, everything squared up. In the hall, above the small table that held the post, someone had put up a clock; Tam remembered the same one being in the first police station he'd ever worked in, white plastic with big numbers, and it felt somehow reassuring, something solid on shifting sands. Below it was a small cork noticeboard, completely devoid of notices. A wave of exhaustion came over him. Thank God his flat was on the ground floor. He put the key in the lock and went inside.

After turning every light on, Tam dropped some ice into a glass and poured from a bottle of Glenfarclas ten-year-old. There wasn't even enough left to cover the ice. That would be the cleaner; she drank like a fish. At least he could dispense with her now he was out of a job. Tam picked up the phone and rang her number – voicemail. He left a message telling her not to come back, and explained that he'd lost his job ... pay it forward. He needed to relax, though, and the off-licence was only down the road, but 'down the road' seemed like a challenge. He would see if you could order whisky from Hungry Horse later. Today was a fuck-up, it was official. He would watch porn on his phone, in bed. It was one of the few luxuries left to him. He downed the tablespoonful of whisky, chucked his clothes on the floor, pissed into the sink and walked into the bedroom. He pulled the duvet over him, typed 'young, hot and horny' into the search engine and exhaled. The front door slammed and he heard feet going upstairs. Did no one work any more?

2 | Nick

'As long as habit and routine dictate the pattern of living, new dimensions of the soul will not emerge.'

— Henry Van Dyke

Tuesday

I opened the front door and there they were, in the plastic covers, all my clothes hanging on the hook that Grandpa put up, and my dirty washing was gone. No one knocked on my door on a Tuesday because it wasn't a visit day; my mother just did drop-and-go. I put them all in the cupboard still in their plastic covers because the covers kept the germs away. I made a sandwich from white bread, and square ham which exactly fitted on the bread, and ketchup which I put on from the squeezy bottle and made into a round and round circle, but not too much or it would come out of the sides when I bit it. I put lettuce on the top, neat Little Gem lettuce which was good for you and didn't have bits and was the cleanest lettuce I had found so far. It all fitted together and that was lunch. Then I had a yoghurt, I had been saving hazelnut which was my favourite, and then I put it empty in the bin, holding it carefully by the little foil bit which opened it in case the yoghurt went on me. I washed my hands just in case, as yoghurt was alive and could breed, which Mother said was good for your insides but I didn't want it growing on my skin. I wiped all preparation areas with Dettol antibacterial spray and I was ready to go.

I got my jacket on not my coat because it would be the afternoon by the time I got to Richmond Park, and I wanted as much air in my lungs and sun on my skin as possible. I knew that there were lots of people in Richmond Park on a sunny day because you could see the bikes and cars, but it was so big that they seemed to be invisible, which I liked. Summer was over, although today was warm and quite sunny. The trees near the house were turning brown and look old, and the ones in the park would soon be bare for the winter and the deer would be rutting which was a word for mating but only with deer, and when they mated they fought and might be dangerous. I sat down for a minute before I set out, to get rid of pictures of rutting and fighting deer from my mind, and then I went out of the flat and closed the door behind me.

I liked Richmond Park most of all because it was a huge park where you could be on your own and I liked to be as quiet as I could, and watch the deer close up from behind trees. Sometimes they would come so near, one at a time, or a whole group, and if you moved or stepped on a branch they would start running away, sticking together. Deer made venison. That was their meat, and you could buy it but you couldn't kill the ones in the park. You could go to a forest in Scandinavia and hunt them. I thought that I would like to point a gun and shoot a deer, but today I was going to concentrate on breathing clean air, and I would take off my jacket and get sun on my arms so they were less bobbly. Clear the cobwebs. *Down the stairs, up the path, round the corner, down the steps into the Tube one stair at a time, keep away from crowds, sit on the edge of the seat, wipe hands regularly. Up the stairs and out into the air.* It wasn't completely fresh here because this was a high street but I took the first deep breath since going down into the Underground. Even when I got off at East Putney it was such a long walk from the Tube. My body had to be full of nearly fresh air now, and I remembered that lungs only had a certain capacity and they had to be full and I almost turned round and went home, but it wasn't time.

Don't step on the cracks in the pavement, don't meet anyone's eye. Get away from the computer and pretend shooting. Toughen up, be a man, stop your snivelling, put your heels on the floor, keep quiet. Tuesdays were always difficult and I pushed Grandpa's face out of my mind. I stopped and looked up and breathed. *Concentrate on the clouds.* It's a coping strategy.

I did try and explain to Grandpa about why I liked computer gaming, I had been doing it a long time, and it had taken a lot of hours to be as good as me. I had a high score and if you had practised that much you should use your skills, and the games on the computer could help me if the *worst* ever happened, maybe more than the correcting. I walked quicker to get away from the thoughts about that.

When I was little I wanted to join the army but now I thought it would be better to be your own boss, make up your own mind and watch carefully to see who was bad and who was good and anyway Grandpa said that I

wouldn't get in. It was probably because you had to be a team player. I didn't like teams. I decided not to try in the end because of the recruitment video. You had to always do what you were told and never question it and when people shouted at you even when you tried your best you had to not cry and I didn't like shouting.

All this thinking had taken me a long way, and I was nearly at the park. I knew the route really well, and I didn't have to think about which way to go.

I could see the gates now and beyond them I was scanning the horizon for herds of deer. There was a small group off to the right in the distance, and I started to stalk them which was in one of my computer games but really it was just following, but with deer not people. There were bushes to crouch behind and you had to have the wind blowing towards you or they might smell you even if you showered a lot. I squatted behind a tree and tried to be as quiet as I could; they were in an opening on the other side of the road that cut the park in two.

When I'd crossed the road after looking both ways, I decided to practise my crawling on my belly like in my war game because no one was around, but the ground wasn't dry and now my clothes had dirt on them which didn't happen in the game. I wanted to rip them off and throw them on the ground. Dirt, germs. They might not wash off. I would put them in a plastic bag and then into the bin when I got home. I was quite close now so I tried not to think about the mud and breathe evenly, think about the deer. I walked instead, looking at the ground: *stay on the flat bits, don't tread on twigs*. I managed it, I was behind the tree and they hadn't moved. One deer, a smallish girl one, was really close, and I was hidden.

'Pssssst…'

Her head went up and there was some grass sticking out of her mouth. She looked straight towards me, but she could only see the tree. I wanted to laugh but instead I bit on my cheek and lifted up my arm. I pointed it at her as if I had a gun. 'Bang. You're dead.' I said it out loud and now she knew I was there and she turned and ran towards the others, who ran with her. They wouldn't come back for a while.

It was hot, even by my tree, even through the leaves, and I started to walk again. I liked to be by the water when it was hot and I always went the exact same way, on a winding path towards the lake. I liked to sit at the edge on my jacket, not that it mattered now, I was dirty. I would sometimes see fish, or tadpoles which were my favourite animal because I used to catch them and they seemed very clean with no hair and being washed all the time in the water. Once I even saw a hedgehog just walking along. It was my most peaceful place. I always brought bread for the ducks, and I kept some in my jacket pocket in a plastic ziplock bag. Once when I was feeding them they came out of the water in a pack and I had to run away.

I was getting near now and I saw a couple sitting in my spot by the water. They looked really young. The girl was blonde and she was giggling, loudly, at everything the boy was saying, bending towards him, and he was speaking into her ear. I would have told her to shut up if she were my girlfriend. I liked quiet girls, even though in my head I would have liked to have a girl touch me, but not giggle at me, and not lean on me either. I did once have a friend called Harriet who wanted to come round all the time, and be in my space, which just meant very close to you. She went to the school for special people with me, and always gave her homework in on time which I thought you should do, because I always tried to do things on time too. She liked me a lot and I knew that because she told me all the time and she didn't mind that I was quiet but she tried to fill up all the silence with what she thought, and even the idea of her naked hadn't been enough for me to want my room full of her all the time.

We had held hands and I had tried not to mind about germs and wash them when she had gone and she tried to kiss me, but the worst thing was when she would try and push my mouth open with her tongue and her mouth spit would get on me. I hated it, I really didn't want someone spitting in me, and I was certainly never spitting into anyone. I wanted to fuck someone, not kiss them. I had seen pictures of naked women, they were everywhere.

Even on the Tube I would think about the pictures on the adverts, and where I could put my penis, what I could do to relieve this endless throbbing in my trousers, but I did know that it wouldn't involve spit and it wouldn't involve lots of hugging. Just fucking. That was the word Harriet had used, but she had wanted me to do lots of other things. I felt physically sick when I thought about it. *Bodily fluids.* Even the words made me feel like scratching myself.

The couple by the lake were locked in a kiss now and the man's hand was stroking up the girl's thigh towards her bottom. That was full of germs.

I crept behind a tree so that they couldn't see me. His hand was now between her legs and she didn't even try to move away. At least she'd stopped the giggling, but now she was frowning and looking very serious. I put my hands over my ears to stop hearing the sound of them panting. I was very sensitive to noise and the only noise I had expected to hear today was ducks quacking, not this, in the place I had come to clear my head. They shouldn't even be here in the middle of the day, and I was worried about her now. She was wriggling and he seemed to be squeezing her breasts really hard. I tried to look away and felt sad and angry at the same time. I was angry with them both, and sad, knowing that this was the last time I would ever come here because of them and their disgusting appetites. Now what would I do with all the crusts and stale bread? I wanted them to shut up, pushing my ears shut was just giving me a headache, and it wasn't really working. I felt goosebumpy and sick and excited. I tried to pluck up my courage to shout 'Go away!' at them, but one bit of me didn't want them to stop.

Their mouths were literally chewing each other up. I was feeling as if I might cry now, *stuck like a rabbit in the headlights*, my grandpa would say. If I touched the front of my jeans I would explode, so I didn't. I wasn't walking home muddy and sticky as well. My hands weren't keeping the noise out properly; I wasn't pushing hard enough in case I burst an eardrum.

The man unbuttoned his trousers and hitched up her skirt. I pulled at the sleeves on my jacket – I hadn't even taken it off yet and hadn't got any sun on my skin. Everything was ruined. Grandpa would have called her a slut and I agreed with him. This was not how I had wanted my walk to go. I wished I could go home, and I didn't think it was fair. Why did my whole routine need to be upset when parks were for walking and ducks and houses were for sex and germs? I looked at them again and that was that. I couldn't help it, I came in my pants, and that really really made me cross. Then, just as I didn't think it could get any worse, the man started moving down, kissing her and I could see what he was going to do, he was going to kiss her between the legs and I snapped. I was almost sick in my mouth and I had to make him stop before I had that picture in my head for ever.

I couldn't get a word out of my mouth, I was too upset, and I was on my tiptoes, hands waving, searching for a way to make them stop and then I saw it, between me and them, a huge heavy stick that had fallen from a tree, and I started to walk towards it, quickly, before he did anything else to her.

I didn't try to hide, or walk quietly now, I marched towards them like the men in my army game, and they

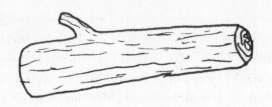

didn't even hear me, they just carried on like animals, on the spot where I sat, where children would feed ducks, where the nice brown dog had once jumped in to get his stick. Now I had the stick in my hand, feeling its weight, and as I got to them I made the war cry like in my computer game and lifted it up above my head. Now they saw me, now they stopped their noises, and the rhythm broke just before he got past her stomach with his kisses.

His eyes met mine, and, although I was not good at reading emotions, I could see that he was scared.

'What the fuck?'

He was in a sitting position now, but his body covered most of hers even now. He was quiet, at last, but I could see that he was poised, working out the situation, and I knew I had to do something quickly. The girl wasn't giggling now. She was pulling up her spotty knickers and covering her pale little breasts. She had red blotches on her neck.

'Fuck off, you perv.'

'If you can't say something nice, don't say anything at all.'

That was also advice from my grandpa and I said it quietly, and tried not to look at the penis between his legs. I was at a loss standing there, and the branch above my head was heavy. Just then the girl started to half scuttle, half crawl away and looked over her shoulder at me. Disgust, that look was, disgust. It made me furious and I finally took action. The wood made contact with the back of the man's head as he turned towards her, and the branch didn't break, and he went face down on to his stomach, and I hit him again on the back of his head. I was good at aiming and that was from playing so much on the computer. I wished I could tell Grandpa and that would be one less thing for him to correct. Now she was getting to her feet and I swung and hit the backs of her legs to stop her. She tried to cover her face and head but that just showed me her body again, and I noticed for the first time that she had no hair anywhere. I brought the club down on her head now, and she fell back, legs apart, and neither of them looked like people any more, or a couple, they just lay there, still and quiet.

I couldn't look at them any more and I threw the stick, like that family did for the dog, into the lake. There was blood on my white T-shirt, and some hair which was long so must have come from her head. I decided to do my jacket up because it was dark and you could see some spots on it but they didn't look red, they looked grey, like dirty marks. I walked round to the other side of the lake and splashed water on my face in case it was also bloody, run my fingers through my hair and started to walk. I smoothed my hair as I went, and looked down at my trousers; they were messy but the mud from earlier covered the blood marks, and the stain from me coming by the tree was covered by the jacket. I felt organised and as if I had done something important. I had stood up for myself, and that was the first time. They wouldn't go to the park and grunt in the middle of the day again.

What they did was wrong. I knew right from wrong and I was calm. *Cool as a cucumber*, my mother said sometimes, and they were a vegetable so they would be calm.

I had known for a long time that when people looked at me they didn't really look. My paleness and being different made them feel uncomfortable so they glanced away quickly. So I walked the route I always took, down the steps one at a time, and, apart from the looks that people gave when I avoided the lines on the pavement, I felt alone and safe. I was tired, and I thought I might have a splinter and a blister but as soon as I put the key into the door I relaxed a little bit because I was safe. I took a bin bag out of the cupboard and unfolded it and put it on the floor, and tore off a second one from the roll. I undressed until I was naked. I was wearing the T-shirt with the mud and blood on it, beige trousers with blood and mud marks on them, and muddy shoes and cleanish socks and underpants. I thought about keeping the socks but I didn't want anything from this morning so I put them all into the bin bag and I tied the top. Neat bow, double knot and I shuffled myself all the way to the door of the bathroom, standing on the other bin bag, avoiding looking at myself in the mirror. I knew I would still be pasty and my arms red and bobbly, and I didn't want to see that. The water in the shower was set just as I liked it, warm, not too warm, but not cold, and I stood and did my breathing exercises waiting for it to be just right before I got in.

I needed to scrub myself, with a brush, until my skin was all red. There wasn't a germ or a sperm that could survive my showers. I had googled cleanliness and my shower gel killed ninety-nine per cent of all bacteria.

35

I stood with the water running over me, and I decided again that I had done a good thing. People could go on walks in the park without having to watch strangers being disgusting.

I got out of the shower and dried myself carefully even between my toes. You had to dry everything, even between your legs. I always did that but today the roughness of the towel made me think back to the park, and I cleared my mind and went and lay down on my bed naked and clean. I was hot, and my panting made me start thinking about them and their panting which made me get hard. I tried to keep my mind off them, but at least I was at home, *in the privacy of my own home* as my grandpa said, and I wasn't upsetting anyone. I pressed down hard, hoping that would get rid of the thoughts, but it didn't and two minutes later the hot white liquid spurted out on to my stomach, while thoughts of her legs and her scrabbling to her feet flashed through my mind.

I reached for the baby wipes in my bedside drawer and cleaned myself. At the back of my mind, nagging worries about what I'd done and being in trouble tried to push in, but I got under the duvet and thought about nothing at all. Tomorrow was another day. I drifted off looking at the list next to my bed. Tomorrow was Wednesday and Grandpa would still be coming to visit. I wished he wasn't.

The light woke me up. I had forgotten to draw the curtains, which had never happened before. I was on my back, as always. It was good for my posture and I had trained myself. My size twelve feet were tucked under the duvet, with my arms resting on the top. Neat and tidy. I got out of bed and straightened up behind myself as I went. Feet into my slippers that were waiting by my bed, dressing gown on, tie the bow, go and make my toast. I love familiar things, and my mother gave me these green and black checked slippers every Christmas, and the dressing gown every year for my birthday.

I was feeling tired. I counted the number of hours of sleep, and it should have been enough so why was I tired? Eight o'clock on the kitchen clock. I had found one which didn't make a noise and had big clear numbers on it and it was on special offer, two for one. I put one in the hall and one in my kitchen. *Tick tick tick* at my mum's house had made me want to scratch my own skin off and grind my teeth. Quiet clocks. It was time to start the day. I dressed, in a white T-shirt, beige chinos, white socks and white Calvin Klein underpants. The same clothes that filled the bin bag from the walk in the park. I needed to ask my mother for a new set. I would tell her that the old ones had a hole because sometimes they got holes from being washed so much. My mother says my clothes are like a uniform, but I had seen this outfit in a magazine and she bought each item in bulk, one set for one week and the ones that are at the laundry. Even the trainers I wear are always the same.

I put the cereal bowl into the dishwasher and my mug next to it. The bin bag of clothes was sitting, tied in front of me, so I took it and the small one from my under-sink bin and I went downstairs. I wish I lived in a house with no stairs, and one that didn't have a paving stone path with cracks in it where dirt and rubbish could get in. I laid my kitchen rubbish in first and then put the bag of clothes

37

on top. I closed the lid tight and made sure the bins were in a straight line. What next? I checked the time again. Grandpa would come at eleven but now I had a gap, so I went back up the stairs, one at a time, and sat down in front of my computer screen, the big one my mother had given me. It had a dual processor and was good for gaming and graphics. That was important. In fact it was the most important thing in a computer.

I had nothing to do so I could google anything at all. The time stretched ahead of me and I struggled to sit still and concentrate but that was because I didn't want Grandpa to come. He kept telling me to 'get on with life' although my life was exactly how I wanted it, but I knew that there was no point at all in saying that if I wanted to stay in my own flat, so I went through the motions and Grandpa had given me advice and a book, and later I would have to do more research into medieval history to get a degree one day from the Open University. That would please my mother too.

I went to Google and wrote *cats* in as a search. If Grandpa was going to get me one I had to start researching them. It didn't take long, though: they were different colours but they weren't very interesting, I wrote down some different breeds and then tried to think of a new thing to look at. I wasn't myself this morning.

What had happened in the park had thrown me out of my routine and I was finding it hard to concentrate. I started to panic and get agitated but I had to remember it was their fault, dirty people in broad daylight.

There must be girls in the world that weren't dirty and wanting sex all the time: pure girls.

Then I suddenly thought of something to google. Grandpa said you could find anything on the internet and sometimes he showed me things to prove it. Lots of things I didn't like at all. Now I thought of something which would be worth looking for. 'Pure girls'. My fingers were trembly on the keyboard as I typed, and then, like a wonderful surprise, pictures started appearing. Blonde girls with plaits, in dresses, in gingham, in socks, in shoes, in white panties that you could just see when they bent over, but they didn't want you to see, and they looked embarrassed. These were the sorts of girls you would want to have in your flat, clean and good and washed. These girls smiled straight at me, and they made me smile back.

One of them looked a little bit like the girl in the park, which made me upset, and I quickly closed that picture, my mind filled with the grunting and panting and giggling from the day before. I could see her face, the disgust looking at me, and the look in her eyes as she saw the stick. I felt sick thinking about it, but the front of my trousers was tight again, and I almost kicked my desk. I hated my body, I knew what was right and it let me down every time.

I wanted to get yesterday out of my head, and then I saw the video links. That was like a story, a different one, about nice girls. I scrolled down until I saw a young-looking girl sitting in a meadow with wild flowers round her. This would do it: I would never think about the park once I had watched this. I reached down and undid the buttons on the front of my jeans to be more comfortable, and my penis almost jumped out of my trousers: relief. The girl smiled, and my hand grabbed hold of the throbbing between my legs. It was all going well, I felt better and in control as she walked through the meadow, but then she seemed hot, and started licking her lips, and taking off her clothes, stroking her breasts, and the panting started. What the fuck? I hated it, but I couldn't stop. As she lay down on the ground, she pushed her panties down and her legs parted and the redness of the blood I had seen the day before flashed in front of my eyes as I came into my hand. As it pumped out of me, my thoughts were a mixture of blonde hair, sweet faces and the crunch of the wood as I wiped the smile off the face of the girl in the park.

I felt peaceful for five minutes, then the tenseness came back, worse than before and I wanted to scream. I had no idea how to do it, but my week had to get back to normal. I sat still for a minute, tiredness washing over me, and then went to the bathroom and turned the shower to cold. I threw my clothes on to the floor, something I never did, and the unfamiliar temperature made me jump. So many routines and parts of my schedule were altering: this was what happened when you had anything to do with people out there. I lifted my face to the cold water, and decided again to get everything back on track. The panic was rising in me, and the cold water helped me push it down.

My grandpa arrived when I was sitting back down at my computer and doing notes to show my mother when she next visited. The notes were on medieval feudal systems, but I ignored the section on *droit de seigneur*; I needed to keep right away from the subject of sex and violence until I felt calm. Our lunch was a baked potato each with butter. I had a raspberry yoghurt and Grandpa had blackcurrant and we ate together and then I washed up the cartons and put them in the empty bin.

After lunch Grandpa talked a bit about kittens, and then patted the sofa next to him.

'Come and sit down with me here, I've got a bad back from digging the garden over. You've always been a strong lad – what about a back rub for your old grandpa?'

I didn't feel it coming, I only heard it, a sort of noise that was made up of all the times with Grandpa when he was teaching me lessons, and yesterday in the park, and my routine changing – they all burst out of me, and I could hear myself from far away, screeching and crying, my eyes balled up and my hands tight, on the very tips of my toes.

I had never seen my grandpa look scared, but he did then. He got up, and backed towards the door, shouting, and I could hear him through my own noise. 'Calm down! I only asked for a back rub – what's the matter with you? Bloody retard, scared the shit out of me. I'll be back with a kitten and see if that calms you down, you freak. After everything I've done for you, ungrateful bastard. You think you're normal, do you, screeching like a fucking banshee. Normal people have jobs, did you ever think about that? Independent my ass. Your life is a joke.'

He could say what he liked: my reaction had scared him and I thought he seemed smaller and not so wise. I would show him: I would try the cat and try and get a job – anything to stop the games and not go home to him or my mother.

I heard the door slam and slowly my noise died away. He was gone and another thing had changed. I had changed things two days in a row and I felt as if I was making progress, but it also made me scared and very unsure what would happen next.

I looked at my list. Wednesday afternoon's first thing was supposed to be de-stressing and that was what I would do. I pulled my chair over to the window to sit and watch the outside. I could hear two cats fighting, but I couldn't see them, and after about half an hour a fox walked slowly past the bins, and disappeared into the hedge.

Through the glass the sun was shining on my shoulders and face, and the afternoon was warm. You could actually start a fire just by reflecting the sun through a piece of glass so you had to be careful, but I decided that sitting here was safer and in autumn with weak sun it would probably be a better way to get rid of pastiness than going for a walk. This might help the bobbly rash on my arms too, so I wound up my sleeves. I began to unwind and thought about my grandpa leaving without any correcting lessons, and that no police had come to ask me about the couple in the park, and I started to feel a tiny bit better.

I heard something above me. Bang bang bang then shrieking, then bang bang again, right over my head. I clenched my teeth and counted, which sometimes worked. I knew exactly what the noise was, my upstairs neighbour's children had come but they didn't live here in the house. They lived with their father and only visited sometimes. They saw their mother less than I saw mine and I was a grown-up, and they were still children and children needed supervision. Why were they here again? No balls in the house my mother had always said. I hadn't really liked playing with balls, but my brother had been there then, and he spent hours bouncing a ball against the living room wall or on the floor. My mother hadn't even been able to hear it upstairs in her bedroom, and she would come in when it was time for supper to find me leaning, banging my head, fingers in my ears, jaw clenched. I didn't like noises. I didn't like noisy people.

I had seen my upstairs neighbour many times since I moved in, but I lived alone and I never talked to her, and didn't look at her if I could help it, especially her face. I didn't like looking into people's eyes. When I had moved in she was already here. Her name was Karen. I had seen it on her letters and she was a doctor. It said Dr Karen Watson. She wasn't young, and she didn't care what she looked like. She wore grey and beige clothes, and she had had the same coat for the whole five years we had lived in the same house and I didn't think she had ever cleaned it. Her hair was messy and looked greasy to me, I wouldn't want to touch it and I had never seen her smile. Her mouth was like a straight line across her face. She carried a very old Asda bag and a brown handbag and she looked like a tired person. She doesn't even do her coat up, and you should or you wouldn't get the benefit, my mother told me that. Her boys had satchels and school clothes which were a bit worn out and never neat and they had an older sister, a girl who tried to say hello to me if I was on the stairs, but I didn't reply. She was very quiet, and the taller brother was noisy and I knew it would be him banging the ball and making a noise. He reminded me of the boys in the playground when I was at school, and that was why I hated it there. I had to spend all my time trying to find a quiet spot where I wouldn't get pushed, or made to join in with things I never asked to do and didn't see the point of.

Calm, I liked to be calm and on my own. Thinking about myself from the outside, which Mother said I should try and do, I didn't smile or laugh if I could help it, only sometimes when I was really nervous. Sometimes I would stand in the bathroom in front of the mirror and smile. That wasn't a real smile, but if I was going to have a job in a place with other people I would have to smile my mother said but I didn't like my face when it was smiling. I preferred to be content, which was a calm version of happy and I was content now I lived here but not when it was noisy like this with Karen's children.

I turned my arms over so that the sun would get both sides, even though the rash was only on the back, but I like things to be even. I tried my cloud shape coping strategy and thought I could see a horse in the cloud just ahead of me. It wasn't working, I still felt very tense and I clenched my teeth together. I just wished the boy would shut up, I couldn't do anything while the ball was banging and he seemed to be shouting at his brother, who didn't reply. I heard the front door close and footsteps coming up the stairs, so I jumped down and looked through the little spy hole in my door and saw the sister. I stayed very still even though you can't see in through the spy hole, only out. The footsteps went upstairs and she opened the door and went in. She must have taken the ball away because the banging stopped, and she had a cross voice then a soothing voice and then I heard the television come on and that was better. It wasn't perfect and I was finding the whole day nearly as exhausting as yesterday but at least my jaw relaxed a little. I hadn't made any plans or done my exercises and Wednesday was nearly over. My head was too tired for plan-making and my body was so tired that I couldn't do any exercises. Everything was going to pieces and I needed to get back on track. I went over to my desk and wrote on a Post-it, TOMORROW, PLAN-MAKING DAY, AND EXERCISES AND CLEAN FLAT. It was a lot for one day so I got another Post-it, and wrote EXERCISES AND CLEAN FLAT. It seemed more manageable and I threw the first one away and stuck the new one on to my computer monitor. Then I took a clean piece of paper and wrote:

WORK WANTED. MUST BE WITHIN TWENTY MINUTES' TRAVELLING DISTANCE. INSTRUCTION ESSENTIAL. PLEASE CONTACT NICK IN FLAT ONE, MY NUMBER IS 07938 557801. CALL BEFORE KNOCKING.

Then I walked downstairs and pinned it on to the noticeboard that I had put below the clock, and went back upstairs to sit by the window. I had made a plan but I had overdone it and now I was feeling overwhelmed.

I tried to remember when I had last seen the children here. It was hot, I remember that, so it might have been in July and now it was September. The sister went to big school next to her brothers' primary school and they had different uniforms but they had all looked very sweaty. I wished they hadn't come, I really had needed peace and quiet today, and I tried to squash down the feeling that someone was deliberately trying to push me off balance. It was a big coincidence though, the park, then Grandpa coming and making me upset, then the children. These were all things that didn't happen often in my routine. A lot of them were firsts, like Grandpa leaving, and they never all happened on the same day. Ever. Just as I was thinking about it all, my downstairs neighbour came round the corner carrying a bag, so now I had no peace below or above me. He looked really strange, not like his usual self at all. He was carrying a bag saying Oddbins in his right hand and had a cigarette in his mouth and I had never seen him smoke before. He didn't have work clothes on, he was in a pair of tracksuit trousers and a dirty T-shirt and I wondered if he had become an undercover policeman instead. I thought he would put the cigarette out, but he unlocked the door and as he disappeared into the house and stepped out of my line of vision I could still see the smoke that had been pouring from it hanging in the air outside. I hate smoking. I know that it is illegal in communal areas, and my downstairs neighbour is a policeman, I know that from his letters too, when I put them on to the table. Why would a policeman be breaking the law and filling up my lungs with smoke? My jaw clenched back up. Smoke would be in my flat too; it would come through his ceiling into my living areas. My flat was the same layout as his: the house was three floors, all the same, with a staircase and hallway out of each one. The house was wide and like a rectangle with the short sides at each end, and low, which would mean that the smoke would probably contaminate every room with carcinogens. I wanted to go downstairs and shout at him, but I couldn't do one more thing today.

I knew that I couldn't go to bed yet. I sat and looked at the sky for as long as I could but it was still only six o'clock. I really didn't like the day I was having, and I did another one of my exercises, breathing in through my nose, and out through my mouth, clenching my hands and feet and relaxing them. I stared out of my window, trying not to think of the smoke which was invisibly filling my flat or the moving and television above me. I looked at the houses, one by one, and noticed which ones were flats, which were being done up and becoming what my grandpa called *gentrified*. The wide street looked quiet, and slowly my panic subsided again. I recognised faces in kitchens and at windows that I saw every day, but I didn't speak to strangers.

It was a quiet road but it was on a bus route. I often counted buses coming along, or I counted the cats which prowled the gardens. I saw a cat waiting on the pavement judging how far away an oncoming red bus was and then suddenly making a dash across Staverton Road. He got to the other side without getting run over. The bus stopped and the doors opened, and I realised that Dr Karen from upstairs with the noisy son was getting off. Wasn't anyone sticking to their routine today? I knew what time she came – never before eight. She looked cross, and tired, and ugly. I watched her getting closer to the house when suddenly with no warning she looked straight up at my window, and at me. Our eyes met and she actually stopped walking and stood still. I hate people staring at me. My eyes screwed up a bit and she still stared, so I rolled off the chair and on to the floor. I stayed there a long time. Nothing was making sense. The sooner today ended, the better.

3 | Karen

'*I hear and I forget, I see and I remember, I do and I understand.*'

— Confucius

Wednesday afternoon

Karen's office was an unimpressive grey eight-by-ten box at the front of a hospital which had been built entirely from concrete in the 1960s. The whole structure was monotone, from exterior to pavement, and it looked as though it needed hosing down from top to bottom. The windows were covered in a carbon monoxide city glaze that robbed the interior of light, and the pallor of Karen's skin, her clothes and her filing cabinet could all have come from a colour chart for a prison. The only beacon of light in this small cell of urban misery came from a computer screen. It illuminated the rapid tapping of fingers on a keyboard.

The phone rang, and the jerk of her body in response would have been obvious even to a casual observer. Karen scraped her frizzy, grey-streaked hair back with the reading glasses she had bought for a pound on the concourse of Victoria station, and looked suspiciously at the unwanted interruption. She had never changed the ringtone, it wouldn't have occurred to her, so the default jangle rang out strident and familiar and set to high volume. She didn't get many calls and had never set up her address book, so there was no clue on the screen as to the identity of the interruption. She hated talking to anyone when she was in the middle of developing an important idea and thought about leaving it to ring, but something niggled at the back of her brain.

Eyes still on the monitor, she took a breath and pressed the green button.

'Hello?'

The voice on the other end sounded young and she knew at once who it was.

'Mum, you're supposed to be picking us up from school today. Where are you?'

She missed the resignation in the voice of her eldest child completely because she was rereading a paragraph.

'Mum?'

'I'm here, Sarah, I thought we agreed that you were old enough to make your own way home now. That's why I bought you a travel pass.'

'I know that, but you said we're all going for a pizza today because you missed my birthday for the autism conference and we haven't seen you since.'

Through the lightbulb moment of academic excitement that Karen was experiencing as she reread her words on the monitor, a feeling of guilt and recognition penetrated her consciousness.

'Of course. I'll be there in half an hour.'

Silence. Not for the first time Karen was flooded with resentment at the constant conflict between motherhood and work, and the lack of recognition of what she actually did every day. She sighed inwardly and spoke.

'I'm really looking forward to seeing you all.'

'School's finished, Mum, so we'll just wait. Can you text us when you're ten minutes away?'

'Yes, see you soon, Sarah.'

Karen put the phone down on the desk. It was only a paragraph that she needed to finish and the kids were safe where they were. She just had to finish this thought and then she'd go.

When she pulled up outside her kids' school there was no one around, just an empty playground. A few leaves were blowing across the tarmac and the doors all looked closed. Perhaps their dad had picked them up instead. She tried to push down the feeling of relief and picked up her phone to call Sarah.

'Where are you? I've driven right across town to eat with you, when I was in the middle of something very important, and you're not even ready.'

'Mum, we stood there for ages and the boys were getting tired, we spoke an hour and a half ago and you said you'd text. We're in the primary school library. We're coming.'

Karen drummed her fingers on the steering wheel and tried to clear her head of the ideas of the day. Research was really a mental process, an intense one, and interrupting it was often disastrous. If they ate close to school the kids could hop on the Tube afterwards and she could go back to the office. She hoped she hadn't suggested them coming back to her place for the night. Easily changed, though: she knew they didn't like her flat. On the other hand they could get a takeaway pizza and go straight back there and she could get on.

They were coming across the playground now, dragging their feet, especially Jamie, the youngest, who was easily distracted and looked bedraggled. There all had black rings under their eyes and Karen made a mental note to speak to their father. It was vital to get enough sleep at this age, for optimum physical and mental development. She wound down the window and beckoned to them. 'Come on, slowcoaches, let's go and have some fun.'

Once they were all in the car, she turned, seatbelt still done up, to hug them, awkwardly. Sarah managed a small squeeze and a pat, and Jack a pat, but Jamie was in the corner and barely looked up. Karen took a decision. She would take them to have pizza near their father's house. It was on the way to her flat and they could decide from there what they wanted to do.

As she drove the familiar route towards the restaurant and past what had once been their family home, Karen felt the awkwardness and lack of familiarity between her and the children. She felt what she always felt when she saw them: the unfairness that if she had been a man with a career she wouldn't have been judged to be a bad parent just because she was committed to her career. It didn't make her sad exactly, but she did feel compelled to keep explaining herself, and with every passing year she felt less able to get her point across. The gulf between them just kept getting wider, and it correlated, as far as she could see, with the amount of time she had spent in the same house as them as a family. Sarah had been eight when Karen had moved out, Jack had been five and a half, and Jamie eleven months. She could still remember Sarah's serious, sad little face, and Jack's screaming as she drove off down the drive. Sarah had been holding Jamie, and he had sat quietly on her hip, too young to understand. All she wanted now was for the times they did have together to be successful, the type of relationship she saw divorced men having with their children, guilt-free and comfortable.

She parked the car, and they went inside, found a table and sat down. 'Have whatever you fancy – have starters if you want, or ice creams afterwards. This is Sarah's birthday treat, after all.'

As she said it, Karen remembered the card she had bought a few weeks ago. It was still in its bag on her desk. She excused herself from the silent table and went to ask a waitress if they could possibly put a sparkler into the pizza or dough balls, or sing 'Happy Birthday'. The girl looked at her blankly and said they didn't have sparklers, but they would sing if she wanted.

Dinner was not a success. Jack didn't have much news for her, even though she asked; he just wanted to talk about Manchester United and a new striker that was going to change the Premiership. Karen knew nothing about football and tried to convince him that school was more important, but she knew she was fighting a losing battle. Her ex-husband had encouraged him to kick a ball about ever since he had started toddling, and he had caught the bug. Silence fell again, and Karen started to wish she could get out of there and back to what she did best.

Sarah looked at her mother over a margarita pizza with extra cheese. She was the eldest, always had an opinion and very rarely wavered from it.

'Mum, did you see my exam results? Dad was really pleased – you know I had to revise by myself because he was working so much? I might be put in the excelling class for English and for maths.'

'Maths is great. Not sure what you're going to end up doing with English, but as long as you're keeping up your sciences. You do need to learn to write, I suppose.' Karen smiled encouragingly. 'What do you have in mind for a career?'

'I want to be a journalist, or a novelist.'

A small sleepy voice from Jack cut across Sarah's provocative statement.

'I want to be a footballer.'

'Well, I can see I need to talk to your father. An education is not a passport to just muck about and please yourselves. You need to think ahead, plan the next step. Always take a moment to decide why you are doing what you are busy with.'

The looks on their faces were familiar to Karen: boredom and a tinge of sadness, and in Sarah's case she glimpsed suppressed anger. Jack fidgeted, and Jamie was hard to read. She tried to explain again.

'Work is our testament – it's what we stand for: it speaks for us. Mummy's work is important for lots and lots of people. It's a study—'

'Finished, and I have homework to do.'

There was an edge to Sarah's voice and Karen noticed that there was half a pizza left in front of each of them. If they wanted to go she would get it put into boxes as a takeaway. She beckoned the waitress over and smiled at her daughter.

'Come on now, *happy birthday to you, happy birthday to you, happy birthday, dear Sarah...*'

Jack was singing a different version involving mashed potatoes and stew, and Jamie wasn't singing at all. The awkwardness was palpable now that they were about to leave, and Karen felt like a complete failure as a mother. She tried again.

'Sarah, I know you spent your birthday on your own...' She fished around in her bag for her purse. 'Here you are, darling, go and buy something lovely.'

Twenty pounds didn't seem to cheer Sarah up, so Karen added another, and watched her daughter's face for a smile. It didn't come.

There was a pause. Karen was close to losing her temper now but tried to keep the mood upbeat. 'So, what's it going to be? Back to the flat? You're all very welcome but I have to work, I'm afraid. You can watch the telly.'

'Do you have *QI*?'

This was the first thing her youngest child had said since getting into the car. He didn't look up; he was too busy cleaning his knife and fork with a paper napkin.

'I have BBC 1 and BBC 2, will that do?'

There was a pause, and they looked at one another until Sarah broke the silence.

'Mum, it might be better if we went back to Dad's if you've got to work. Jamie looks really tired. He doesn't like being out of his routine, so if you're busy Dad can help him with his homework. I usually do but I've got my own, and it's getting late.'

Karen dredged her memory. She had a feeling Charlie had already told her there was a reason that they couldn't

54

be at home with him tonight, but she wasn't sure. She couldn't remember, but if there was he could always get in touch later and she could make a plan. Better that they were in familiar surroundings, she told herself, and decided not to dwell on the thought that she could have tried a bit harder to convince them to stay with her. Jack, her classic middle child, stood up and started to walk towards the door.

'Jack, come back here, what's the matter?'

Sarah replied while Jack stood kicking the skirting board. 'He missed out on football club, and basketball, actually, Mum. Dad said you had the forms and the teacher never got them and I tried to sort it out but you need a signed permission slip and he didn't have one.'

Karen remembered then, her insistence on seeing the forms, her promise to get them back. She had a sinking feeling that they weren't far from the birthday card on her desk.

'Alright, let's get these pizzas to go.'

She watched as Sarah smoothed Jamie's hair and steered his arms into his sleeves. She felt a muted pang of something deep inside, just before her mind turned back to a thought she had been halfway through earlier. Yes, she needed to get back to it, and far better for the children to get some sleep and wake up fresh.

The car journey only lasted a few minutes. More awkward kisses and they parted on promises of seeing each other that weekend for Jack's social football on the Common. Karen decided that the lecture to her ex-husband about subject choices and getting enough sleep could wait until then.

'Love you all, see you Saturday.'

Charlie was bearing down on the car from the garden path, and Karen gave a wave and got the kids out just in time. Duty done, she drove off, mind clearing as she went. Behind her on the pavement Sarah stood with Jamie, her arm protectively round his little shoulders, while Jack zigzagged up the path to the front door as their father watched her drive away, his hand on the top of his head, exasperation clearly visible.

Her laptop was in the back, and she could work at home. A half-bottle of Pinot Grigio awaited her, and she had eaten. She felt a sense of freedom and almost excitement thinking how close she was to a breakthrough in her research on how to maximise the potential of autistic people in society and work situations. She hit the High Road quite quickly – it was a route she drove often – and then sat in the inevitable jam leading to the turn-off for the road back to her flat. Ten minutes later she had a clear drive ahead. She put her foot on the accelerator.

Nothing.

She was stuck, and with a sinking feeling she looked down at her petrol gauge. Three times this month – what was wrong with her? Everyone else could manage to keep fuel in their cars, but she seemed incapable of it. She could hear her husband's voice: *You think you're above the normalities of life – mothering, cooking, parenting. It's pathetic: your children need structure, your car needs petrol. You will never be happy.*

People were starting to beep their horns, trying to get round her, and she couldn't think where the nearest garage was. Two big Polish guys got out of a white van and offered her a push on to the pavement. This was an important day: her many ideas, the strands of her paper seemed to be finally forming a cohesive mass in her mind. She needed to get home, and she could deal with the car in the morning. She steered up on to the pavement, got out, and waved away the guys who had helped her, manners lost in her frustration at the situation. They got back into the van, and shouted something at her as they drove past. The next car to pass her actually put his window down. 'Ugly bitch, try smiling, it might never happen. Haven't you heard of petrol stations?'

Shrugging it off, she started to walk. It was too far to walk all the way, but she might see a taxi. Ten minutes passed and she didn't see a single one. Finally she sat down at a bus stop and waited. When a bus finally pulled up, she was thinking about her idea and running it through her mind, over and over. She didn't want to lose her thread before she got home.

'Staverton Road, please.'

There were several people behind her and the lady driver behind the window just looked at her expectantly.

'Sorry, how much is it?'

'You need your Oyster card, love.'

'What? I don't have one. Here, I have money.'

'We don't take cash. Don't you have a contactless card?'

'Um, no, I don't think so...' Karen had no idea what the driver was talking about.

'Then you need to go to an outlet that sells Oyster cards and get the next bus.'

By the time she had managed to find a shop, make the purchase, get on to another bus and get home, Karen was shattered. She picked up her bags and dragged herself towards the house. She had left her light on again; she could see it from the road, and as she looked up she caught sight of a young man in the window of the middle flat, below hers. He was apparently sitting on a chair, staring out into the dusk. He looked straight at her and they locked eyes. The tight formality of his posture, the way he cocked his head on one side, and the immediate discomfort when he realised she was looking at him, stopped her in her tracks. Then suddenly without warning he threw himself to one side and was gone. Karen shook her head, and carried on walking.

Opening the door, she grabbed her mail. Who had a postman who took the trouble to make letters look this neat? Above the cheap IKEA desk which passed for a table, mail repository and general dropping point, she noticed that there was now a perfectly centralised clock. Plain, black and white. Cheap, but telling the correct time and ticking silently away. Below that, centralised again, was a noticeboard. Small, functional and cork, it had one solitary note pinned to it.

WORK WANTED. MUST BE WITHIN TWENTY MINUTES' TRAVELLING DISTANCE. INSTRUCTION ESSENTIAL. PLEASE CONTACT NICK IN FLAT ONE, MY NUMBER IS 07938 557801. CALL BEFORE KNOCKING.

Without giving it much thought, Karen turned to go upstairs, and as she climbed the two flights to her front door she thought about the glimpse of the young, neat man looking out of his window on the first floor. His hair had been just a little too perfectly combed with a straight parting, collar buttoned up to his chin, reactions just a little too jumpy. Karen registered all this and lodged it in her mind for later.

She could hear her children before she could see them. What the hell? Her heart sank, everything seemed to be conspiring against her today. She opened the door. Sarah was sitting at the table with Jamie, helping him with his homework, and Jack was on the sofa watching television. Karen put on her best game face.

'Hi, guys, what are you doing here?'

She realised she probably looked less than enthusiastic about seeing them, but she could only do so much.

'Dad had plans, and said it's impossible to stay there tonight. He dropped us off and went.'

Karen was furious. She plugged her dead phone in and waited until it sprung into life. Charlie, her ex, had sent a text.

Jesus, Karen, you know it's my work dinner tonight. I'm up for promotion. We discussed this. I have a work conference all this week and the kids need to come to you to do homework unless I can get away early. They haven't actually spent the night with you in over a month and I need a bit of flexibility for the next few days. Let me know when you get back. They all have homework and it isn't fair for them to be ferried from pillar to post, not to mention that I'm now going to be late. Thanks for nothing.

It came back to her now: the conference, the promotion. Karen took yet another deep breath and resigned herself to a long night ahead. She had some DVDs that had come free with the Sunday papers a while back, and they could watch those when they had finished their homework. It was already after six and she needed to get this new idea down as soon as she could.

'Right,' she said, 'I need some peace and quiet because I have a very complicated problem to work out. I'm right here if you need me, just let me know if you need any help with anything. Lucky we've all had a lovely dinner. Did you bring the leftover pizza with you?'

Sarah nodded, and pointed to the boxes on the side in the kitchen. Not for the first time this evening, Karen felt redundant, and turned on her laptop.

Eventually the children cuddled up together on the sofa and *The Lion King* seemed to please everyone. Karen managed to tune out the annoying little monkey and the Disney songs and was soon engrossed in the world of data and extrapolation that she understood best.

It was four the next morning before she stopped typing her proposition, but she didn't feel tired, she felt jubilant. There was no one to tell, though. The children had drifted off in reverse order of age and Sarah had lifted Jamie into bed, Karen had carried Jack, and Sarah had watched the news before she went to bed. Information collated, ideas crystallised, Karen had finished. She emailed it to her work address so that she could add this work to the main body of her paper tomorrow, and rubbed her eyes.

It had taken a long time as a practising children's epidemiologist for Karen to identify the field she was most passionate about. The first big row that she had ever had with her ex-husband was when she had been invited to be part of a panel exploring how everything from toxic chemicals to social factors shaped the health of children from birth to age twenty-one. It had taken place in Boston. Charlie hadn't wanted her to go; the children were tiny, in fact she had been pregnant with Jamie and even Sarah had only been in Year Two. Karen had realised then that her career was more important to her than her family, and she had made it clear to Charlie that he would have to pick up the slack. He hadn't liked that, and it had been the beginning of the end. His one-night stand with his secretary had been a symptom, not the cause of their break-up, Karen knew that.

That first Boston conference had given Karen an insatiable appetite for statistics and cause and effect. Eventually she had distilled her vast theoretical knowledge down to one subject: autism. She had become obsessed with its causes, and then with how social factors could help those on the spectrum to lead productive lives. She lived and breathed the apparently endless facts and figures. She gobbled up the latest estimates of the increasing number of people diagnosed, and now she was concentrating on the lack of specifically designed routes into employment for autistic children. The lack of career opportunities and lack of appropriate teachers who could maximise these children's potential kept her awake at night. Karen was determined that there should be a formula for this growing part of the community which would maximise their contribution and happiness and, where possible, keep them in the workforce. It was her passion, and kept her focused on the path ahead, even though it might keep her away from her kids. Karen saw it as self-sacrifice. Others seemed to think she was being selfish.

Even discounting the discredited studies, no one could deny that autism was a rapidly increasing problem, with at least one in a hundred children on the spectrum today (up from one in two thousand in the 1980s). You had to be sensible about it, of course, there was a lot of over-diagnosis, but Karen had seen so many skilled children with Asperger's going to waste, and she wanted to write the definitive paper identifying early markers, methods of coping, and eventually career and education paths that really would make use of the incredible skill-sets that some of the high-functioning Asperger's children demonstrated. All she needed now was a perfect case study to back up her findings and she would have everything she needed to present her paper.

On her way to the bathroom, Karen passed the mirror, caught sight of herself and looked away quickly. She might have a sound intellect, but she couldn't remember the last time she had put on a slick of lipstick or mascara. Sacrifices had to be made. She smiled as she thought that might be a good epitaph for her, then wondered who would be there to read it.

Karen put this maudlin train of thought to one side and, after a lukewarm shower and a cup of coffee, she curled up on the sofa and set her alarm. The couple of hours she had allocated herself for sleep passed much too quickly and she awoke disorientated and feeling a bit paranoid from tiredness. She crept into the bedroom and woke up her children. Jack kept falling back to sleep, but Sarah was up straight away and gently levered Jamie's legs over the side of the bed and pulled him into a standing position. 'Arms up, Jamie, come on, time for school.'

Karen had lent them a T-shirt each to sleep in, but they still looked a sorry sight in the day before's school uniforms, underwear turned inside out. At least their homework was done. If Charlie was trying to be Father of the Year and make her look bad, he could at least have sent them with a change of clothes and clean underwear, or a toothbrush.

Jack had been handed back his football by Sarah as an incentive to hurry up, and was bouncing it on the floor repeatedly. Suddenly, the banging was answered by something like a broom handle from below, and muffled shouting. Karen had lived in the house for five years, ever since her marriage had broken down, and never before had she heard a peep from the flat below her. Now in the space of twenty-four hours she had seen the occupant staring at her from his window, read a note from him about a job, and now apparently woken him up.

She did the best she could, making them all brush their teeth with her toothbrush and untangling their hair, then called a cab to get the kids to school and herself to the hospital. Five minutes later she had disgorged them all at the gate to the playground, a five-pound note for the canteen taking the place of breakfast at her flat. She watched as Sarah tenderly led Jamie towards the primary school entrance and handed him over, Jack running in ahead of them to join his friends, and then for the second time in twenty-four hours she drove away from her children. As she left, she realised that she had never noticed before just how dependent her youngest son was on his sister, and she wondered whether it was because he missed his mother. She dismissed the thought, reminding herself that they had a primary parent at home, before her mind filled up with the day ahead.

As she sat at her work station, the morning sped by. Surrounded by case files, she worked her way through pictures and biographies of familiar faces that she had interviewed over the years, trying to place them on the spectrum. Familiar pathologies and symptoms swam in front of her eyes, but she had been involved with most of these case studies for too long for them to be viewed as objective by her peers. She needed a fresh case, but had no idea how to find one.

Twelve-thirty came around and she was no further ahead. Stomach grumbling, she headed for the canteen. She filled her tray with a balanced slow-release mix of chicken salad on wholegrain bread, a banana and a sparkling water, then looked for somewhere to sit. Every table was full, and she had no option other than to sit perched on the end of a group of lively-looking young people who obviously all knew each other.

Enthusiasm was not a familiar emotion for Karen, but she had been as close to it as she had ever got this morning. Things could have gone worse with the kids, and she felt excited by her work. Now she sat, deflated, as the easy familiarity of normal human interaction surrounded her.

'How the hell are we going to fill this position?' said a young man to her left. At a guess she would have pegged him as of Ethiopian extraction: he had a handsome aquiline face with fine bone structure, long limbs, and a confident bearing. Anthropology had been the subject of her first degree, many years ago. She half listened and tried to think of a way of introducing herself and throwing her achievements of last night into the conversation. There was no opportunity, but she did work out that the team she was sitting with were a mixture of pathologists and morgue workers who had lost their jack of all trades. He had done a bit of everything as far as she could tell – prepared the bodies, cleaned up, sterilised the instruments – and everyone at the table seemed to agree that they would struggle without him. He had apparently left to work at a local coffee chain.

'More money, less gore.'

The easy laugh that accompanied this gruesome observation grated, and Karen finished her banana and headed back to the lab. Once again, something niggled at the back of her mind, but she couldn't pin it down.

4 | Tam

> *'The world breaks everyone, and afterward, some*
> *are strong at the broken places.'*
>
> — Ernest Hemingway

Thursday, early evening

Tam had no idea what time it was or which end of the week he was at. His flat smelt of a mix of stale sweat, cheap whisky and unchanged bed. He pulled on some tracksuit trousers and a T-shirt that he found on the floor where he had thrown them the night before and headed across the hall. He needed a drink, and he was sure that he had thrown away a bottle a couple of nights ago which was a quarter full. He was on a mission to retrieve it.

He opened the front door and looked out on to the dark, uneven pathway leading to the bins. It had been warm when he had started his porn-and-curry binge, but now the evenings were drawing in and the wind had a real feel of winter about it. He should have put his shoes on. Fuck it… He tiptoed as best he could, the cold hitting his bones and making him feel even older than life's general rejection of him already had.

He lifted the heavy black plastic lid. A neat white bin

bag tied in a double knot was on the top. It was bizarrely clean for rubbish and it wasn't the first time he had seen this. Someone had far too much time on their hands, or OCD. Who the fuck positioned the detritus of their life across a bin in a perfectly straight line?

He pushed it out of the way, dug down below another smaller, equally neat bag and found the bag for life he had chucked away earlier in the week, untied, grubby, and overflowing with the containers from a takeaway that he had lived off for a couple of days after he had handed in his resignation. Things must be getting better, as he was now working his way through a pizza from Franco Manca; the sourdough crust made it almost healthy. Averting his eyes, he gingerly reached inside and his fingers made contact with the glass bottle. He lifted it out, curry sauce and all, and tilted it into the light of his mobile. About four fingers in here, enough for a pre-dinner relaxer.

He let the bag go and put the other two back on top of it. As he turned around, the mix of rain, oil from the takeaway which had got on to the path and the lack of balance that had come with his hangover made him lose his footing and down he went with the bottle. He made a vain cartoon-like attempt to grab it and ended up on his knees surrounded by glass. It made a hell of a crash.

'Fuck fuck fuck!'

Tam heard a window above him open, and a furious-looking woman put her head out of the top flat.

'What the hell are you doing? Get away from our bins. This is a private house and you have no right to be here. Go away before I call the police. I'm trying to work.'

It was not a great tableau, even Tam could see that. He was barefoot, soaked, unshaven and surrounded by the remains of a cheap bottle of scotch. He looked up before he thought the situation through. As their eyes met, he saw a flicker of recognition. They had passed each other enough times on the way in and out of the house or in the hall to at least be recognisable to each other. Even in London with your head down, you couldn't completely avoid human interaction.

'Oh, I'm sorry,' the woman said. 'I didn't realise it was you. I thought it was a fox, or a tramp. Well, I mean I heard the crash, before I realised.'

If a pause could be awkward during a one-sided conversation with a man by a bin on his knees, then this one was, and after a nervous cough or two she shut the window.

Tam picked up the bigger pieces of glass, mainly to avoid impaling himself on them, and dumped them in the bin. He got to his feet, tiptoeing gingerly and empty-handed towards the house. His new-found conscience was waiting in the hall.

'Do you want to borrow a dustpan and brush?'

Tam rubbed his chin, the gesture of a man searching for answers that eluded him. He shook his head, simultaneously exasperated and lost for words, and looked properly for the first time at the woman in front of him. *Mousy* would probably be the word that sprung to mind. Wiry hair scraped back and held in place by a pencil, which wasn't doing a great job, a bobbly sweater that had seen better days and had never been near a sheep's back. *Don't light a match near that one, council house special, she'll go up like a Roman candle.* Pub banter about a long-forgotten barmaid popped into his head. He smiled at the thought. Under the acres of man-made fibre it looked as though she had a fair pair of tits and her legs weren't bad. No make-up, so at least you could see what you were getting.

'No, I'll clear it up later. Thanks.'

The disapproval on her face was clearly visible and Tam sighed. He wasn't going back out there with no shoes on and covered in mud. Fuck that.

His mouth was dry, and, like a man in the desert who glimpses an oasis, desperation overcame him. 'I haven't got anything in, at the flat. Do you have coffee?'

It was the best Tam could do; he couldn't ask her to give him a drink, they'd only just met and it would only reinforce her opinion of him.

'I'm working,' she said. 'A very important project. It's really a vital piece of research.'

Tam didn't have the energy to argue. He crossed the hall and let himself in, his tracksuit trousers sticking to his knees. He peeled off his clothes, pulled a small piece of glass out of his foot, went into the bedroom, lay down and pulled the covers over his head. He was well aware from past experience that his grizzly chin and broad shoulders and general air of needing to be fixed were irresistible to a certain breed of woman, and he had a feeling he had just aroused something which he would be sorry for awakening later. Fuck it, he would worry about that when he woke up.

The knocking was insistent and coming from somewhere close by. He came to, the usual sequence of events kicking in. Head pain, swimmy head, mild nausea. He remembered now: he couldn't complete the sequence because he had no more booze and his usual hair of the dog would have to wait. Tam swung his legs over the side of the bed and listened. The knocking was on his door. He padded over, sweat starting to form on his upper lip, and opened up.

Through a mist of sleep and dehydration he made out the mousy neighbour from earlier.

'Thanks for clearing up the glass, I've finished my work for now. Do you still want some coffee?'

Tam knew it. He hadn't cleaned up, so it had to be a ruse to knock on his door, unless they had a secret house elf that he hadn't been told about. He had been holding the door half-open so that the hard-on in his boxer shorts was semi-concealed. He hadn't done a very good job, and her eyes dropped, her cheeks going bright red.

'I'll be up in five minutes. Thanks.'

Tam shut the door as politely as he could manage and looked down at his crotch. Well, at least things could only improve from this point. Nothing like starting from a low base.

He thought about pulling on the same pair of tracksuit bottoms that he had taken from his floordrobe for the last two days, but from somewhere deep inside he mustered the energy to shake his head clear and strip before heading to the shower and turning on the taps. This self-pitying bender had gone on long enough. He turned on the television while he waited for the water to heat up, and scratched his balls. The news was focused on a pack of deer and the scene was Richmond Park. He tried to follow the story: a couple in their twenties, making out by a pretty lake in peaceful Surrey, had got their heads bashed in earlier in the week, for no apparent reason. What the fuck? No leads, no forensics, no apparent plan from the Met. Typical. This was exactly what his kind of police work was for, old-fashioned plods who could follow clues, and understood people's motivation. Instead, there were ever-multiplying awareness seminars and blue skying.

He needed something to take his mind off this; if he started to watch he wouldn't be able to stop. His fingers were already itching to take notes on the scene and to google articles. He jumped under the shower and began washing away the strain of the past few days from the top down, even turning the water to cold for the last five minutes. Kill or cure. Ten minutes later he was in clean boxers, a semi-clean T-shirt and pair of jeans, and deck shoes, knocking on his top-floor neighbour's door. It occurred to him that he knew her name, from the letters he saw every morning: Dr Karen Watson. Thank God for the postman with OCD.

She opened the door, looking as uncomfortable as she had been downstairs, and a blast of chilly unheated air hit him from the interior of her flat.

'Hi, coffee brewed?'

Karen stood, half-hidden behind the door, and looked him up and down with her head on one side. An awkward ten seconds later she stepped aside and let him in.

'You look different – much better. Have you been ill?'

Tam considered telling her he had, but shook his head. 'No, I lost my job and I've had a bit of a messy few days.'

'Oh, my God, I'm so sorry, how awful. I can't even imagine how painful that must be. If anything like that ever happened to me...'

Her words trailed off, and Tam shook his head to better understand her unexpected burst of emotion. He looked at her as she fiddled nervously with the fraying sleeve of her jumper. He had told people about bereavements in the line of duty with less reaction, and he could now see her eyes were welling up. He must have completely misread her.

He looked around him, to give her a moment, hoping to see a pot of steaming coffee somewhere, and was struck by the starkness of the place. She had kids, he had seen them coming in and out, visiting he assumed as they weren't here often. There were no signs of them. Not a toy, or a homely touch. The sofa looked as though she had bought it in IKEA ten years ago, and there were two mismatched chairs. Awkwardly, he walked towards one of them, but as he passed Karen she made a noise somewhere between a cough and a sob, and he looked at her. There wasn't much to look at, a tired, uncared-for woman of a certain age, and he began to regret climbing two flights of stairs on wobbly legs. This was a bit much on a hangover and no food all day except a slice of cold pizza, and he wasn't good with emotions even when he was feeling strong.

'Are you OK?'

He was still frozen in the middle of the room, and reached out towards her nervously as she now had tears streaming down her face. What the hell was going on? Tam thought that maybe patting her shoulder would help; he had been on a course where they had said CPC, close physical contact, was helpful in situations of distress. As his arm reached her shoulder, she dived towards him, head on his chest, and sobbed against his only cleanish T-shirt, burrowing into him like a puppy who had never been stroked.

He flattened the back of her wiry hair with his big rugby player's hand as best he could, as she wept and apologised, and then their faces were very close together and her hand was on the back of his head, pulling him in. He hesitated for about two seconds, closed his eyes, inhaled and found that her breath smelt minty and her hair of supermarket shampoo, and there was a pleasing scent of Simple soap, so he bent towards her and he kissed her. It seemed like the gentlemanly thing to do.

Tam had heard the expression 'the quiet ones are always the kinkiest', and had even heard about dams breaking, but he had never had his clothes ripped off with such speed, or been devoured by a starving female before. He regarded himself as a game guy, a man's man, always up for what was on offer, but as he was being kissed, and stripped and nibbled and licked, he was begging Karen to slow down and hang on a minute, as she sank to her knees and took him deep in her mouth. He tried not to give in, but she seemed to have made a study of where to put her hands and her tongue, and her enthusiasm was so obviously real that he couldn't help himself. He warned her that he was going to come if she carried on, and her reaction was to redouble her efforts and use her other hand to play with his balls. That did it, and as he came in her mouth he saw stars. Hearing her swallow made the whole experience even more visceral, and when he emerged from this completely surprising state a few minutes later he had to resist the urge to apologise, as Karen was on her knees, still fully dressed, and they were still strangers. From somewhere far away came the thought, *never piss on your own doorstep* ... God knew what it meant but it seemed appropriate.

He supported his frame on the arm of the sofa for a minute or two while strength returned to his legs, then he gathered his thoughts and spoke.

'Can I make the coffee? It seems the least I can do.'

Karen got up, and the awkward silence that had preceded the blow job resumed, as she didn't answer and got a small, disappointing jar of Nescafé out of the cupboard. At least she wasn't crying – that had to be a good sign, Tam thought to himself. Fuck it, he felt physically better than he had in ages; she had swallowed every bit of tension in his body.

He walked over to her as she busied herself with the kettle, put his arms around her from behind and kissed her neck. His knees still felt a bit weak, but even he could work out that she might not be feeling quite as satisfied as him yet. Her body language seemed off, one arm making the drinks, the other clamping her bobbly cardigan around her body, which suddenly he realised he would quite like to see. She turned round, holding his coffee, which he accepted, and he took a deep slug.

'Right, your turn.'

He led her, both arms crossed across her middle now, to the bed, gently put her arms down by her sides, stood her in front of him and sat down. He took off the cardigan and undid her blouse. He had been right the first time he saw her: she had beautiful breasts, with big, firm pink nipples. He could tell she hated the scrutiny. She couldn't meet his eyes, but it had been a long time since he had seen a naked woman and he swallowed hard before taking off her jeans. His invisible neighbour had been hiding her light under a polyester bushel, and he leant forward and took her nipple gently between his teeth, pulling her towards him.

This time they took it slowly, and although they still hadn't said more than four sentences to each other their bodies didn't seem to mind. They fitted. He found himself thinking of those salad sets where the vinegar and the olive oil slide together to make a perfect whole. His size matched hers, and his mouth fitted all parts of her, and she was tight around him and when he woke up early the next morning she was asleep on his chest, something that he had hated all his life but which for some reason now seemed perfectly natural.

Tam felt wide awake, and had an overwhelming desire to spring clean. Karen's flat might be bare but his, he thought, was a pigsty. He crept out of bed, grinning to himself, and pulled the duvet up over Karen's shoulders. She didn't stir. There was a pen and a pad by the computer, and he wrote, *Thanks, Tam*, then screwed it up and wrote, *See you later*, then screwed that up too and wrote, *Thanks for the coffee, see you, Tam*.

That would get over the awkwardness of her not knowing his name. He had noticed that even when she was coming she hadn't a clue what he was called, or he was pretty sure she would have shouted it. He grinned to himself again, picked up the two rubbish bags by her door, and headed quietly downstairs.

The fresh air hit him like a bucket of iced water and his deck shoes left his ankles vulnerable. He ran, bag in each hand, towards the bins. There was not a trace of the broken whisky bottle from the night before, or the takeaway containers. Even the patches of oil that had helped him fall ass over tip last night were gone. Maybe they did have a house elf after all. It was mesmerisingly clean, not a sliver of glass on the path and it looked as if someone had wiped the bins down and straightened them up.

Tam opened the lid. The bags that he had thrown around the evening before in his search for booze had been repacked, at angles of ninety degrees to each other, and right on top was the translucent white one which he vaguely remembered seeing as he dug for his takeaway bag. If he had still been a copper he would have sworn that the T-shirt he could now see inside was splattered with blood. Old habits died hard, and he picked the bag up carefully, tucked it under his jacket and headed back inside to the flat. His nose could smell something off, and his nose was never wrong.

5 | Nick

*'I read that when cats are cuddling and kneading
you, and you think it's cute, they're really just
checking your vitals for weak spots.'*

— Kandyse McClure

Friday morning

I was pleased when I woke up at 6.30 in the morning,
it's a good time to wake up. It's quiet on Staverton Road
then, birds tweeting and the sound of distant engines are
the only noises you can hear – well, apart from my own
breath, which I try not to concentrate on. In and out, it
seemed loud to me and I was worried I was getting a chest
infection; there are germs everywhere. I quickly googled
'signs of chest infection' and counted. I only had two of
the symptoms on the list. I had agreed with Mother that I
was not allowed to panic if I had less than three on a list
of symptoms for any illness. Mother had explained it – the
reason was that most illnesses had similar symptoms and
I could misunderstand and get really worried and think I
was ill when really I wasn't. Even thinking about it made
me start to think I might have symptoms I didn't have, like
'itchiness' or 'excessive need to urinate'. Keeping calm was

very important or stress might follow, which caused so many symptoms you could hardly list them. Shortness of breath was one effect of stress and it was scary as it could also indicate a heart attack. The thought of my heart made me feel like scratching my legs. I started to worry that my position in bed might be making my heart pump harder than it should have to, and that might be putting a strain on it right now. I'd spent hours looking at films on the computer of operations where the surgeons opened someone's chest and worked on a shiny, slimy heart that had been stopped by a machine before they connected it back up or sometimes put in a new one from someone else and it pulsated rhythmically. It all looked a bit hit and miss.

The fact that the whole of my existence was reliant on that one muscle in my chest that could realistically pack up at any time made me nervous. People could be really fit and eat only healthy food and still have congenital heart problems and drop dead. I wish things were a bit more secure, healthwise. There is almost nothing you can do to stop your body getting ill, or responding to situations in a way you might not like. It's like being a servant to a master who is completely unpredictable. That's why I had a routine, so I was busy and my mind was occupied.

I did my breathing exercises and thought about the kitten but that didn't calm me down, I wondered whether cats could have heart problems too; that would be another thing to worry about.

Last night I made my Thursday phone call to my mother and all she wanted to talk about was me getting a cat. Again. I decided that, even though I didn't find them very interesting, if everyone thought I should have one I would try. Mother kept using words like *company* and *responsibility*, and I didn't want either of those things, but it was better than a person, it was just a baby animal. I would try.

It wasn't Wednesday but Grandpa was coming around specially to deliver my new cat. It was a tabby one. Mother told me that she was coming with him, so I had spent yesterday's session on the computer searching and had put together a document on how to care for a kitten and printed lots of pages. Kittens needed a lot of looking after and I was feeling very unsure how I would fit it in and keep to my list.

I had gathered up all the information, and emailed Mother a list of things I needed to get and things that had been recommended by *www.catprotection.co.uk*. There were a lot of things, and I knew that having a cat was going to be hard even though Grandpa thought it was for my own good and was only getting it to make me more responsible in the eyes of the world, which was very important even though I didn't understand how they would see that I had a cat because it wasn't going outside and I didn't have visitors unless you count Grandpa and Mother and they already know.

I would have to do a whole new list, on the kitchen wall, and I would have a whole new set of things to do. It was making my palms itchy and I felt sweaty and upset. My routine was just right, and I could fit everything in, but just when things had settled down, now there was the afternoon in the park, which I hated thinking about and couldn't visit any more, and this. I had discovered that cats need worming and microchipping and got stressed but this one was going to come with those things done, and injections. I hated injections so I didn't want to see that. Grooming the cat wasn't necessary unless you got one which had long hair. I had already told Grandpa to make sure it had short hair. Grandpa had selected a tabby cat, just a normal one, so no grooming and no hair on the sofa, just maybe a few hairs that fell out like they do with a person. I didn't want to have clothes covered in hair.

I remembered I had also put a note on the board downstairs asking for work. I could feel my face screwing up, and my hands, and I leant hard against the wall on my tiptoes.

On top of all this, Grandpa had told me on the phone that the kitten was going to urinate and defecate in a plastic tray that he was bringing with him. I had to scoop it out, it would come with a scoop, and then put it in the bathroom and flush it away in the toilet I use myself. The thought of it made me feel like vomiting. I read an article which said a cat is cleaner than a person but that might be the people you see on the Tube, who don't wash or sanitise. More and more I decided I wasn't looking forward to the cat. It was all adding tasks and the cat hadn't even arrived yet.

The issue of what to call my cat had also thrown me. I had to name it, Mother said, because it was going to be mine. I first wanted to call it Cat but Grandpa told me that Mother would think it showed a lack of imagination and think I had no feelings towards it and had not connected with the animal properly. It couldn't be Cat, then. I made another list.

My list of cat names wasn't that long but I had googled popular cat names and these were some I liked. The cat was a boy so my ideas were for males:

Blackie, but only if it was a black cat.

Whiskers, the second most popular name for a cat.

Richmond, but I had thought of this before what happened in the park so I crossed it out.

Staverton, Grandpa's suggestion, I don't like it and it would remind me of Grandpa, so I crossed it out.

Bob because it's short and for a boy.

Kitty because it's short for cat but it sounds like a girl because I knew a girl called Kitty, so I crossed it out too.

After my usual morning free time I sat looking out of the window until I saw Grandpa's car pull up outside. He looked up and signalled for me to come downstairs. I could see that my mother was in the front seat and that was another new thing because they didn't usually come together. I reminded myself that this was just one day, for the kitten, and not another change to my list. The day ahead had already gone out of my routine and was close to completely ruined so I concentrated on getting this over with and seeing what happened. I slowly stood up and walked towards the door, where I exchanged my slippers for my outside shoes. Adidas, my favourite shoe brand. I liked the stripes on the side.

I looked at the time in the hall, it was 10.10. Good, plenty of time until lunch and if Grandpa left quickly I could just try and do the exercises I should have done on Wednesday but was too tired. Then I could just ignore the cat and watch television later. I was trying to stay fit inside the flat now. On the way down the stairs I took a decision and decided to call the cat Tabby because I would remember it and the cat turned out to be even stripier than I thought when I saw it, which was good, the name was a good choice.

'Morning, Nick,' said Grandpa in his chirpiest voice. I had asked him once why he sounded like that sometimes, very bouncy and loud, and he said, 'Feeling chirpy, Nick,' which isn't even a thing, and I said, 'Morning,' back, and stood away from the basket. My grandpa looked at me, I looked at the pavement.

My mother got out of the car, looking worried, I knew that look, and she said, 'Hello, Nick, this is exciting. I hope the kitten keeps you company.'

I didn't want to look as though I was panicking, so I did my practice smile and just said, 'Yes.'

Everyone was quiet for a minute and I tried not to worry about Grandpa coming inside; Mother was there and he didn't correct me when she was close by, but I had a kitten to get used to. I wanted a short visit. Grandpa spoke to me. 'Give us a hand. I have to say I never realised a little animal would need this much gear.'

I tried to explain about the list and the research so that Mother would be impressed, but Grandpa was looking at the pile of things on the floor.

'Yes, I know, Nick, I was only joking. I forgot you had a humour bypass. Do you want to take the stuff, or the kitten?'

'The stuff.'

We carried everything up the stairs and my mother followed and as I went through the hall I saw it was 10.45.

My note was still up, I stopped.

'Mother, look at my note. I am looking for a job.'

'Nick, I'm so proud of you. Well done. Let us know if you find one.'

We got the kitten into the flat and Grandpa put its carrying basket on the floor and undid the leather straps. We waited, and after a bit the little animal came out. It was really small and as its head emerged it made a little sound as if to say, *Help*, but it was just a squeak not a word.

I wasn't sure what the right thing to do for a small kitten was, but it stopped outside the cage, looking at the floor, and began scratching at the carpet with claws that looked very sharp, before Grandpa scooped it up in one hand and held it out. 'Here you go. Hold him.'

I hadn't realised you had to hold them, it hadn't been on the list or on the website, and I didn't feel at all like having it in my hand now that I had seen how its claws had made runs in the carpet.

'Come on, he's yours, you can't just stare at him.'

Grandpa held the cat in his palm while I tried to pluck up the courage to take it.

'He might scratch me.'

Mother frowned at Grandpa and smiled at me. I knew she was trying to make me feel better, but smiling doesn't make someone who doesn't want to hold a cat feel like they want to hold it. I concentrated. There would be no point in going to all this trouble if I couldn't do what everyone else did with their cats.

Grandpa doesn't like people who don't make up their minds, or who are babies, or won't do what they are told, so just as I was going to hold out my hand he picked the cat up into the air and put it on me, and it clung on to my jumper, and then, while I was concentrating on not waving my arms or flicking it off, it lay down on the bend of my elbow. I looked down at him and little dark blue eyes stared at me. It weighed nothing and it smelt cleaner than I had thought it would. I knew my grandpa was watching, so I stayed still and tried not to think about germs.

'He's nice,' I said finally.

'Yeah, he's sweet. What's his name?'

'It's Tabby, because he's a tabby. I found it on the computer.'

'It suits him. Let's get him sorted.'

Grandpa unpacked his bed and I unpacked the bowls and the litter tray and Mother made cups of tea for me and her, and wiped down the side with Dettol spray. I felt as if everything was going well. Perhaps this cat was a good idea after all.

I sat on the chair and the kitten climbed down off my arm and I drank my tea and the kitten went to sleep, on the floor, not even on the bed Grandpa had got for it to sleep on. I asked Grandpa to move it, but he told me it could sleep anywhere it wanted and laughed but it wasn't a nice laugh. If it could sleep anywhere, then what was the point of the bed? I decided I could try and move it later. Grandpa filled up the tray with grey grit, and left the scoop next to it. It could be outside the bathroom, I didn't think the germs could get to the kitchen from there. We watched *Homes Under the Hammer* together – well, Mother was watching me and Grandpa and we were watching the programme – then we had a sandwich which was chicken and avocado and brown bread, and baked crisps, and a juice. Tabby was quiet and seemed quite easy to live with so I relaxed a little bit and thought my day might be alright.

'We have to go, Nick, leave you two to get acquainted. Places to go, people to see. You look white as a fucking sheet, Nick, you eating? You're very pasty, like I said before. I think you need to get some colour in your cheeks.'

'Leave him alone, Dad – look, on his list it says he goes to the park on Tuesdays.'

I wanted to explain that I wouldn't be going there again, and about getting sun through my window, but I decided to be quiet. The cat was enough for one day. I would just tell them I was going to go out.

'It's alright, I will go for a walk tomorrow, I'll get fresh air.'

'Alright, then. Just pay attention to the cat. You know, stroke it.'

I felt upset when I heard Grandpa say that. I looked back at the kitten. I wanted to move it on to its sleeping cushion.

I felt uneasy until the door closed behind them. Mother gave me a smile, and said she would see me next week. Grandpa gave me a wink, which I hated.

I sat still for a bit; the kitten didn't move and I didn't really want to wake it. Eventually I had to go to the bathroom and when I came back the kitten was stretching. I decided to get my routine back on track so I pulled the bin bag out of the bin and tied it up. I put my left trainer on ready to go outside, and then went to put my right one on. As I picked it up off the floor, I could smell something bad. The kitten hadn't used the litter tray, it had made a mess on the floor next to my shoe. I threw the shoe away across the room and put my hand over my mouth and nose and opened the window. I pulled off my other shoe, laces still done up, which you are not supposed to do, and ran to the sink and scrubbed my hands until they were sore. I put on my washing-up gloves, trying to ignore the stink in the room, which was overwhelming me.

Tabby had only just arrived, and so far I had stared at it for three hours while it slept and now I had a flat that stank and I had to somehow get rid of the mess on the floor. I filled up a bowl with water and washing-up liquid and carpet cleaner like Mother had done once when my brother was sick on the carpet, and got out my cleaning wipes and some toilet paper. I picked up what I could and dropped it into the toilet, gagging, then took a cloth and rubbed and rubbed, then put bleach where it had been, then more water, then more bleach. The carpet looked paler but the smell was less. I would have to throw my shoes away, you can't have one shoe, and the one which was close to the mess must be covered in germs. I undid the bag and with the gloves on I picked up the trainers one at a time and put them into the half-filled rubbish bag that I had been about to take down. My heart was pounding so hard I thought I would faint. Last of all I put the gloves I had used in too.

In my socks I went downstairs, re-tied the bag neatly and laid it on top of the bin, trying to be calm, and I tried to breathe slowly. As soon as I went upstairs and opened my door the smell hit me, it hadn't gone, and I got out the air-freshening spray and sprayed everywhere. I sat on the sofa and tried to think. How could one little animal make everything such a mess and put a whole life's routine out this much?

No sooner had I sat down, Tabby started to jump up on my leg. It had its claws out and it hurt a bit, they were very sharp. I told it to stop, calmly, and asked it to get down but it didn't seem to hear and I was panicked now. How was I supposed to control it if it wouldn't take simple instructions? Just as I was about to call cat protection for advice, it landed on my lap. This meant I was completely stuck and I sat there, rigid, while the kitten pushed into me, and put its claws in and out, and made a noise like a mobile phone vibrating. This was not relaxing. I sat rigid, held prisoner, and I couldn't even turn the light on or get a glass of water and I had only had two today, so I could get dehydrated. I tried to lift it off, but it was attached by its claws.

I didn't like cats.

When Tabby eventually woke up it was nearly five o'clock. The sun had gone round the other side of the building and I hadn't turned the light on. The cat had wasted my whole day and now it jumped down, as if it had lived in my flat all its life, and started miaowing really loudly for such a tiny body. I had seen cats do that on TV and they always wanted food, so I prepped its food carefully, with my hand over my mouth as I dug it out of the tin. It stank of old fish guts and I tried not to be sick in my mouth. I kept my yellow rubber gloves on so at least my hands wouldn't get contaminated. I also filled its water bowl while it ate. When it had finished the whole tin, it repeated the pooing of earlier, this time in the litter tray, which smelt just as bad, and I had to empty that, and, although I thought about putting it in the toilet like Grandpa said, I decided to get another bin bag and go downstairs again. I didn't want to share a toilet with an animal. By the time I got upstairs, it was asleep again. I was exhausted, and happy that I didn't have to worry now it was sleeping. I decided not to put the television on in case it woke it up. Sleeping cat was the least trouble, and I decided I liked it best like that.

I needed to achieve something other than looking after the cat today, so I sat down to continue my research. There was something comforting about being back on my chair, in front of the computer. I could forget about the cat, and try and breathe calmly. It would have been even better if I could have looked out through the window and watched the world go by, but most of the light was gone now, and I had missed the quiet time of the day. Watching people in the rush hour made me anxious, nothing but running for buses or horns blaring. This was another disturbing day. I started to itch but I stared at the screen and slowly calmed down.

Just as I found a really helpful website, the phone rang. It made me jump and I then looked over at Tabby in case he woke up. He didn't. It was probably Mother wanting to find out how things were going with the cat. I left it, but it was stressful letting a phone ring. It stopped after fifteen rings and I sat for a moment then did my centring exercise and breathing, checked the kitten was still asleep and walked to the kitchen to prepare something to eat. I would make pancakes, white ones – that always soothed me. I loved mixing the milk into the powder and I loved the taste. The smell from the kitten was in the kitchen area as well, and I started to worry that there could be germs in the air. I washed my hands and the bowl for the pancakes

and the spoon in very hot water with soap. Then I washed the frying pan, then I made the pancakes.

I got them to the table and sat down. Better. Just as I was lifting the fork to my lips, the phone started ringing again. That was twice in fifteen minutes. I didn't want to speak to my mother and I didn't pick up. I could be busy with the kitten, or outside at the bins. Mother knew I hated being rung over and over again and she never usually did it.

I had strategies, I had learned them at school, and I knew I had too much stress on me at the moment. Whoever would get a cat to relax them I had no idea. I was doing everything right, trying not to panic, but then the phone started ringing again. This time the persistent ring tone carried on echoing through my brain even after it stopped and I couldn't even sit still, my hands were waving around, and I twisted up against the frustration of it all.

Fifteen rings. It was like torture, surely Mother should know that. Ring ring, it started again and it felt unbearable. My elbows were really itching now and the little bumps on my arms felt enormous. I could be developing stress hives; my blood pressure was probably very high. I thought if Mother was ringing this often perhaps it was an emergency. Grandpa could be dead, which might mean I would never be a proper man because he hadn't finished showing me everything, but I did think I might be calmer if he wasn't visiting. I couldn't think of any other emergencies that would need this many phone calls. I covered my ears with my hands. It had to stop now, it was driving me mad.

From behind me I heard a miaow.

I walked over to the phone and for a moment I considered smashing it on the wall, but I knew that would upset Mother so I didn't. Usually I was coping, I was coping just fine.

I picked up the phone and I listened. Nothing. I waited and then said, 'Hello?'

A voice I had never heard said hello back and before I could say wrong number I heard my name. The day was getting worse and worse and I listened to see what they were ringing to say, on my tiptoes, in my smelly flat.

'Is that Nick?'

'Yes, this is Nick.'

'Hi, this is Karen Watson, your neighbour from upstairs.'

I knew I was supposed to say something but I didn't. I had never had a day like this, never. Mother said to me sometimes, 'I am speechless'. I knew what she meant, and felt myself backing up until the wall was behind me. I leant on it.

'I saw your note, downstairs.'

She paused. I said nothing, trying to work out what she meant, and then I realised, I had put up a note. It was my note. I couldn't deal with this today but I tried to be polite. It was on my list.

'Yes.'

'You're looking for work and I might be able to help. I work at University Hospital and some of my colleagues in the mortuary are looking for an assistant.'

I wanted this conversation to end. I waited, but she wasn't going away.

'What do you think?'

Her voice was a bit sharp, like my mother when she was talking to Grandpa. I leant harder against the wall.

'I don't know.'

'Don't worry; if you're at home I could drop by and tell you more about it.'

'I can't, I have a lot on, I've just got a cat.'

'That's nice. Are you still looking for work, though?'

I wanted to say no but for some reason I said yes because it would be wrong to lie. I can keep secrets, Grandpa had taught me that was alright and sometimes it was the right thing to do for your own good, but I can't lie. I tried to think of a way to get her not to come, but she was talking all by herself and the end of what she said was that she was coming to my flat.

I put the handset down and sat down on the sofa next to the cat. I felt like passing out. The room was blurry from me nearly crying. It was a mess. There were things everywhere and I didn't know where they belonged. I needed help.

The cat seemed to want things from me that I didn't enjoy. There might be something wrong with it, as I hadn't read anything anywhere about cats being this demanding.

It tapped me with its paws, and scratched the sofa and started to walk around sniffing the air curiously. It started running as if it was chasing something across the floor but nothing was there. It even chased its own tail. It didn't listen to any instructions to stop or slow down and in between the running it would lie down for a little while and do the mobile phone noise. It was crazy, and full of energy. It ran around everywhere, pulling, pushing, making noises and making me feel out of control. Then it pooed again, in the tray. The flat smell was enough to put me off fish for ever. How could one tiny kitten make this much waste? I went to the toilet every morning myself, but this was ridiculous. I grabbed it and put it back in its travel box. Then I took it to the bathroom and closed the door. I couldn't breathe. I put the tray outside the window on the window sill and closed the window. The flat still smelt of cat and fish. I thought I'd better call Grandpa and tell him how hard I found it. I tried to remember what Mother had said: *A kitten is company, a friend, sweet, cute.*

I hadn't seen any of that yet.

I sat back down, put the television on, but in the broken world I had wandered into today the first thing I saw was a picture of the park and the two people who had been doing disgusting things by the lake. I turned it off. Quickly. Sweat was running off me, and the cat was still in its basket in the bathroom. I opened the door and lifted it out, put it next to the wall and opened the leather straps.

That was when I heard a knock on the door. I tried to flatten myself against the wall, tripped over the cat basket, and the pile of books on the shelf above hit the floor with a bang. She knew I was in here. The kitten miaowed and I thought I might scream, something I never did, but which had already happened once this week with Grandpa. I didn't scream, though; instead I stood still.

My neighbour pushed the letterbox open, and shouted in, 'Nick, it's Karen, your neighbour.'

'It's not a good time at all at the moment.'

'Don't worry, I won't keep you, I just wanted to say hi and give you some information about the job. Also, I love kittens.'

I thought carefully about what to do. I didn't want Grandpa or Mother to know I wasn't coping, but she didn't know either of them so she wouldn't tell. She was a doctor, so she wouldn't be lying. She had a job. I needed work. I walked towards the door and slowly pressed the handle up and then down, which is how you open that door.

I wiped the sweat off my face but I only opened the door a little bit to start with, so that I could see her. She looked as grey as ever to me. This time she was drenched from the rain and she made some remark about how she hated umbrellas. She didn't look me in the eye, which was a relief, and I tried to stick to the list in another way: make conversation.

'Umbrellas can be practical,' I pointed out.

She was taking out a bunch of papers from her Asda bag, which I could see had the University Hospital logo on it. I knew it was their logo because it said the name underneath the curly UH.

'So, about this job. When would you be available to start? They are very keen to get someone in as soon as possible.'

I thought about it, then I remembered my mother saying, *one thing at a time, Nick*, so I asked her, 'Do you want a cat?'

This stopped her talking in the middle of her sentence and she frowned. 'Your new cat? Didn't you say you just got the cat?'

'Yes, but I don't like it. It's under the sofa but I don't want to get it out because it scratched me earlier, it makes a mess everywhere and it has too much energy. It's called Tabby, you can have it, I will get it.'

She laughed, and I didn't, and then she started talking again, but she came into my flat, past me, her coat dripping on the floor and her hair flopping in front of her face. She went into the living room without asking.

'You can have all the stuff, the bed, the tray, the food, all of it,' I said. 'I can have a job but I can't have a cat and a job and I think a job is better.'

'Don't be silly, cats are very independent. You can leave Tabby here in the day, with some food and his tray. He's probably just nervous. I love cats, but I can't have one, I sometimes work all night, at the hospital.'

She reached under the sofa and pulled the cat out. You aren't really supposed to do that because kittens can't retract their claws and they could be ripped out of their paws which I didn't want to see, but I didn't really care about Tabby so I didn't tell her that.

Karen sat down on the sofa. I started to put the cat's things into a bag.

'Nick, I can't take the cat. I wish I could. I will ask around and see if I know anyone who wants one. Do you want to hear about the job? It's in the hospital where I work, in a place called the morgue. It's the place where they keep bodies when people die in the hospital or on their way to the hospital. Do you mind dead bodies? Are you scared of them?'

I didn't know why anyone would be scared of dead bodies. Did they have germs? What if they had been ill and you got their illness?

'I don't think I am scared of dead bodies. Can you get germs from them?'

'No, Nick, it's sterile, you wash the bodies with surgical gloves on, and it's cold. They are kept in fridges and it's just a big science lab really. I just wanted to check, but you will be able to tell really quickly if it is too much for you.'

'I think it will be a good job for me if it's clean and in a hospital.'

I was going to have to find a solution to the cat, but I could think about that when Karen had gone. I just wanted to be on my own. My arms were wrapped round my middle, and I had sweat running down my back. I needed to stay calm or Karen would think I wasn't coping and change her mind about the job. This was too much pressure.

'How many hours a week do you think you could work, Nick? I could give you a lift in until you are used to it, and they will show you the ropes? It's from eight until twelve-thirty Monday to Thursday to start with, and you can do a week's trial, would that be good? Just part-time.'

'Part-time, yes, that's good. I have things to do every day of the week so that way I could still fit them in.'

I felt fine every time I thought about the job. It was a big step but I wanted to do it. It was time for Karen to go now.

'You will be responsible for washing the bodies, preparing them for their families to come and say goodbye, wheeling people down from the wards to the morgue, assisting with autopsies, whatever is needed. I have a job description form here, and you should look it over so you know what you will be doing. I can come back when you have signed this confidentiality form to pick it up, and I'll bring the contract.'

I didn't want her to visit every day of the weekend so I made a decision.

'I will sign it now, and I can start on Monday if you want me to. I just need you to go now, and not come back today. I have things to do.'

I had said it, out loud, and I picked up the paper, and Karen showed me where to sign, and I signed and she left. I sat by the window trying not to look at the dirty cat tray outside in the rain, and tried to think what to do next.

I decided to lie on the bed and close my eyes. I tried to make some sense of the last four days but I just felt fear and panic and wanted to run away, from the pictures in my head, from the mess and the smell and the kitten who had now seen that I had moved and climbed up the side of the base then the mattress with its claws and started to knead the pillow. It wouldn't leave me alone.

I got up and went to the computer, I needed to calm down. I googled 'pure girls' then clicked images; I had decided not to watch videos ever again. The problem was, for me, that I liked the girls lying in cornfields, or on beaches with plaits, but it was hard to resist wanting to see them moving. I was looking at a girl in a gingham dress when suddenly a message popped up between her parted legs, flashing at me.

DO YOU WANT TO FUCK ME? I AM ONLY TWO MILES AWAY.

This was the final straw, and I was up on my tiptoes, hands twisted, trying to make it go away. How did she know where I was? How did she know who I was? I banged at the keyboard with my fist and sat back down, desperate now just to stop the images and the flashing sign. Just as I found Control Alt Delete, Tabby jumped and attached himself to my leg, through my trousers. I tried to pull him off, while the picture of the girl called Meg in her pretty dress carried on asking me the same question. Her perfect little breasts and the skirt which just covered her panties mixed up with the pain in my leg and my worries about the germs on my trousers.

My head was starting to spin and there were whole sequences of unrelated images playing in my brain that I didn't want there. I realised I was sobbing. The pressure in my head was making the floor vibrate, my eyes pulsating behind my eyelids.

Sweat was trickling down my forehead again. I hated sweat and I needed a shower. It was all because of the cat. It was on a campaign to make my life hell. My nostrils were full of the new smell of the flat, everything was out of place, there was cat equipment everywhere, strangers were turning up at my door and my life was on the television. I couldn't cope and Grandpa would see that next Wednesday and tell mother and she would make me move back to her house, and Grandpa would have to correct me then, for my own good.

I wanted to say it out loud, I CAN'T COPE WITH THIS CAT, but I didn't. Instead I paced up and down my living room saying, 'Right decisions, I must make them.' It was something I had seen on a documentary on BBC2. It didn't help.

The miaowing was getting louder, or my ears were getting more sensitive. The cat seemed to have a built-in megaphone. I really, really wanted it to be quiet. I told it to be quiet one last time, then I picked it up to put it in the bathroom for the night. It wasn't the way you are supposed to pick up a cat, I knew that from the website. I picked it up underneath its head and put my thumb on its throat to make it be quiet. It worked. Under the fur its bones and its neck were tiny, and I could feel gulping as I pressed my thumb in further. I just needed a minute to think. Peace.

I sat on the sofa holding Tabby out in front of me, and its little feet jumped around a bit. It was trying to scratch me. Then its neck went click in my fingers and it went completely still. I picked up its sleeping cushion with the other hand and lay Tabby on it. He was quiet, and calm. The rain had stopped and I watched people and cats coming and going while I sat with my pet, keeping each other company. The phone didn't ring, and no one came to the door. I took off all my clothes and put them into another bin bag. If I kept on going through clothes like this Mother would not be happy. I would have to get back in control. It was sensible that my clothes all might get worn out at once, though; they were the same age because she bought them all at the same time. I left the bin bag of clothes next to the pile of cat equipment, except the litter tray which I left outside the window for now, and added all the printing I had done on kittens to the bag. I didn't tie it up because I was going to put Tabby in there before I left in the morning. I went into the bathroom, then I had a long hot shower.

Tabby was still on his cushion and I decided I liked him better like this, he was nicer. Perhaps working with dead people wouldn't be such a bad idea. I carried him to the bed and got into my pyjamas, and lay in my usual position. I fell asleep next to him, thinking about the job, and my still, calm kitten, that I now liked very much.

6 | Karen

*'I put my heart and my soul into my work, and
lost my mind in the process.'*

— Vincent van Gogh

Saturday morning

Karen lay in bed and thought about the past few days.
She felt satisfied and as if her normally uneventful life was
taking on a new dimension. She had woken up yesterday
to the sound of her neighbour closing her flat door, and
realised that she had spent the whole night sleeping next
to him. That was new. She hadn't had any sort of physical
contact with a man for over two years, and when she had
it had always been at his place or an anonymous hotel.
Now she found herself living under the same roof as a
man she had spent the night with, which could make her
life more complicated but at least Charlie couldn't call her
a dried-up old spinster and be completely right any more.
Friday had disappeared as she worked out how best to
incorporate Nick into her study. She had worked from
home, not even getting dressed, and now she had a plan.
It might be Saturday but there would be someone at the
hospital morgue, there always was. People didn't die on

schedule and she wanted to take Nick's forms there as quickly as she could before they gave the job to someone else. This was so much more exciting than her night with Tam, as she had discovered her night-time companion was called. Nick could be the guinea pig she had been searching for to complete her thesis. Diagnostically, as far as she could tell so far, he sat exactly on the line between functional and non-contributory, and Karen's passion was to get those individuals into society, working, studying, living a useful life.

She jumped out of bed, showered and dressed. Nick's forms were in her handbag and she was filled with a new sense of purpose. At the bottom of the Asda carrier she always used to transport work papers she had a little stub of lipstick that had absorbed tissue and crumbs, but now she stood in front of the mirror, dipped her little finger into it and smeared it on to her lips and her cheeks. She would feel a little bit better if she saw Tam on the way out now. She decided not to tie her hair up; it looked wild and she shook her head gently. A little woolly and streaked with grey but, she thought, less severe. She headed downstairs with the hint of a smile on her face. She would show everyone. She would be vindicated and Nick would be the catalyst of her redemption. She could see Charlie's face when he had to apologise, and her children congratulating her, while Nick worked happily and successfully at a job that he would never have got without her and she won the respect of family and friends with her brilliant thesis and important work.

One flight of stairs down and she passed Nick's door, hesitated, then knocked.

'Nick?'

There was no answer from inside, not even the faint miaowing of the kitten. He must have popped out. She needed to make firm arrangements for Monday. Perhaps they could go in together – once she had retrieved her car and filled it with petrol. She felt slightly more benevolent towards the human race this morning; although she understood that what she had shared with Tam was purely a one-night stand, for some reason she still felt less judgemental towards the shortcomings of others. Perhaps it was the release of sexual tension; she must remember how useful it was going forward.

She opened the front door, and her mood descended from what were the heights of joy for Karen to instant misery. Her ex-husband was standing outside leaning against her car, arms crossed and an expression on his face which slowed Karen's pace almost into reverse.

She was still five feet from him when he shouted, 'What the fuck is wrong with you?'

Even through the shakiness which his fury always induced in her, she retained a little of the earlier unusual cheer. 'Nothing's wrong with me. What do you mean?'

'You think nothing's wrong with you? Do you know your children's names? Do you have any fucking idea what is going on in their lives? Jack walked off the football pitch halfway through his game this morning. Apparently you promised to come and watch his social side, having already failed to get the forms in for the school club. He looked out for you when he scored a goal and when you still weren't there he legged it. You're a joke. The great scientist. You should stop doing experiments on strangers and start looking at what's under your nose. You're damaging your children while trying to fix people who probably had mothers just like you. You're pathetic. Sarah told me your last words were, "See you at the weekend, at football, I promise." Nice touch, the promise – kids tend to believe those even from absent parents.'

Karen remembered now. She had got so caught up with the possibilities for Nick and her unexpected night of lust that it had gone out of her head. She stood, head down, trying to think how to explain. The images of her children congratulating her on academic success were receding fast. From round the corner Karen heard rustling. She hadn't realised it, but she had started crying and her nose was running. She grubbed around in her bag for a tissue and by the time she had found a crumpled one that had seen better days Nick had appeared in front of her. He must have been at the bins. She had seen him before on a Saturday, wiping them down and putting them straight after the bin men had been on a Friday. Now he stood in front of her, looking agitated and stepping first to her left and then to her right. Karen realised it was because she was blocking the doorway.

'Sorry, Nick.' She stood to one side and blew her nose, then started dabbing at her eyes. The remnants of the lipstick she had smeared on ten minutes before were on the tissue.

'So who the fuck is this, then? Very cosy, and since when did you wear lipstick to work?'

Nick was hurrying towards the door.

'Are you her boyfriend? She likes guys who can't step on the cracks in the path; you're right up her street. Did she mention she had three kids, and an ex-husband?'

Nick was standing on the step in front of the door with his hands clamped over his ears. His key had fallen on to the paving stones below and he didn't have a free hand to pick it up with. Karen turned, and unlocked the door for him, handing him back his key, which he took after he'd pulled his jacket sleeve down to cover his hand. Karen understood: germs. When he was safely inside, Karen turned back to her ex-husband.

'Typical of you to pick on someone vulnerable. Don't you understand? My work is vitally important. I am trying to help a vast swathe of misdiagnosed people with my research. There is an epidemic out there of illnesses which are being put under the all-encompassing umbrella of autism and there are a huge number of permutations and symptoms that haven't even been classified yet. There are hundreds of thousands of people; students, mathematicians being lost to society once they are labelled autistic. Do you understand that some of the great minds of history would be classified as autistic today? Albert Einstein, Michelangelo, Mozart, Hans Christian Andersen – they would all be considered on the spectrum, and probably drugged up to the eyeballs on antipsychotics or playing endless computer games. Don't you understand that sacrifices are necessary to rectify that? I work as hard as I do to make life better for millions of people. I'm proud of that. What am I supposed to have done wrong? Not told the kids a bedtime story? I was *working*. I made sure they got to school, I fed them – just leave me alone.'

It was the first time Karen had ever tried to explain to her husband what she felt or what she was trying to achieve. For a moment it seemed to have helped, as he was silent. Her relief at being able to put into words the rationale for the long hours in front of her computer, the weeks of research, to express the reasons behind it, gave her courage, and she stood, momentarily defiant, and waited.

'Have you ever heard of balance, you stupid, stupid woman?'

Charlie was shouting now, and from the window on the first floor Karen heard a high-pitched screeching noise which she knew instinctively was coming from Nick's flat.

'Karen, you have children, you have responsibilities, don't you understand that? Play God all you want, cure the whole fucking human race, but has it occurred to you that for someone with so many letters after their name you're incapable of making anyone happy, even yourself?'

Karen was frozen now, as the tirade got nastier and nastier and her husband got closer and closer. He was almost on top of her now, flecks of white spit on his lips, and he was so close she had to bend her neck to look up at him, like a snake hypnotised by a mongoose.

'Look at the state of you, look in the mirror. You're a fucking embarrassment. The best thing for everyone concerned would be if you just disappeared. You're a frigid, ugly old bitch with ice for a soul and I wish I'd never met you.'

Karen sensed Tam before she saw him and shame filled her. He walked up the path in her peripheral vision while Charlie carried on shouting, oblivious to the approaching newcomer.

'Excuse me,' Tam said, putting down his shopping on the path.

'Just go round us, mate, we're talking here.'

'Yes, I caught some of it. Karen, are you alright, can I help?'

'What the fuck is going on in this house?' shouted Charlie. 'It's very cosy all of a sudden. Why would *you* be able to help? Just mind your own business and fuck off.'

'I think abusive men *are* my business.'

Tam's arm was between them now, and this intervention broke the lock between her and the father of her children, the man she supposed she must have loved when she was twenty and they had first got together and who still had the power to make her doubt everything about her choices. She dropped her shoulders and her whole body felt weak, as if it was about to crumple into a ball.

'This isn't over, you stupid cunt. I need some backup with the kids, I'm drowning. Email me a schedule and stick to it, and turn up for parents' evening next week. You're supposed to be an academic even if you've never published an original thought in your life.'

Another wail came from inside the house, followed by repetitive banging.

'That's enough,' said Tam. 'Karen, come inside.'

As she turned towards the door something hit her hard in the back then landed at her feet. Car keys.

'I sorted the car out for you too, as you seem to be the only member of the human race who can't put petrol into a tank. It was sitting on the pavement on my route to work all week collecting tickets and I couldn't drive past it one more time. You're lucky they didn't tow it away. How've you been getting to work? Cabs, don't tell me. Can't pay for Jack's football club but you can go backwards and forwards to the hospital in a taxi. Don't worry about the money for filling it up, or the tickets, I'll pay those as well, shall I? Fucking stupid bitch.'

Charlie carried on as Karen let Tam lead her through the hall and to the door of his flat. He sat her on his sofa and made her a cup of sweet tea. She was going to explain how bad sugar was for you, what it did to your pancreas, but she stopped herself. She sipped her tea and then for the second time that morning she started to cry.

'I think I should go and check on Nick. I was talking to him about a job and...'

She trailed off. Tam was standing in front of her holding out his hand and pointing at his ceiling. 'Silence is golden. You can go later,' he said, as he pulled her towards him and kissed her.

Karen was lying on her back in Tam's bed. She couldn't see Tam's head, it was under the sheets, between her legs. She couldn't respond enough to be stressed about the intermittent buzzing from her phone, in her bag by the door. She was a pool of molten jelly quivering like agar without a thought in her head, and when he lifted himself up in one smooth movement, and pushed into her, his mouth closed over her moaning one as she came, and she couldn't even hear the renewed banging on the ceiling above them.

Later – Karen had lost all sense of how much later – reality returned to her, this time in the form of a cup of coffee. Tam brought it to her, or what was left of her, spreadeagled across his bed with no worries about modesty or where she should be. She seemed to have lost direction completely. She sat up and shook her head briskly. She looked at Tam, who was staring at her with a huge grin on his face.

'You're full of surprises. That is the best time I've had in bed for years.'

Karen opened her mouth to speak but he interrupted her.

'Drink your coffee, it's a Saturday and you're all mine, nowhere to go at the weekend, or do you just ignore those conventions too?'

Karen remembered then, about Nick, and the morgue and the job.

'Oh, God, can you hand me my phone please?'

Tam walked over to the door and dug into her bag, took out the ancient Nokia and handed it over.

'A message from Jack, one from Sarah, and one from Pete in the morgue saying he'll be there till two. Oh, and two from Charlie, my ex-husband. You met him earlier.'

'What's the story there? He looks like a real charmer. What was he so upset about?'

Karen hated talking about her ex-husband nearly as much as she hated discussing her work, and she hesitated. It had been a very long time since she had shared anything with anyone and she was out of the habit. She hardly knew this guy, even though they might have spent a few hours of their respective lives making each other happy in some very intimate ways. She took a deep breath. Even as a scientist she would have to acknowledge that her life had been delivering little in the way of contentment, except where her work was concerned. Perhaps it was time she tried again, took a chance and tried to engage with the human race. She wasn't convinced but she would give it a go.

She chose her words carefully.

'I am very dedicated to my work. It frustrates my ex-husband and I think it's beginning to affect my children. It's difficult, but I can't just give it up. I know how important my work is; it has implications for far more people than the five in my family. Important discoveries demand personal sacrifices.'

Tam was standing over her, and his head was slightly on one side, with a gentle lopsided grin on his face. 'Well, I think we've sorted out a bit of the work-life balance this week, and as for the kids, they're yours; everyone prioritises their own kids above their work, don't they, so why doesn't he just give you a break? I'm sure he knows how much you love them and that they come first.'

Karen didn't really remember getting dressed, or the furious push that was almost a slap she delivered to Tam as he tried to put his arm on her shoulder to slow her down. She was going to the hospital and she was going to drop these forms off, Saturday or no Saturday. She had spent the last couple of days clearing the backlog of paperwork and tidying up her case files so that she could use all her time to concentrate on Nick and finishing her thesis. Fuck men. Fuck opening up. She slammed his door, crossed the hall and went upstairs. As she left she could hear Tam protesting,

'For God's sake, what did I do? One minute we were talking like grown-ups and then you just up and leave and nearly take me out on the way through. What's going on? Did I say something?'

Karen took the first flight of stairs two at a time and stood outside Nick's flat. She waited for a moment and collected herself. Tam might have been good at sex but he was an idiot. Men had no idea what it was like to be a working woman and a mother. She took a breath and knocked decisively. Nothing. She wasn't giving up this time.

'Nick, I am taking your confidentiality form to the hospital now. I have also downloaded the contract, and you can sign that if you want so that I can tie everything up today. It's only a zero-hours contract but it will be made permanent if you're a good fit. Are you still happy to start on Monday?'

She tried to contain her temper. She could sense that Tam was in the hall below her listening, and she could see that Nick was at the computer, back to her, because she was now bent over looking through his letterbox.

She waited.

'Nick?'

'I will come on Monday. The cat ran away. I can start but please stop coming to my door. I am busy.'

Karen understood. She hated interruptions, and she hated unexpected interruptions most of all. Nick sitting tapping away on his keyboard had focused her mind. 'OK, just pick up your pen and sign where I've made a red mark and I will leave you alone. Meet me downstairs at 7 a.m. on Monday morning. I'll give you a lift in and show you where to go.'

After a minute Nick pushed the contract, signed, back under the door and she picked it up. She didn't even bother to go and shower; she almost ran downstairs, ignoring Tam who was still standing at his open door, and went down the path to her car, trying to look dignified, and in control and unbothered by what had just happened. She got into the front seat and dug a scrunchie from under the handbrake. She gathered up her hair, which was still loose, and reversed towards the road…

If there was one thing that reminded Karen of what was important and restored a feeling of order when life got on top of her it was driving into her own parking space at the hospital. Seeing her name, the initials and her title seemed to calm her, and restore her faith in herself a little. She put all thoughts of Tam's admittedly pleasing face out of her mind, and slotted her car in next to the shiny new BMW belonging to the head of neural science. She locked up and followed the signs to the morgue, called the lift using her ID card to overcome the restricted access to the lower floors, and walked alone down the sterile corridor, holding the contract, the confidentiality agreement and Nick's CV. She recognised the chatty forensic pathologist from the previous day's lunch in the canteen and stopped him.

'Hi, I don't know if you recognise me; we were sitting on the same table in the canteen yesterday? I emailed you about my neighbour, and you sent me through a job spec and a zero-hours contract.'

His face was blank, but that wasn't a surprise to Karen. She rarely made much of an impression on men, despite the unexpected evidence to the contrary of the last couple of days. He hesitated, probably hoping for more clues.

'I have a neighbour who needs a job, and I showed him what you sent through and he can start Monday.'

'Well, there's nothing like getting straight to the point. Does he have experience? Although he is our only applicant so the question is only a formality.'

'I don't think he does have experience, but he's very neat, diligent and clean and he can do the hours. I can give him a character reference and a lift in on Monday morning so that you can meet him and go through everything.'

'Wow, that's above and beyond. We're really struggling down here without an assistant; we had to have someone in from an agency today and he freaked out and went home after a young road-traffic victim came in DOA. You've saved the day. I'm sorry, my name's Pete. I should have introduced myself yesterday. I didn't even realise you were listening.'

Karen smiled. 'Don't worry, I wasn't there long, I just happened to overhear and looked for your details in the hospital directory. Just to let you know that Nick is quiet; he likes routine. I think you'll be fine together. I think he has Asperger's, mildly, which means he'll be extremely organised, and brilliant at the job; just treat him gently.'

Karen's conscience, which had been niggling at her, was assuaged. She had covered the thorny topic of Nick's differences, and hopefully that would mean everyone would understand the boundaries and take it slowly with him.

'As long as he can do the job and muck in, we'll take him.'

Karen walked away, mission accomplished, completely unaware that Pete was still talking. Small talk had never interested her and she needed to get on with her planning. She had done more than enough human interacting for one week. All she knew was that she needed Nick close, where she could watch him and his reactions. He was the perfect case study, and this way he would be under her nose both here and at home. Life was beginning to make sense again.

7 | Tam

'*Selfishness is not living as one wishes to live, it is asking others to live as one wishes to live.*'

— Oscar Wilde

Saturday morning

Tam stood by the open door of his flat, baffled. He hadn't seen that coming at all. He rubbed his stubbly chin and did up a couple of buttons on the crumpled shirt he had pulled on after Karen had stormed out of his flat. He felt strangely squashed. If you had asked him to pick a sexual mate out of a line-up, Karen wouldn't even have merited a second glance, but he realised that he had been strangely drawn in by her need, and in particular the need she had suddenly seemed to have for him.

He kicked himself mentally for letting his guard down. She had made all the moves, and from pinning him on the bed and riding him like her life depended on it, to the headspinningly impressive moments, two of them, when he had come in her mouth, it had been a passionate and almost happy couple of encounters which he had hoped would become a habit. He thought they had fitted together, as bedmates at least, and she had given him no reason to think she didn't agree. Quite the opposite, not that he was complaining. It had been a long time, and feeling attractive and horny and desired had galvanised him into action, he had to admit. He had cleaned his flat, got his hair and beard trimmed, taken his washing to the launderette and begun to take an interest in what was going on out there in the big bad world. Karen had helped, and he had felt he was helping back. It had been a good feeling.

There hadn't been a lot of talking, just a lot of really surprisingly good sex and some mutual sleeping, but it had been cathartic, and in its own quiet way also healing. He had felt as if something had been delivered to his door in plain brown cardboard, and on opening had turned out to be something he had always wanted without even knowing it.

Perhaps that was why he found himself staring down the driveway after her, angry and disappointed, as her car reversed and then drove away without even a backward glance. Fuck it, women – there were plenty more out there. He had tried a new way of looking at things, and it hadn't worked out. He went back into the flat, which smelt of sex, had a shower and chucked the condoms from earlier into the bin. He took out the bin bag and went out to chuck it away.

He had been weighing up his work options. There didn't seem to be many employment opportunities for raffishly attractive men in their forties with a broad pair of shoulders and a good nose for trouble, unless he became a private detective. He walked towards the bins in his bare feet. The drizzle of the day before had been replaced by a weak sun and blue sky, and Tam vaguely contemplated googling 'How to start up a private investigation business' when he had finished his chores.

He lifted the lid and his morning irritation disappeared as he looked inside. The bin had been emptied the day before and now contained only one bag. Again it was white and translucent, and had been laid on the bottom of the spotless receptacle neatly at ninety degrees. Tam decided he really needed a hobby; he was becoming obsessed with his neighbours' rubbish. He put his bags down, leant in and lifted the bag out carefully. This time, instead of folded clothes, he could make out the shape of a small cat, in a sleeping position, laid carefully on a cushion and another pile of clothes. What the fuck? Next to the bins, with a note bearing the legend PLEASE TAKE THESE THEY ARE FREE, was a pile of cat equipment. He might be frustrated by a lack of police work but bloody clothing plus a possibly dead cat and discarded cat equipment merited further investigation. It would take his mind off Karen, anyway. Maybe it was a toy belonging to her absent kids – not that he had seen much evidence of anything as homely as that when had been up there. His nephew had once had to bring home a pretend baby which cried and needed its nappy changed; maybe it was an animal version of that. He put down his bag and tentatively prodded the cat-shaped object. This was no toy. It was definitely a real cat. He didn't know what the rules were for disposing of dead animals, but something was very wrong. He thought about the bag in his flat with the clothes inside it. He hadn't opened it since he had taken it out yesterday morning and dumped it in his freezer and now he was taking a dead kitten on a cushion in to join it.

He needed to call in a favour. He put the cat bag on the path, dumped his rubbish and carried the white bag, being careful to keep it flat, inside. He even looked left and right. He wasn't used to being spooked but the combination of so little sleep and coming off a bender, not to mention Miss Marathon Sex Sessions, was starting to mess with his mind as well as his body. He wasn't eighteen any more.

Tam opened the door of his flat and carried the cat-containing bag into the kitchen. He opened the lid of his under-stocked chest freezer and put the bag on the worktop. He flattened the bags of frozen peas, which were the only things in there, and laid the bin bag on top. You could freeze DNA and all that happened was that it became easier to analyse. He took out his phone and went through his work contacts. Who did he know in forensics?

As it turned out, his twenty-three years of work at the Met had left him with just one solid contact. Danny Morris had never been interested in promotion and he had stuck to his own methods of doing things in the face of endless initiatives and faceless chains of custody. He conformed just enough not to jeopardise a case, but still had a nose for trouble. In short, he was a kindred spirit. Tam was pretty sure that a dead cat in the bin and a bag full of clothes was not going to add up to much; it wasn't as if any crime had actually been committed, but at least this way he could get rid of the bags, and when he dropped them off with Danny he could divert on the way home and do some overdue shopping at Iceland. He had a niggle that wouldn't go away, and Danny would understand exactly what that meant.

He picked up the phone and dialled Danny's direct line. It felt weird tapping out the familiar first seven digits for the Met after all this time. Strange how the everyday could so quickly become the past.

He got an answering machine message, which he had been expecting on a Saturday. Danny wasn't the kind of guy who would have answered his phone at home. He would call back, though. At least Tam felt that he had taken control of the situation, and now all he could do was wait.

Tam was bored. Itchy feet, that was what this felt like. He should probably sit down and make a plan for starting a business or getting a start-up loan, but he had always hated the admin that came with any job, and that had been part of the problem. He pulled on his jacket, put on his shoes, and tried not to wonder what time Karen would be home.

As he opened the door, he realised that the pavement-jumping guy from upstairs who was now apparently Karen's pet project was hunched over the table by the door. He had taken a couple of days to put two and two together, and was embarrassed that he could have been living in the same house as someone he didn't even recognise on the street. The commissioner would love that, after all his talk of community and traditional policing. Tam waited as he scooped up the letters and flyers from the doormat and bundled them together, then methodically straightened them into a pile and moved the biggest to the bottom and carried on until they made a neat pyramid. He put them on the table below the clock, centred them, looked at them again and seemed satisfied. In one hand he held the red elastic band that had bound them together, plus some takeaway menus and a couple of flyers. He opened the front door, ignoring Tam completely, which wasn't difficult as Nick's eyes were on the movements of his feet and avoiding the cracks in the path as he headed for the bin.

Tam watched as he took a folded recycling bag from his pocket and dropped the rubbish into it. He folded it over neatly and laid it on the top of the bin. For a moment Tam held his breath. It had to be him. The cat and the clothes... there couldn't be two anally fixated OCD nutters using these bins. Nick seemed to notice nothing, not the missing bag nor Tam watching him from the front door. He put the lid down carefully, and walked off down the path, carrying the tower of items that had been next to the bins. A travelling basket, two cat bowls, various cat toys and the note Tam had seen before taped to them, saying, PLEASE TAKE THESE THEY ARE FREE. Tam watched as Nick put them down carefully by the gate and then turned left and out of sight.

Tam had a long day stretching ahead of him, and as he had already done the hardest bit, dressing, he decided to practise his rusty detecting skills and see what this strange guy with his letter-tidying habit and strange relationship with the bins was up to. There was definitely something going on here and he was the man for the job. Perhaps this could be his first case as a private detective and the guys at the Met would see that he had cracked a mystery using nothing but his nose and the instincts honed over years of being a copper. This was exactly the type of thing that just never got investigated any more. There were no policemen on the beat, no curious neighbours, no concerned citizens.

He followed Nick at a discreet distance – probably unnecessarily discreet as it turned out, as the younger man seemed completely locked in his own world – and waited to see where the afternoon would take them.

It was not a challenging few hours of sleuthing. Tam was able to keep up easily, and when it came to Tube stations he just hesitated for a couple of minutes at the top of the stairs while Nick made his way a stair at a time down into the depths. It was a lengthy procedure and getting on a Tube was interesting as sometimes Nick let three or four trains go without getting on them and there didn't seem to be any logic to this process because they were all going to the same place. When he eventually jumped on to one, it was at the last minute, and Tam started to wonder if there was a cunning plan to evade him, but as Nick's eyes never strayed in his direction he decided something else must be at play.

It was equally baffling working out when Nick was going to get off. Tam tried to combine looking at yesterday's *Evening Standard* casually with being poised to exit at the last minute. At one point they had gone from Victoria to St James's Park, then back past Victoria in the other direction to Sloane Square. Baffling. Maybe he was a spy with a really good cover. It was as if he couldn't decide whether to go home or carry on, and the more times they changed trains, the more agitated he got.

Two hours after Tam had ambled off after Nick down the path, they arrived at Putney Bridge station. Nick had finally jumped on to a District line train heading from Sloane Square to Wimbledon, and Tam had sat poised on the edge of his seat for six stops. Putney was always busy and Tam had to concentrate to keep track of Nick, as he ducked between oncoming bodies, and zigzagged the cracks.

Nick kept his head down the whole way to the High Street, and walked quickly until the pavement emptied out as they went up the hill, and Nick turned right on to Putney Heath. There was hardly anyone around at all, and Tam hung back, wishing he had a dog to help him blend in more. If anything Nick seemed even more in his own world now, muttering to himself and pulling at his sleeves. He seemed to know where he was going, and almost marched towards the wooded area ahead and down the hill. He had replaced dodging the cracks in the pavement with searching for dry patches of ground and almost jumping from one to the next. Tam kept well behind him as they were pretty much the only two making their way through the thick woods.

The walk ended where the Heath ended, with the A3 in front of them, six lanes of speeding traffic. Tam was very out of breath and had long ago stopped wondering where they were going. Instead, he could feel a burning in the back of his calves, and the shock of change from woodland to motorway was disorientating. They weren't done yet, and Nick turned left and walked along the pavement until he hit the Asda superstore and the underpass.

Once they were on the other side of the road, Tam now struggling for breath, Nick turned left, and with a gait somewhere between demented dancer and uncoordinated puppet he reached the gates to Richmond Park. Tam hung back as Nick went forward towards them, stepped back a few paces, went forward again and stopped. He repeated this strange ritual half a dozen times, after which he turned abruptly back towards Tam. Was that a moment of recognition, Tam wondered, or was he used to people staring at him?

Nick walked up the road a few yards and sat down at the bus stop. Thank fuck, they were getting the 190 bus back to Hammersmith. Why the hell couldn't he have taken that on the way here?

Tam sat at the back of the bus and waited to see whether Nick acknowledged him or showed any signs of recognition, but all he seemed to be doing was talking to himself. This private-eye business wasn't all it was cracked up to be. Between Karen and the route march this afternoon, though, at least he had kick-started his fitness plan.

He let Nick get off the bus first, then hung back at the bus stop until he saw him turn on to their road. He gave it five minutes, walked after him and bought himself a bottle of single malt at the off-licence then turned for home and let himself in. His flat no longer looked tidy, and he had only spring cleaned yesterday. Getting rid of his cleaner had been a mistake, although now he could make a fresh start with someone who wasn't an alcoholic. He would advertise; if his flat was clean he could concentrate on sorting out the rest of his life. He looked out of the window. Karen's car still wasn't outside. Tam poured himself five fingers of malt, decided against ice as the only bag he had was now under a part-frozen cat and some peas, chucked his sweaty shirt on the floor, and sat down to write a note for the newsagent's window.

CLEANER WANTED. START ASAP. LOCAL.
TWO MORNINGS A WEEK.

He added his number, and turned the news on. Still no leads in the case of the couple bashed over the head in broad daylight. He should have used his sleuthing skills there; he had been at the gates of Richmond Park earlier. He sipped his whisky and watched the families of the young couple appealing for information. The niggle in his brain was turning into a really nasty itch.

8 | Nick

'About morals, I know only that what is moral is what you feel good after and what is immoral is what you feel bad after.'

— Ernest Hemingway

Sunday morning

I had made a new list, just for the job days. I needed to because some days were full up now, and I tore up the old one and put it in the bin. Things would be different from now on, and I had to be on top of my routine. I was so happy that the cat wasn't here any more. I had tried to imagine getting ready, with the cat and all its stuff around me and the smell of the tray.

It made me feel like retching. I had put the kitten in the bin and the flat was back to normal except for the litter tray outside on the window sill. I just wouldn't look at it until I was ready to touch it.

Karen my neighbour was making me want to scream. A long time ago, when I was little, I used to scream when I wanted something because I couldn't find the words and if someone tried to put a scratchy jumper on me, or a stiff coat, all I knew to do was throw it on the floor and scream.

She was making me feel like that again. I didn't like being this close to someone who knew me. She was making me feel invaded. She was outside fighting with her children's father yesterday, and I could hear all their horrible words, then the policeman had come in his out-of-work clothes and taken her inside, and they had sex in his flat. It was obvious, moaning like in the park and then banging on the wall below me, just when I wanted a peaceful day and had got rid of the cat and all its mess. It was like having my mother living in the same building even though I had made it clear she couldn't just knock on the door, and she must have read it because she had posted me a note saying, *Be downstairs tomorrow morning at 7 a.m.*

She had told me this twice already and I am always on time, and I could easily get down there by setting my alarm. I was glad she was giving me a lift as long as I didn't have to talk to her or listen to her talk, or have the radio on. I would be able to work out how to go on public transport after I had been in her car once. I was very good at remembering directions, I had a visual brain and that was not a guess; a doctor had told me that as a diagnosis.

It was a good time to get a job now that the cat was gone. I was doing my best to get things back to normal but now even watching television was ruined by the story of the sex people in the park, so being out of my flat would be good. In the evenings I could watch other programmes but in the day the sex couple seemed to be there every time I turned the television on. No one seemed to be pointing out that they deserved it. It was against the law to have sex in the open air when other people were there and didn't want to see it. I had googled it.

When Karen couldn't take me, the journey to the hospital would involve walking and a bus ride. I didn't get on trains often as the smell of other humans was horrible. They pressed against you and I hated that so I always waited until there was a train or a bus with very few people on it. Mother and Grandpa were happy about the job. Mother didn't like the idea of a morgue because she doesn't like anything to do with death since my brother died. I still think it's a good job, and I am still starting tomorrow which is Monday. Grandpa was so happy that he had hardly asked about the cat. That was a closed book, as my grandpa would say.

I sat by the window and waited for Sunday to pass. I had to sit by the window on the right now, so that I didn't see the litter tray. It had filled up with water, and the grey litter had swelled up, full of germs. I had locked the window and checked that it was tightly closed. I would have to ask Mother to help, or my neighbour. I didn't want to ask either of them but I couldn't do it, I knew that much. I watched television but not the news channel, and I had fish and chips for supper which I only ever had on Sundays and I had to walk round the corner to get that and I finished it all. I would work very hard tomorrow to burn it off. Grandpa said it would make me fat round my middle, and strangle my heart with fat. Visceral fat that you can't see from the outside. It was still my favourite meal, but I only had it as a treat. Having a job in the morning, I gave myself a treat and Mother had told me to. She wanted to come and eat some with me, but Sundays are a quiet day.

* * *

The alarm went off at six a.m. I lay there as always for five minutes to wake up properly, then I got out of bed and put my slippers on to go to the bathroom and do my stretches. I put my slippers on the mat outside the bathroom, had my shower and dressed in my clothes, a white shirt and beige trousers. I combed my brown hair into a side parting and brushed my teeth until the buzzer went on the toothbrush. If you brush them longer you can hurt your gums.

Walking down the stairs, carefully putting two feet at a time on each step, I felt less happy than I thought I would. My hands were in balls by my side, and I couldn't get my heels on the floor. I was not good with change. I had a lot of change at the moment, which made me very stressed and I had to use my special techniques to cope with it. Usually my routine held me together, but it wasn't my routine any more. The last week had upset me. Changes never happened without this feeling coming with them. My head felt as if a mini-earthquake was happening. I nearly turned round and went back upstairs but Karen was waiting at the bottom. I could see the top of her head. It was only 6.50, so I didn't really know why. I wasn't late. Grandpa always says punctuality is the politeness of kings.

As I went down I decided that this had been the worst week since I moved into the flat. I didn't understand why any of this was happening to me. I had been given rules to live by and I had stuck to them. I was going to stick to my job and my flat only from now on until I felt settled again. If I couldn't go to the park without seeing sex, or carry on living the way I always had without a pet, feeling like this would keep on happening.

I was at the bottom of the stairs now, and I went straight to the front door because we were going out. I glanced at the doormat but the postman hadn't come yet so I would have to sort the letters when I came back. I would have to write all this down, adjusted to my new hours, but I wasn't sure of them yet. I felt a bit of panic pushing up, so I opened the door, and said hello and started to walk down the path. I had to think of Mother and Grandpa as well, and fit them in. Now that I didn't have the cat, I would ask if they could come together. I didn't want Grandpa to come any more by himself, and I had made him leave last week. I had a job now, and he had said lots of times that if I ever got a job he would eat his hat, which he hadn't done yet. I would ask Mother. Grandpa wouldn't like it, he always said, 'I know what you need,' but he didn't. Not always.

I had the picture of Grandpa stuck in my head all the way down the path, and I didn't even look to see if anyone had taken the cat things away from the pavement. Karen didn't have a clicker to open her car, so she had to use a key. I waited and got into the front seat. She was talking, but I couldn't get in and listen at the same time.

The journey to the hospital was a blur. The radio was on, and Karen was asking me questions, and there was traffic and noise outside. All the things I had hoped wouldn't happen were happening. It was too much noise and it felt like a dentist's drill in my ear. I put my hands over my ears and decided I would go in with her, see the job and then go straight home before things got worse. My foot was tapping, she was talking, my hand was rubbing against the opposite arm, and I turned away towards the window, with the noise creeping in through my fingers. My computer had said that the journey would take twenty-eight minutes. It lied. We arrived at 7.50 and it seemed like the whole world had arrived with us. People rushing, greeting, noise, stretchers – this was horrible.

'We are going through Accident and Emergency. You have to know where it is so that you can get back here if you need to collect anyone.'

I wanted to tell her that I was good at directions, but I didn't want my voice to add to the noises so I followed her. She had tried to take my arm, which had made me even more determined to get out of there. I didn't need another mother.

Karen started to walk through a series of security doors, which opened when she put a card on a pad. A green light beeped every time she did it and we must have walked through eight germ-covered doors. I saw that there were dispensers for hand sanitiser every time you went through a door, and I used it. That was very helpful, as the whole place looked dirty. I didn't like the beep of the door each time, but the crowds and the noise and the stretchers and the shouting and the sounds of people being sick got less with every set of doors, until it was quiet.

We took the lift down two floors. Karen kept smiling at me but she had stopped speaking, which was a relief.

The corridor was long and empty, her shoes on the tiles making the only noise. I was wearing my Adidas trainers and they are quiet. It was cold down here and the feeling of being underground was new. The sign above the long corridor in front of me read MORGUE. She stopped beneath it, so I stopped too, and she looked at me and said, 'Are you ready?'

'Yes,' I replied. My hands started to sweat. Was I supposed to have prepared something?

Just behind the doors two men were sitting around a table in a side room drinking tea and eating Hobnobs which I know because they are Mother's favourite biscuit.

'Morning, Karen, is this Nick?'

I looked at him, but kept my head bent as far forward as I could. I didn't like to meet people all at once. I looked up enough to see that he had dark hair, and his ears poked out through it on both sides of his head. His eyes were tiny and he had a pointy chin. He looked like a rat.

'Morning, Pete, morning, Mark. Yes, this is Nick, my neighbour. He's ready for work and keen to know all about the job.'

They both stopped what they were doing and looked straight at me. I didn't like that, so I looked back down at the floor.

'Hi, Nick, welcome. You've arrived in the nick of time!'

They both laughed and I knew it was a joke from the laughing. Karen joined in. I didn't.

'Right, the best way to get going is to get going.'

They all laughed again, I was pretty sure I was not even going to make it through the day if things carried on like this.

The one called Pete was talking at me.

'I'm a pathologist, and my friend here is a mortuary technician. I should tell you straight away that you will be seeing very little of us. You need to be able to work independently, once you know what you're doing.'

This cheered me up quite a lot. Then Karen said she would see me later and if I wanted a lift she would be outside by the car when I had finished, and drive me home in her lunch hour.

'If I don't like the job then I will get the bus.'

Everyone laughed again and my hand started rubbing my arm again. The patch I was rubbing was getting sore. Then it was just us, Pete and me. Mark stayed at the table.

'Follow me, Nick.'

We walked down a long corridor and came to a small seating area, with curtains in the middle of a wall.

'This is where relatives wait before they identify a body. We've got capacity for thirty in the fridges, and then extra capacity in the freezer area, but we rarely need that much space. It's actually surprising how few people die in hospital; it mostly gets busy during flu epidemics or a big road accident.'

I hoped I wouldn't be here for a big road accident. I didn't say anything though and he just carried on talking.

'This curtain covers a window that looks on to the viewing area, and when relatives are here we pull the curtain back so that they can do the identification. All the bodies have to undergo post-mortems unless they are old and die of something obvious or natural causes. We can only do three a day down here due to space and the number of available pathologists, so we are sometimes against the clock. You'll be a massive help, as long as you're happy to muck in and get your hands dirty.'

He chuckled again, and I waited. I had been told you had gloves and that I wouldn't get my hands dirty. I hoped that Karen hadn't lied about the job, just to get me here. Pete kept walking, round the corner, and pointed out another room. 'This is the drying room. People sometimes get brought to the hospital in an ambulance after an accident and are DOA, covered in blood, or water from ponds or rivers, and this is where we dry the clothes and personal effects. Over here are the fridges.'

Pete walked towards a metal wall, with labels on, and handles. It looked like a giant drawer unit. He pointed at the front of one of them.

'This label has the name of the deceased, the date of birth if we know it, and contact information, again if we know it. We also write cause of death once the PM has been done.'

I began to think that this was much too much information to be giving me all at once. My head was still too full from the journey and noise to take most of it in, and I was missing my routine. I was beginning to think I should have started a week later, when I had got over the previous week and all its problems. I decided to ask about the gloves, but Peter didn't really give me any gaps to talk, and he was walking fast again down the corridor.

The next room held two shiny steel trolleys, and each one had a showerhead at the top and a row of knives and ladles and saws next to them. It was all very clean and smelt like my bathroom after I had bleached everything. It was empty and quiet, which I liked, until suddenly Pete beeped, loudly. He looked at a box in his pocket then started talking again.

'Nick, I have to pop back to the relatives' area for a minute. Wait here. I'll bring Mark and he can show you the ropes.'

I was glad when he had gone, and I waited. It was so quiet and so metallic. There was nothing here that wasn't needed. I felt as if the world above with its chaos and its shouting was gone, and I started to feel at home. I decided that this might be a very good job as long as I could avoid Pete and Mark, and wear gloves, and I walked over to the instruments to have a closer look.

Pete didn't come back; Mark came. On his own. He showed me the fridges again, and the freezer room where bodies were kept if they weren't identified and stayed for a long time. There was even a scanner which could scan a body in thirteen seconds. Mark told me about a man who had died and no one knew why so they scanned him and a bullet had been in him near his spine for twenty-two years, and it moved so he died. It was all very interesting but I wished I had brought my recorder. I had got it for my birthday and it would have been useful today and Mother would have been pleased.

Mark took me over to the freezers and pulled out a drawer. Inside was a bag, a black bag, with the shape of a body. I thought it was nice, the way it was neatly put into a drawer, out of the way, and the bag had a label on the side of it. It couldn't get lost, because it was in a plastic pocket which was sewn into the bag. You really couldn't fault it, they had thought of everything. There was even a body-lifter which was for people to get lifted on to the slab for a post-mortem. Mark showed me how it worked, but without a body.

I decided I wanted to stay. This was peaceful, and I was going to be good at this. Mark gave me my own set of tools, which held a comb, and scissors, and glue, and various types of make-up, but thicker than normal make-up, and Mark asked me to touch it and it felt more like putty and I asked for some gloves, which was better, then I asked whether Pete was coming back.

Mark told me that Pete was dealing with relatives, doing an identification of a road-traffic accident victim, and he was going to start to show me how to prepare a body. He closed the drawer he had opened, and pointed me in the direction of the steel trolley behind me. He pulled back the sheet and there was an old man there, his mouth slightly open, and he seemed quite peaceful. He was wearing pyjamas. I hoped someone had checked that he was actually dead, then I remembered it was a hospital so they would have. I waited until Mark spoke again.

'Right, I'm going to go and give Pete a hand. If you could go into the scrub room, put on some Wellington boots and a robe and give your hands a good wash, I'll be back. This old boy needs a wash down – put the pyjamas on the side here – and his beard and hair combing. You alright to do that? I hear you're not squeamish.'

I had to sign a form to say that I would keep the identity of the bodies confidential and never talk about what happened at the morgue outside it. This was the last thing and then Mark had gone and I was on my own. On my own and surrounded by quiet and peace and people who weren't suddenly going to ask me questions, or make me anxious. I started to take off the pyjama top, and my hands were shaking a bit, but I soon realised that he wasn't going to move or react and I calmed down. I was very good at personal hygiene, and Mark had pointed out the antibacterial body wash and the cloths. I filled the bowl with steamy water, and liquid soap, and I started to give him his last wash. His face came up really nicely, although the eyes wouldn't stay shut and the mouth kept coming open, but I kept going. He stopped smelling like a person who hadn't washed and started smelling like soap. Better. Cleanliness is next to godliness, Grandpa says.

I was happy when Mark came back, pulling another trolley. He was impressed, I could tell, and told me I was the first mortuary assistant who had shown bloody initiative. I knew that was good; Grandpa was always telling me to show some and now I had.

Mark did the bottom half of the old man, and I was glad as I didn't really want to do that, and I concentrated on getting his hands really clean, and his arms and chest. His family would probably see his hands. Dignity, that was what Mark said. I cut his nails, without being asked, and combed his hair and his beard and trimmed them.

'You aren't scared, are you?'

Mark chuckled again, which spoiled the mood and my feeling of being at peace had a ripple in it for a minute. We turned the old man over, and soon he was washed on both sides, and smelling good, and in a gown, and in a bag and in the fridge. It was organised and quiet and I read out the details we had to Mark, and he wrote them on the label, and on the door, and then he read them back to me.

'Usually, when we get a new bloke down here, they tiptoe around for weeks, jumping at their own shadow. Once, when I was new, I was bringing a body down in the lift and she sat straight up under the sheet. Nearly shat myself. It can happen. Nerves are funny things.'

I didn't think I would like that. If it happened I might not come back. Otherwise I would be fine, and at least he had told me it was nerves.

Mark turned towards me. 'Do you fancy a cup of tea?'

'I don't like tea.' It was eleven o'clock and it seemed better to keep working. Mark asked if I wanted to come and sit in the coffee room while he took a break, but I didn't. I remembered what Karen had said: always try and be helpful. Ask what you can do.

'Is there anything I can do while you have your break?'

Mark pointed me towards a huge bucket of instruments. They had been used. He showed me how to work the autoclave; it was a bit like my microwave. You wash the instruments, then put them in there and steam sterilises them. I wished I had one at home; you would know all the germs were dead when you used one. Mark had put strawberry Vaseline under his nose, but I didn't want any. How could you tell when someone was clean if you couldn't smell? I could smell strawberries now when Mark was close, explaining the autoclave, and it made me feel sick. It smelt like the sweets Grandpa used to give me when I had been good, when I lived at home. I shuddered, not from the bodies but from the sweet strawberry and the way it made me feel.

I stood still waiting for Mark's footsteps to disappear into silence, and stared at the bucket of instruments. I had half an hour, all on my own, and I breathed out. I picked up the bucket to move it to the sink and autoclave area, and as I did I caught the corner of the sheet covering the body Mark had wheeled in from the identification. I had been expecting another old person, but the face that was now half uncovered was young, and pure, and beautiful. Blonde hair was spread out behind her on the pillow, and she looked as if she was asleep.

I pulled the sheet back and realised I was holding my breath. She was wearing a flowery dress, and she had a light tan as if she had just come back from holiday. The sheet had knocked a lock of hair across her face, and I gently pushed it back into place. She looked like Meg from my computer: pink lips that were slightly parted, and white teeth just showing. I stroked her cheek, and then ran my fingers over her lips. She was perfect, like a wax model. This was how I had always imagined my perfect woman and here she was, quiet and soft to the touch. I was calm and happy; the feeling of being in charge came over me again and I ran my hand over her, just her neck and then for a moment my hand cupped her small cold breast. I had never felt so much or wanted anyone like this before. I put my finger just inside her lips. Even her mouth was dry – no saliva, no nasty words, just softness.

I went to put the sheet back on her, and as I did my hand brushed over her stomach and I jumped. There was a hard line of stitches all the way down her middle. I covered her up, and picked up the bucket, but the smell of her hair and the feel of her lips stayed with me. I wondered if this was what it was like to be in love. I spread the sheet back over her, and it made the outline of her body. The whole time I was autoclaving she just lay there quietly with me, and I felt content and as if I had found my place in the world. *Find your place in the world and you will be happy* was written on a sign in the coffee shop near my flat, and I had never thought it made sense until now.

The morning went much too quickly, and I walked behind Karen, who had come to collect me at twelve-thirty. We went to the canteen because it was lunchtime, and we got food on trays that you had to choose, and I didn't like how people in the queue were so close, and decided I would bring a healthy sandwich. I needed to have lunch and everyone was wearing gloves, even the people who handed out the trays, so I managed to push down thoughts of germs. I had chicken and vegetables and water and yoghurt. I was going home on the bus and I was glad; Karen had to work the whole day but I was doing half-days. Now that I was back in the noisiness of the world I wondered if I could change my mind and work all day instead. I would ask after I had actually got the job permanently. Karen had explained I was on a trial.

We ate lunch at the same table. I noticed that the tables were cleaned with the same spray as I use at home, so at least ninety-nine per cent of all the germs would be dead. We sat in silence for a bit, then I had finished and decided to go. I thought I should tell Karen, so I said, 'I am going to the bus now. I don't want a lift. Thank you for telling me about the job.'

'I hope you stick at it. I know it's a tough place to work but Mark and Pete both thought you did really well.'

'It's very clean at the morgue.'

'You like things being clean?'

'Yes. I have a schedule, at home. I have a routine and a schedule and I am going to put my work on to it now. Cleaning and putting out the bins is on the schedule.'

I was keen to go home. Work was finished. But Karen wasn't.

'How old are you, Nick?'

'I'm twenty-four.'

'How long have you lived on your own in Staverton Road?'

'I have been there four years. My mother bought the flat for me.'

This was ruining my morning. Everything had gone really well at the job, and now I was getting annoyed. I stood up.

'Well, see you back at the house,' Karen said. 'If you want a lift in the morning just let me know. Is this your first job?'

I tried to remember the list – make eye contact, be polite – but I was too tired so I just said yes.

Karen looked at me and I realised that I was almost hopping from foot to foot. 'I understand that completely, I like being on my own too.'

'Why would you have children, then? If you have children you should be with them, shouldn't you?'

When I said that, which was true, she put her head down and stopped talking. I didn't like having to think about her life, or what she was doing. I started to walk towards the door and didn't say goodbye.

I heard her say something else. It sounded like, 'Apparently, yes.' It made no sense, so I didn't turn round.

I can't remember the journey home now, and I can't remember what I did in the afternoon. I can remember googling car accidents to see if I could find a picture to print of the girl who looked like Meg, and I can remember that as I sat looking at pure girls on the computer I closed my eyes at the end and remembered that lock of hair, and the feel of her lips. I came all over my desk and I didn't even care. I also googled symptoms of being in love, and I had more than two. I was in love, and it was a good feeling. I sat quietly knowing that in the morning I would go to work and see her again.

9 | Karen

'He alone who owns the youth gains the future.'
— Adolf Hitler

Tuesday morning

Karen woke up to the faint echo of a dream that she couldn't quite pin down but it only lasted a moment. She pushed the imaginary from her mind and turned her thoughts excitedly towards Nick. She had thought carefully about it and he really was the case study she'd been looking for. He was the right age, the right background, had finished his education, and most incredibly of all he lived under the same roof as her and now worked in the same hospital. She allowed herself a satisfied stretch of happiness, and started to think again about everything coming together, the forgiveness of her family and the plaudits of her colleagues. How could it go wrong now? All she had to do was to keep collating information here and at work and she would soon have enough material to prove that there was a valuable and neglected section of the population who could be a massive resource, working, contributing and having real quality of life. In order to accurately record the data and make it into a study, she would have to see Nick at least three times in a twenty-four-hour period in a mix of home and work environments. Karen didn't envisage much of a problem in achieving that; the issue was more likely to be making sure she didn't alienate him, or she would get very little co-operation and even less data. Writing a research paper was a technically challenging issue, and it needed to be done properly.

It was 6.45 on Tuesday morning. She would jump out of bed and catch Nick before he set out for work. That way she would be able to chat to him in the car and do the first entry in the log when she got to the office.

She was particularly looking forward to hearing his reactions to his day in the morgue. Detachment from emotion was one of the main signs of being on the autistic spectrum, but its effects on behaviour in situations traditionally regarded as extreme had never really been studied in any depth. It was not as if you could just put a vulnerable subject in close proximity to death just to see what happened to him or her, but by this strange turn of fate she had managed it. She showered, dressed and headed out of the front door, looking forward to the day ahead for the first time in a very long while. Walking down the first flight of stairs she felt confident and optimistic, but as she came towards Nick's door she realised that Tam was collecting his post. Before she knew what she was doing, Karen had flattened herself against the wall, and was trying to breathe as quietly as she could.

It wasn't until she heard Tam's footsteps coming up the stairs and across the landing towards her, that she fully appreciated the picture she was presenting. Hands clenched in balls, mouth in a rictus pose, body squished into the corner of the landing, eyes tightly closed.

She heard Tam clear his throat right in front of her and opened her eyes.

'Are you alright?'

His voice was deep and attractive, and suddenly Karen wasn't actually sure how she felt. She knew that from most people's standpoint she probably seemed as different to them as Nick did to her. Her husband was always telling her what a joke she was, and now she was trying to prove him and her children wrong, along with the scientific community. Now, her confidence receding, she wondered whether putting a young man on the autistic spectrum to work in a morgue so that she could write a paper to make herself seem more credible was really defensible. Was she doing it for Nick and so many others like him, or for herself? Self-doubt was not something that Karen had ever indulged in and suddenly she felt furious, as if something precious was being snatched from her. She felt uncertain, shaky even, and, when she opened her eyes and looked at Tam, all remaining conviction that she was doing all this for the higher good fell away.

Tam put his hand gently on her arm and Karen shook it off, turned her back and knocked on Nick's door. No answer.

She knocked again, harder.

'I don't think he's in. I saw him going up the path half an hour ago.'

Before she realised it was going to happen, Karen was sobbing. Huge retching sobs, for herself, for all the hours she had put in to prove her worth when no one was watching, for her husband and her children, and for Tam's gentle hand on her.

'Whoa, what's the matter? If I upset you the other day I apologise. I'm a bit blunt at the best of times; it comes with the job. Plods, you know… I didn't mean to make you feel bad; parenting is complicated. That's why I've never done it, I suppose. Come down to my flat for a coffee, and calm down.'

Karen relaxed; the crying had made her feel better, and she wiped her nose on her sleeve. Her shoulders still convulsed now and then, and she let Tam put his arm round her and lead her downstairs.

'Come on, I know how to make you feel better.'

Tam was unlocking the door and smiling at her over his shoulder now. Something deep inside her fought back and she shouted in his face, furious now.

'Don't tell me what to do, or what I need. I'm perfectly alright, and I need to be at work.'

Turning, she rushed out of the door, down the path and into the car. Nick must already be at the hospital and she needed to see him. She wasn't about to turn into a 'little woman' and blow her life's work just so that Tam could have a handy shag whenever he felt like it. She spun her wheel, turning to get on to the road, and glanced once into her rear-view mirror, to see Tam standing in jogging bottoms, looking perplexed, staring after her. Karen sped off. For once she was taking control. She pushed down her doubts, and the series of images from the past few days of people in her rear-view mirror as she drove away.

On the drive to the hospital Karen made a plan. Three observations a day was going to mean she would have to stick close to Nick. If he was going to insist on using public transport, then she would follow him, to see how he coped with crowds, and the rush hour, and proximity to other people. It would sort out the problem with the car constantly running out of petrol anyway, and she would get a bit of exercise. She didn't let herself think about Tam once, and that felt like a personal victory.

She parked her car, and went straight to her office. She hung up her coat and turned on the computer. It was hugely important to Karen that she had her own space, even if her ex had called it 'the cupboard', or 'that fucking shoe box you call an office'. The nameplate on her door and the sign in the car park were the only two pieces of tangible proof that she existed at all in the eyes of the world. She sat down and cleared her mind. Everyone breaking new ground had the same doubts, she was sure of that. She opened Excel and drew up a spreadsheet for the visits, then opened a new file and prepared a document ready for her observations.

She got up, went to the lift, and while she descended she planned how best to approach Nick when she got downstairs. The doors opened and Karen walked down to the kitchen. Pete was leaning against the counter, waiting for the kettle to boil. Karen began to understand why they needed an assistant. Pete smiled.

'Hi – Karen, isn't it? Thanks for sending Nick to us! He's quiet, but he's doing great. Does whatever we ask, no fainting, no puking. Seems to actually enjoy the work as much as you can tell. Even ate his breakfast down in the body room next to the freezers this morning. Honestly don't know how we would have managed without him;

Mark's off today, so Nick's been thrown in at the deep end. I don't usually like leaving guys down there alone when they're new, but when I told him I'd be gone for an hour he didn't mind at all.'

'Thanks for the feedback, Pete, I'm glad it's working out. I'll go and see if he needs a lift home later.'

'OK, see you, Karen.'

If Karen had been interested enough to look, she would have seen the second perplexed male face of the morning staring after her, but her mind was already with Nick in the body room. She turned right, and in front of her was a cold, apparently empty white-painted hallway. There was no sign of human life, and Karen walked alone towards the area Pete had indicated. Past the relatives' area, the sluices and the drying room and towards the freezers. If that was where Nick was eating breakfast then that was a good place to start.

Karen came round the corner and there he was, clearly visible through the glass panel in the middle of the double doors. Poised over a steel trolley, the angle of his tall body obscured all but the feet of the corpse below him, arms spread and his right arm raised above the body.

Karen's immediate reaction was pride. No one instructing him, no one giving him tasks to do; here was her subject, taking the initiative and dealing with a difficult situation on his own. She shrank back behind the doors and watched as his hand rose and fell, and she thought to herself that he must be washing the body. There was something in his hand, which Karen couldn't see clearly. Nick was intent on what he was doing and she waited to see what he would do next. This was exactly what she needed to observe. Concentration on one task to the total exclusion of all others was one of the ten characteristics she had already classified as being transformable into useful social skills, allowing these subjects to contribute and function in society. Karen suddenly made out what he was doing. He was brushing hair, the strands of blonde rising, held up by static, from his hand. Long, translucent white-blonde hair, suspended in the position Nick lifted it into, then relaxing and falling slowly back towards the head of the cadaver.

Karen decided not to disturb him but to log the visit and come back at lunchtime, but, just as she was about to turn, she caught something out of the corner of her eye, and looked back towards the body room. Nick was bending towards the body now. Karen thought he must have noticed something out of place, but he kept on bending until his face was close to hers, and then he smoothed her hair back from her forehead, and he kissed her.

He kissed her on the forehead first, and then the cheek. The last thing Karen saw as she backed down the corridor was his hand pushing the sheet down from her body, and his mouth covering hers.

Karen retraced her steps, heart pounding, walked straight into the lift and hurried, head down, to her office. Shutting the door behind her, she scuttled to her desk. The question she had burning in her head was simple. What should she do?

Karen thought back through the many experiences she had of children and adults on the spectrum. She knew that if children were already suffering from Asperger's, the way they were treated when young was incredibly important. Abuse of any sort, physical or sexual, was incredibly difficult for these children to process, and their adult behaviour became skewed as a result. It was true for anyone, but Asperger's sufferers didn't have the emotional tools to distinguish between good behaviour and bad. That was often cited as a reason why there was such a high proportion of Asperger's sufferers in the prison system; the original condition was exacerbated by trauma, and, as with any vulnerable group, autistic children were more likely to end up in care, or in boarding schools, and were at a higher risk of abuse. You had to love the human race; the weakest were always most likely to be attacked.

Karen needed to find out whether Nick had gone through any childhood trauma that had made him more detached than was usual when you were at his level on the autistic spectrum. He seemed to have a pronounced detachment for his intelligence level. Karen compared him to Temple Grandin, someone who had achieved great things by using every coping strategy at her disposal. She had tried therapies and drugs and even a cattle press to subdue her anxiety. That was the gold standard for Asperger's achievement, whereas Nick did not seem, from what she had seen so far, to have had the benefit of much intervention at all. She would wait and watch, but interacting with a cadaver was not a good sign. Karen decided to ignore the voice in her head telling her that leaving him in the morgue was not a good plan.

When 12.30 came round, Karen took a deep breath and headed back towards the lift. It was set at the back of a little-used corridor. Death was not something that sat well with the patients, which Karen had always found odd. Surely the possibility of death was all around us, and having it hidden, and whisked away like a magic trick, seemed like denying something fundamental.

She stepped out into the corridor for the second time, and it was a different place entirely. Pete was standing chatting to an orderly outside the break room, coffees in hand, and Nick was walking towards them, eyes down.

'Hi, Nick.'

Karen got no response, so went towards him. As she got closer his agitation at her arrival was clear; his hands started flapping and he half turned away.

'Don't worry, I just popped down to see if you were getting on OK. Do you want some lunch or a lift home? I can run you now and then come back to work.'

The closer she got, the more agitated Nick became. 'I get the bus from the corner, twenty minutes because they can use the bus lane, and then I walk to my job. I don't need a lift, and I have work here this afternoon.'

With this Nick picked up a sandwich and drink from the side and walked back towards the freezers.

'Nick, don't forget to clean up if you drop crumbs.'

Pete was grinning as he said it, and Nick didn't turn but his head was nodding, and his steps got a little faster.

'Jesus, he may not be very communicative but he is a hell of a worker. Honestly, you have to show him once, and he doesn't need to be shown again. We've even asked him to stick around till three today, to have a really deep clean of the drying room. He's taken over all the body prep, watched an autopsy, and not flinched at any of it. Best guy we've ever had down here, even if he reminds me slightly of Marty Feldman in *Young Frankenstein*.'

149

The guys laughed, but Karen didn't find it funny. Nick was coping and these guys seemed to find him good to have around. Still, Karen thought she had better cover herself and enquire further.

'Can I ask, has he been a problem in any way? Has his work been up to scratch?'

'Yeah, I just said, his work's great and he's willing to do anything. Just likes to be left alone when you aren't giving him an instruction. That's fine with us.'

Karen smiled tightly, then headed back to the lift, bad-taste pathologist humour following her up the corridor. Perhaps Nick was just taking their lead and getting it slightly wrong. At the end of the day he was working with cadavers, and there was little harm he could do to them. She knew it was him she should be worrying about. He was functioning, even excelling in a job, and surely that was the most important thing. The little voice whispering in her ear that trouble was coming and something had gone wrong that might well be her fault had stopped by the time she got back to her computer. Her study would be groundbreaking, and sometimes hiccups along the way were just that. It would be Pete she would be interviewing to collate the data for the work-related part of the paper, and he didn't seem to have any misgivings. She headed back to her office, and completed the morning log to read: *Observed Nick paying detailed attention to his work, leaning over body to make sure it was meticulously cleaned.*

Karen began to think that made much more sense, wrote up the lunchtime visit, did some research on different reactions to childhood trauma and headed home at 6.30.

She had tried to keep an eye on the car park through her window but she had still been busy at 3 p.m. and she could see how he reacted on public transport in the morning. She was already excited about her journey in tomorrow; she would be up at the crack of dawn to make sure she didn't miss him.

She walked in through the front door with her mind still full of her day, feeling she had made some progress. She stopped for a minute outside Tam's door, feeling she should say something, but she didn't know what would help, and she didn't want to take the lid off her feelings again; it was making her confused and she needed all her concentration to get this paper finished. She would have plenty of time for a personal life when she had got her findings down. People were suffering right now due to a lack of clear, defined diagnosis, and she had no time to waste.

On the way upstairs she put her ear to Nick's door. She could hear him cleaning. She had never heard the hoover on in the evening before, and it surprised her. Most autistic subjects hated loud noise; perhaps being in a work environment was changing some of Nick's behaviours. Making a mental note to add this to the evening log, which she had been battling to see how she would fill, Karen almost skipped up the remaining stairs to her room.

What the fuck was going on here? As she crossed the landing she realised that noises were coming from inside her flat. The smell of cooking pervaded the landing, and laughter, children's laughter, and now male laughter, was coming from inside.

She froze, again. The overriding temptation was to creep back down the stairs and return to her office. It could only be the children and their father. What the hell was he doing in her flat? He probably wanted to give her another lecture. Racking her brains to remember what day she had said she would have the children, she was starting to retreat when the door was thrown open and Jack stood there, grinning, his mouth covered in chocolate, and the guy behind him wasn't his father – it was Tam.

'I lost a tooth.'

'He lost a tooth because Tam tied cotton round it and then the door handle and slammed it.'

His big sister sounded disapproving and delighted all at the same time, while Jamie wandered over to the sink and started washing his hands methodically with a bar of soap.

Karen realised she was still standing in the doorway, bag in hand, coat on.

'Sorry, the kids were bored and charging around a bit, and the guy from the middle flat was banging on the wall so I came up to calm the situation down, and they were hungry so I made pancakes. Hope you don't mind…' Tam looked awkward now, shuffling from foot to foot. 'OK, I should get going now that your mum's here. I've probably ruined your dinner with the pancake feast.'

The familiar looks of disappointment returned to her children's faces, and Karen dug deep inside herself for a reaction that would help.

'No, stay. Let me get my coat off and we can see what to do after that. Sorry, you all took me by surprise.'

Squeals of delight met this announcement from Jack, while Sarah bent forward to awkwardly hug her mother and Jamie carried on washing his hands.

'Dad is coming to pick us up at nine; we're going to France on a day trip tomorrow with him and his new girlfriend, so we have to be up really early. It's inset day at school so we have the day off. I can cook supper if you like; I've learned how to do spaghetti bolognaise.'

Sarah's young face was eager, looking for approval, already wearing the shadow of the serious, earnest woman Karen had grown into. A flicker of recognition that there must be more to life than work, resistant as she had become to the idea, ignited dimly in Karen's brain, and she hung her coat on the rack and smiled at her daughter.

'Great! Spaghetti it is. I don't think we have the ingredients, so you might have to go to the shop.'

'No problem, I can go to the Co-op. I need mince, Dolmio sauce, some garlic and the spaghetti. Ten pounds will be plenty and I could get Coke and ice cream for the boys if you like.'

Karen was about to embark on a lecture about balanced meals and the dangers of sugar but she met Tam's eye, and saw that he was waiting for her reaction.

'Great, yes, get ice cream and Coke … and the spaghetti ingredients.' Karen put down her bag, and let her daughter squeeze her before she ran out of the door. The boys were around her legs and she was led, and pulled, towards the sofa to watch cartoons. She looked at her watch – 6.20 – and tried to do a mental approximation of how long she had before the children would be collected. She had seen people hyperventilate before and she could now understand why. Jack climbed on to her lap, and Jamie sat on the end. Tam chose this moment to put a whisky and water into her hand.

Karen sipped, and tried to remember a situation where she had been this close to her children since they were babies. Jack was twirling one of her curls round and round his finger now and making a noise like an aeroplane, while Jamie kicked the table in front of them rhythmically. The panic in her eyes must have been visible to Tam as he lifted his glass and mouthed cheers.

'Hey, boys, come over here, I bet I can beat you at arm-wrestling.'

Karen relaxed as Jack jumped down and ran to the table, and she sat at a safe distance keeping score for them in the battle which Tam was letting him win. She knew that mothers were important, empirically, and she knew that she had become distant and remote from her children, but images of Nick, alone downstairs, were already creeping into her mind. She sipped on her whisky, and smiled at Jack, who was now fully engaged with Tam. It didn't come naturally to her, smiling, and Karen wondered how she could be so good at analysing patients and compiling data, but no good at showing her feelings or developing her relationships with her own offspring. She often comforted herself by reading about successful historical characters in science or even the arts. Their personal lives were always difficult; perhaps that was what it took to make breakthroughs.

Sarah came back, and asked for a big pan for the spaghetti. Karen didn't have one, and Tam was dispatched to find one. Boiling water, a splash of olive oil and some salt. The spaghetti went in, everyone laughing at Sarah's bravery around the hob and steam, and oohing and aahing at the miracle of spaghetti softening from stiff to soft as it made contact with the water. Karen watched Jack go up on his tiptoes trying to see what was happening, before Tam scooped him up and lifted him high enough to watch.

Sarah showed them how to brown mince, then when it was cooked she poured in the sauce from the can. Karen watched her as she lapped up the claps from her brother and the high five from Tam. She drained the end of her whisky, and patted Sarah on the back. The rhythmic kicking of the coffee table carried on behind them, but was lost in the general hubbub.

They were still scraping the bottom of the ice-cream container when there was a ring on the bell. For the first time ever, the children seemed disappointed that their father had arrived. Tam buzzed him up and Karen bit her lip to stop herself from saying something as her life was taken over. She preferred him to wait in the car, but he arrived at the door, and looked genuinely pleased as the children all talked at once, spaghetti sauce was wiped off mouths, and the three of them all hugged their mother and thanked Tam, who ruffled their hair and did up their coats.

'Come on, Jamie, up you get, we're going. Thanks, Karen.'

Jamie got up and went back over to the sink. He had certainly taken the 'wash your hands' rule to heart, Karen thought. Tam shut the door two minutes later, while the children shouted up the stairs and Karen shouted back from above. She stood in the hallway as Tam came up behind her and put his arms round her gently.

It was too much. She closed her eyes and let him kiss her neck. Sex had always been a release, a physical tension built up in her, but all it meant tonight was that there was going to be even less time left for writing. She had very little sexual tension left after the unexpected encounters with Tam this week, but she was grateful that he had been good to the children.

With the hugs of her children still warm, the softer tone of her husband still in her ears, and Tam's arms round her, she could still feel nothing.

She allowed herself to be led to the bed, undressed, and when the time came she kissed Tam back. As soon as she could feel he was ready, she pulled him between her legs and concentrated all her efforts on making him come as quickly as she could. It worked, and when he had finished, groaning from deep in his chest, he kissed her gently on the forehead, staring into her eyes and gently pushing a stray curl away from her mouth. Karen wondered whether he could tell that no one was home, and that the only face she could see was Nick's.

10 | Tam

'I love sleep. My life has the tendency to fall apart when I'm awake, you know?'

— Ernest Hemingway

Wednesday morning

Six a.m., for fuck's sake. Tam rolled over. He had woken up with a hard-on, and the scent of Karen was still fresh on her sheets. She must have got up to go to the bathroom. He called her name, and in the distance he heard the door slam. That moron from the middle flat.

He had lain dead to the world for the last nine hours, but was still feeling a bit rough around the edges from the whisky the night before. He rubbed his eyes. She wasn't here. It was a tiny flat and he was pretty sure he would have heard some sign of movement or ablutions by now. He crawled to the edge of the bed, pulled back the curtain and looked out on to the path and the road. Nick was scurrying away from the house, darting from left to right like a gecko. He smiled to himself. Why Karen would take so much of her time obsessing over someone like that was beyond him.

It had been a good evening. Chilled, relaxed, and Karen's kids were pretty nice when you got to know them.

He'd never wanted to be a dad, but it felt strangely good having a positive influence over children who had already been potty-trained and weaned by someone else and who seemed polite and up for a bit of arm-wrestling. He had even imagined taking them out for a pint when they got older, but he was getting ahead of himself. It had just been a relief to have a normal evening and see Karen semi-relaxed. He had begun to think she did nothing but work and fuck like a hooker.

Even the dad seemed to have calmed down a bit since their first encounter on the path outside. Tam would probably have been less than amused to be left with three kids to raise if he had been in his shoes; it wasn't natural.

His train of thought was interrupted by the door slamming again, and he looked up to see Karen, fully dressed, hovering in the doorway, then scurrying down the path after Nick. What the fuck was she doing? Following him? She didn't get in her car, and Nick was clearly visible in front of her, on the straight pavement, heading for the corner and the bus stop. That boy must wonder why he always had someone behind him who looked vaguely familiar. To be two minutes behind him Karen must have been poised, waiting for him to leave. The image of her on the landing the day before popped into his mind.

Women – what was the cliché? Can't live with them, can't live without them. Well, he would see her later, and at least they were finally getting somewhere after a failed start. Tam had been on his own a long time, and had never been great at commitment, so this was a good and unfamiliar feeling. He gathered up his things, which seemed to be scattered across Karen's flat, and went into the shower. He came out smelling flowery but clean, pulled on his clothes and went downstairs. He thought about tidying up but decided that might look as if he assumed they were a couple, so he threw the ice-cream container away and went downstairs.

He plugged his phone in and looked at his messages. One from Danny at the Met, yesterday, and one from Karen this morning. Tam clicked on voicemail.

Morning, it's Karen, your neighbour. I've gone to work. I wanted to apologise for last night. I will talk to the children and make sure they don't bother you again. Thank you for looking after them but it really wasn't necessary. I have a lot of work on and they come to my house to do homework, so I would appreciate it if you could respect that. I'll see you some time...

Her voice trailed off, and was gone. Tam was annoyed at himself for feeling as if he had been kicked in the gut. That was it, his guard was going back up where that schizo was concerned and it wasn't coming back down. 'Fuck her, seriously – no, actually...note to self, don't fuck her ever again,' he muttered to himself. He made himself a coffee and sat staring at morning television. *Homes Under the Hammer* was actually making him feel like moving. He didn't want to pass her on the stairs every day. Those poor kids, he thought to himself: she's a cold-hearted bitch and they deserve better.

The realisation that he was upset enough by her curt voicemail to revert back into a life of takeaways and whisky coincided with a news report. There they were again, the couple in the park. The guy had died the day before, and the girl had suffered 'life-changing injuries', which didn't sound pleasant.

Tam took a deep breath, shook Karen out of his head, and dialled Danny's number. 'Hi, mate, sorry I didn't call you back yesterday. Do you fancy a drink after work today?'

Tam had decided that trying to do the right thing was seriously overrated. He arranged to meet Danny at 5.30 p.m., lay down, pulled the duvet over his head and went back to sleep.

When he opened his eyes it was four in the afternoon and he thought about shaving. Instead he opened the freezer, took out the frozen cat, picked up the bag of clothing he had found in the bins, and put the lot into one of those bags that stopped things melting when you shopped in Iceland. It was a chilly day, so he would be fine as long as the sun didn't get any stronger. He texted Danny that he would come past the office, he needed to ask a favour. They arranged to meet outside, which was a relief. Tam couldn't have taken a re-run of his last visit to the politically correct hotbed of police affairs.

So it was that at 5.30 on the dot a crumpled-looking Danny, in a zip-up fleece which expanded comfortably over his paunch, took possession of the 'forensic evidence' as Tam liked to think of it, from the bins outside the house.

'I'm just going to nip these upstairs, mate, and put the cat in the cold room. Normally if someone turned up here with a frozen pussy I'd make a joke and tell them to fuck off, but as it's you and you have the best nose for trouble

I've ever come across I'll make an exception. I don't need to tell you that we already have a big issue with the chain of evidence: this stuff has been in a bin, then in your flat, now here. What do you think it's going to prove?'

'I'll explain it all to you in the pub. Just get it safely tagged and logged and I'll give you the whole story. I have a hunch.'

'Say no more – your spidey sense has always been good. I'll be back in ten minutes.'

Tam waited two, and then headed to the pub. He texted Danny the immortal words, 'At the Albert. I'll get the drinks in.' He felt almost like a copper again.

Danny was twenty-five minutes. By the time he arrived, Tam was on his second pint. It had been intended for Danny, so he got another round in.

'You're drinking fast. I can't keep up with you.'

The blonde barmaid behind the bar seemed to be looking in his direction every time he glanced her way and Tam smiled ruefully, picked up the two empty glasses and headed towards her.

'I haven't seen you in here before,' she said. 'Your friend's a regular. Sweet guy – think he needs a girlfriend, or a mum or someone to do his washing? You ready for another drink?'

'Long week, and I need to blow some cobwebs away – and by the way my sweet friend has a wife and a kid; he just prefers the pub. As for me, give me another drink, it might help me relax.'

She smiled at him, leant forward just a little too much, put her hand on his and said, 'Let me know if you need any help with that.'

Tam sat back down and began to explain to Danny about the weird guy who lived above him, and the neat letters in the hall, and the clock, and the bag of clothes in the bin, and finally the cat. Danny was looking doubtful. Telling the story out loud, even Tam began to see that it sounded like the ramblings of a bored policeman with too much time on his hands.

'It's not my area, of course, mate, but let's see if the blood is in the system or even if it's human – might be the best way to start. I don't know what I can do with the cat. Let's just keep it in the freezer for now. I think I'll just get one for the road.'

'Don't worry, mate, you're doing me a favour, let me get the beers.'

Tam knew blokes were supposed to be heartless bastards, but he was the one who had behaved well with Karen and she'd been the bitch. If she didn't want him, then the best way to get over her was to get on top of someone else. Wasn't that what real men did?

'Two pints of IPA, please, love, and a drink for you. Sorry, I don't know your name.'

'It's Molly. Thanks, I'll have a gin and slimline. Don't suppose you're at a loose end later? I get off in half an hour.'

She managed to make almost everything she said sound sexually charged, and Tam felt himself getting turned on. 'I'll walk you home if you like.'

Molly smiled and raised her eyebrows. 'Yes, please. I hope I can trust you to behave.'

She giggled, and Tam was torn between leaving the pub and trying to sort things out with Karen, and staying. He decided to stick to his guns; he was flogging a dead horse

with Karen, she obviously wasn't interested, but he was also painfully aware that Molly's giggle was probably a clue to just how noisy she would be if they ended up in bed, and he felt exhausted just at the thought. His body clearly disagreed with him, and he pulled his jumper down before he picked up the pints and walked back to the table.

'Looks like you're in there, mate. I envy you, footloose and fancy free. Bloody hell, how old do you think she is? Can't be more than twenty-two, you lucky sod. Look at those tits.'

Tam had been looking; they were so pert and bouncy that it seemed impolite not to, and every time Molly pulled a pint they took on a life of their own, like blancmange when you carried it to the table, not that he had seen that for years. Come to think of it, he hadn't seen twenty-two-year-old breasts for years either. Tam sighed. He had tried grown-up life, however briefly. Now he would go back to cheap Pinot Grigio and faked enthusiasm for the evening. He hoped she didn't live in a flatshare. Shared bathrooms, now that would be depressing, but it was better than taking her back to his place to bump into Karen, judging and looking at him like a failure.

'Your phone's ringing.'

Tam picked it up, a little spark of hope igniting that he could just go home, put on the television, Karen would knock at the door, say sorry or even act like nothing had happened and they could cuddle up on the sofa, but it wasn't her number. He picked up. 'Hello, Tam speaking.'

'Hello, my name is Marta, I am a cleaner and I see your postcard in the shop window.'

'Oh, yeah, hi. I need someone for four hours twice weekly. Actually I'm in a pub at the moment; can I speak to you later?'

'Yes, I speak to you later.'

Tam couldn't hear properly, and her accent was pronounced. He'd sort it out in the morning. He said cheers and hung up. He was achieving a few things now. The evidence was delivered and it would be nice to come home to a clean flat twice a week. If he was going to get into freelance work or a new routine, he needed order to be maintained on the home front. For now, though, home seemed the least attractive option. If he was going with Molly, she'd better get a move on. He was on his fifth pint and now he was less worried about any squealing Molly might be doing later and more worried about not falling asleep. He needed to get the thought of Karen, and for some reason her kids, out of his head, and if he drank any more he would be lucky if he got it up at all.

An hour later, he was lying on his back with Molly on top of him, facing away so his eyes were on her back and her impressively curvy bottom. The experience was somewhere between painful and sexually exciting. She must go to the gym a lot; her inner thigh muscles were really strong, and every time she plunged back down he wanted to shout, 'Gently!' This was probably the position that fractured guys' penises, and he concentrated on getting it over with.

It was made worse by her continually asking questions. 'Do you like this? Shall I bend forward? Faster? Slower?' Then there were the instructions. 'Put your hand here. Harder, play with my breasts, talk dirty to me.' He flipped her over, stopped worrying about what she was saying, kissed her hard to shut her up, and looked down at her firm young body. That did it, and he came in two minutes flat. Tension always made it more of a release, but even as he was coming he felt sad for the loss of what he had done the night before, when he had been looking into Karen's eyes, and Molly's frenzied cries of 'yes, yes, yes' did nothing to cheer him up.

He woke up twice during the night with Molly enthusiastically giving him a blow job. The first time he kept his eyes closed, grabbed her hair, and manipulated her like a blow-up doll, pushing into her mouth, which to be fair she seemed to enjoy, judging by the moaning. The second time, her liberal use of teeth during Round One, which he hadn't really noticed at the time, had left him in pain and taken away all his enthusiasm, and he rolled away on to his tummy and dropped off, to the plaintive sounds of Molly saying in his ear, 'What about me, babe?'

He couldn't have cared less.

Tam woke up disorientated and feeling as if he needed a shower. The room was not tidy, in fact the bedside table was a testament to the youth of its owner. Tampax mingled with half-used make-up containers, a couple of tissues of unknown origin and a bottle of lube. Lovely.

He couldn't get out on his side as he was leaning against a grubby wall, and he didn't want to wake her up. Apart from anything else he couldn't remember her name, and his dick felt as if it had been in a mangle. Something was digging into his cheek, and he picked a false nail off his face. It was covered in glitter and matched the ones on her hand. Gently, Tam slid the sheet off his body, and started to shuffle towards the bottom of the bed and a clean getaway.

Just as he was nearly there, she grabbed his head, which was now parallel with the top of her thighs. In the morning light he realised that she didn't have a single hair on her body. That hadn't registered in the dark drunken hour before he had fallen asleep. He had watched enough porn to know that pubic hair was a rare commodity these days, but Karen obviously hadn't got that memo and he'd been glad. The next thing he knew she was pushing his head towards her crotch, and sleepily murmuring his name. Tam stretched out his legs, made contact with the floor and jumped up. He had his limits, and she hadn't even showered since the night before. He looked around anxiously for any evidence of used condoms. Nothing. He was officially back to being a complete idiot.

The journey home, in a Tube filled with normal people apparently living normal lives, was a long one. Women talked to toddlers, read books on Kindles, ate wilted kale from Pret and recoiled as he came through the carriage. He smelt bad, even he could tell that, and he knew from past experience that when you could smell yourself that was not a good sign. He closed his eyes and vaguely remembered a bottle of tequila being produced from the barmaid's bag when they got home. The single life was not all it was cracked up to be. He seemed to be sweating pure alcohol, and the screams of 'fucking bastard' and 'you were shit in bed' still echoing in his ears weren't making him warm to the fully functioning smug marrieds or maybe just smug commuters surrounding him. He felt exhausted and would spend the next two months praying she was on the pill, and didn't have any STDs. His second youth was not working out any better than his few days of monogamy.

When the front door of his house was finally in sight, Tam lifted his heavy eyelids and glanced up at Karen's window. He wasn't sure, but he thought he saw her jolt with surprise as she saw him. Did he imagine the look of disgust on her face before it disappeared behind the curtain?

What the hell was she doing looking out for him at eight a.m.? Tam got the key in the door, leaning against the wall for support as he did so. Just as he was turning it in the lock, the door opened from the inside and out came Nick, staring at the ground. He seemed even more agitated than usual, if that was possible, and as soon as he saw Tam he jumped back into the hall and slammed the door in his face.

'Fuck this, open the fucking door.' Tam was furious, and had no sooner got his key back in the lock than Nick opened it again and rushed past him, talking to himself, head down and carrying a rubbish bag. He zigzagged towards the bin, smoothing his hair with one hand, and lifting the lid of the bin with the other. Tam watched as he adjusted it a few times, and then carefully closed the bin, and zigzagged back to the front door, slamming it behind him.

Tam was exhausted, and needed some sleep. But old habits died hard, so he walked to the bin, opened the lid and stared at the white translucent bag. He could see the outline of a Shreddies packet, and the triangle of a sandwich container. It looked like rubbish, general household waste, but he had started down this road now, and the bin men were coming tomorrow. He picked it up, just as Karen came scurrying out of the front door.

She had already seen him from the window, that much was clear by the way she studiously looked straight ahead, but even she hesitated when confronted with him looking like an alley cat and removing rubbish. It only took a moment; her mouth opened as if she was about to speak, then she closed it again and looked down. Walking purposefully to her car, she drove off without a backward glance.

Tam had to resist the impulse to shout something after her like 'fuck you', or give her the finger behind her back. Instead, he went inside, carrying the spoils from the bin, and put them down, ready to be examined later. Then he had a shower, a long hot one, trying to avoid his damaged dick, and went to bed and lay carefully on his side. His life was turning into a series of random nights in different beds with crazy fucked-up women.

11 | Nick

'We can easily forgive a child who is afraid of
the dark; the real tragedy of life is when men are
afraid of the light.'

— Plato

Wednesday morning

Work had made fitting in all my week's commitments very
difficult and I knew I had to make more cuts. My teeth
were grinding together, and I could feel how agitated I
was getting, but I couldn't calm down. I had looked at my
schedule the night before and decided that exercise was the
only area where I could save time. I was going to order a
skipping rope on Amazon, and put 'Leave in the hall' on
the delivery instructions. It could come tomorrow which
was Thursday and I could start using it in my bedroom.
It was probably not a good idea to go to the park at the
moment anyway even though I missed the deer. It made
me feel upset. I had tried to go last weekend but when I set
out I kept wanting to just go home, and I couldn't decide
whether to keep going and I got on the Tube, then back the
other way and then eventually I got to the gates and I saw
posters of the man and woman who had been having sex

by the pond and I felt so agitated and worried that I just didn't go in, I went home on the bus. I still wanted to go to the police and tell them what the couple had been up to, and what I had done to stop them, but people weren't all like me and they couldn't always see what was right. I had learned that a long time ago.

My grandpa and my mother still had to visit every week, that was important, and if I tried to change it they wouldn't understand. Work was important and I was good at work. I would keep going to the morgue whatever happened. I liked looking after the bodies. I felt relaxed around them and I could do everything that I was asked to do by Pete. It was a calm place, and I sometimes wished I could sleep there instead of coming back to all the noises and interruptions of the house. Last night I unravelled both the sleeves on my jumper and bit my lips and chewed all the skin off round my nails, but I spat it out in case it had germs. Upstairs it sounded like an army was marching. The children, the neighbour from downstairs, the doors closing and opening, people running up and down the stairs. I tried putting on the hoover, but it just made more noise so I turned it off again. It went on for hours, while I sat with my back against the wall and banged my head against it. Eventually the front door closed and they got quiet, then there was new banging, above my head this time, rhythmic against the same wall my head was on. Sex. I realised then – the neighbours were having sex again; they were doing it all over the house. I grabbed a cushion and screamed into it.

This morning, for the first time in my life I woke up and realised that I was on my side, on the floor, against the wall. I was cold, I hadn't had my shower and I hadn't cleaned my flat or even emptied my bin, but my bed must be tidy, because I had made it yesterday before I went to work. My grandpa says, 'Always make your bed'. I needed to go to work today. I worked Monday, Tuesday, Wednesday and Thursday now, because I was a good worker, and today was Wednesday. I tried not to worry about my list, I had told Grandpa I would be at work and he was going to come at the weekend, instead of Wednesday. Before I left I had to change and brush my teeth. I had no idea how many germs I must have breathed in during the night. I had never slept anywhere outside my bed before, and my whole body ached. I needed calm and I wanted to be in the morgue.

I stood up, and straight away I couldn't keep still, my mouth was clenched. I thought about putting the clothes I had slept in into the dirty clothes basket for my mother but the germs had probably had time to breed now and she might not know how to kill them, so I peeled them off, all of them, and put them into the bin bag, then took them out again because I had thrown so many clothes away since that day in the park that I wouldn't have any left soon. I could take them myself to the launderette for a boil wash when I wasn't working and then I could send them to my mother afterwards for a normal wash. I spent an extra ten minutes in the shower, with four soapings and four rinses. I needed to get out of the house and get to work and I couldn't take a lift with Karen; it would be too much.

I managed to comb my hair, holding the comb in both hands, taking it slowly. *Breathe*, I could hear my grandpa saying in my head, *breathe and take it slowly. It won't hurt if you don't panic.* I wanted to cry. I picked up my knapsack, did up the clasps, and picked up the bin bag. I couldn't even tidy the flat, or put the dishwasher on, and I didn't know what time it was, I just knew that I needed to leave. It took me twice as long as normal to get down the stairs, every step was a challenge, and, as soon as I got one foot down, the other one went back up, and then my downstairs neighbour got in my way just as I was going out. I was looking forward to the cool of the morgue, and as the cold air outside the front door hit me I calmed slightly, and laid my rubbish on the top of the bin; it felt like order and made me a little bit less panicky.

My progress was slow down the path and my head was jerking around, but I put one foot in front of the other on tiptoes, avoiding the cracks, and little by little, by keeping my eyes on the pavement, then the Tube steps, then the pavement, I arrived at the hospital. As I went in through the entrance the volume of people made me turn around for a moment and then I noticed Karen, the neighbour who was responsible for me feeling like this, coming through the car park. I had managed to avoid her at least and the thought of her trying to talk to me pushed me on through A and E, which was the name for Accident and Emergency, and to the lift and down, into the calm below.

But things just kept getting worse. It was not calm. The floor from the lift was messy, that was the first thing I noticed. There was a nasty path made by the wheels of a trolley, it could have been mud or blood, I couldn't tell, but I didn't want my feet to get in it. I let the lift doors close, then open again, and on tiptoe I walked around and between it, avoiding contact like the cracks in the pavement.

The mop was in the cupboard and I hung my coat in the rest area – luckily the wheels had gone straight on –

and I filled the metal bucket with hot water and bleach. When Mark came round the corner I was mopping, three times over each section of the stain, making sure every trace was gone.

'Jesus, Nick, you scared the shit out of me. What are you doing? We need you down at the autopsy room. This can wait.'

I looked ahead, and the trail led all the way down the corridor and was cut off by the double doors.

Mark walked away, and I stood rooted to the spot, panic rising. I hadn't really had to deal with anything like this yet, and I started mopping more quickly to get to the room without having to confront the sticky path ahead. I could see up ahead that it got worse towards the doors, I wouldn't be able to avoid it, as there were drops everywhere and then a big pool of the same, as if they had stopped there. I started to sweat.

'Nick, get your ass down here!'

I hated that word, and I hated being shouted at. I suddenly had an idea and kicked the bucket of hot water towards the worst of the mess, but it made things even messier, and the brown liquid started flowing back towards me. I ran to the rest room, head buzzing, and heard Mark shout again. Then I remembered. I had seen a sign upstairs which said 'Chapel'. When I was at school I had gone to the school chapel to be calm, and I needed to be calm now. I jumped from the doorway of the rest room, and got ahead of the water. Following the path I had already mopped, I tiptoed and zigzagged back to the lift, pressed the button and the doors closed. I got out and followed the signs to let myself into the chapel, and sat on a wooden chair which looked very clean. I started to cry. Every part of my body was moving and frantic, and I remembered another day when I had been in this hospital, and it was a long time ago and the same panic was all the way through me. I curled my knees up and hugged them to my chest, and thought about the last time I had come here.

I was fourteen, with a face full of spots which I hated because they were full of germs. Mother told me I was going to see a doctor about my skin, so I had agreed, because I was having to change my pillowcase every time my face touched it because the germs from my spots were breeding there. She hadn't wanted to come, and so Grandpa had come to the house, and in the morning he talked to me about what to say and what I mustn't say, in case they locked me up. I didn't understand why anyone would lock you up for talking about spots, and I didn't understand what the games Grandpa played with me had to do with it either, although sometimes I did worry about germs, and it made me feel sick. Grandpa had germs on him too, everyone did. I had learned that in science.

When we got to the hospital we went to Reception and Enquiries, and Grandpa asked for Psychiatry, and I said it should have been Dermatology because I always did my research, but no one listened.

I was high on my tiptoes, knees bent, and we went along lots of corridors, but not the same one as goes to the morgue, and Grandpa told me again which things not to say and we came to another reception and someone told us to sit on chairs. After a long time, a man came out and called my name, and I pulled at Grandpa's arm, but the doctor told me to come on my own, and there would be a nurse chaperone. I didn't like it at all.

I can remember it now. I had to spit in a cup, walk in a straight line, look into the doctor's face and keep eye contact, tell them my mother's name, my father's name, stick out my tongue, and answer lots and lots of questions about how I was feeling. I was mostly feeling like I wanted to go home. Did I love my mother? Did I have friends? I wanted to tell them that one spot, the one on my chin, kept coming back and I had looked it up and it needed antibiotic cream, but they didn't listen.

The questions went on, for hours. I stopped listening. My father didn't have a name, because he wasn't someone I knew. I didn't know what missing someone meant. What is the name of a young sheep? I knew that, a newborn sheep was a lamb, then at a year they were called hoggets, so that one was right.

I had to have a needle in my arm, and it was clenched so tight and I was screaming so loud that they couldn't get the needle in. My muscles were taut, I heard the nurse say so, and still no one came to get me. After a while of being still, they told me they needed to keep me there for observation, and not to get upset or they couldn't let me go home, so I tried to be calm, and I closed my eyes for the needle, and then they showed me a bed where I would sleep but I told them I didn't have my pyjamas and I had no slippers, but Grandpa had given them to the nurse. I hated him even more then. Tricking was bad, and lying, and he had done both.

I didn't sleep and I kept my slippers on in and out of the bed. I wouldn't get dressed into the dirty clothes I was wearing the day before, and I had to take a pill just to walk to the car still in my night things and go home calmly. I didn't speak and I couldn't even look at Grandpa; when he said he would calm me down I went to my room and I jammed a chair under my door handle and put my hands over my ears and screamed into my pillow. The white walls calmed me and my bed was clean. I wouldn't eat for a long time, I had to wait and see if any of the germs in the hospital had got into me. I was very lucky, they didn't. I wanted to be on my own in my own place with my own rules and no one forcing me to do things.

From then on, I knew to try as hard as I could not to get agitated. My nails were bitten down to below the quick, which is painful, and my teeth were clamped together. I walked on my tiptoes everywhere now, and I didn't go any-where with Grandpa unless I had to. I knew he still had to correct me, and I knew he was trying to make me a man, but one part of me didn't believe him any more when he said he was on my side and everything was for my own good.

No one talked to me about the visit, but I saw Mother whispering to Grandpa, and then one day she left a letter on her desk when she was out shopping. I saw the name *Stephen Stanniforth* and I remembered.

Hello, Nick, I am Mr Stanniforth.

I remembered the questions, and the nurse, and the needle, and I picked up the letter and began to read. I am a very good reader, I have a visual mind.

Dear Mrs Peters,
Thank you for bringing your fourteen-year-old son Nicholas to see me recently for a psychological

assessment and evaluation. I conducted a series of tests and a full physical examination, which was hindered to some extent by Nicholas's resistance to being touched and to removing or lifting up any of his clothes.

It would be fair to say that I have no physical concerns, other than his being underweight for his age, and his inability to make eye contact or walk with his arms straight at his sides, or with his feet flat on the ground.

It was difficult to assess the apathy about which you are concerned, as Nicholas was in a highly agitated state due to his anxiety at being in a strange environment with a group of people with whom he was unfamiliar. He seemed genuinely baffled by the series of questions regarding personal attachments and emotions, and was unable to answer most of them. He seemed unable to empathise; even with hypothetical situations where it was suggested that harm befall you, or his grandfather, he seemed solely concerned with practical considerations such as who would then do the shopping. He showed no emotion when I asked him about the death of his brother.

I concur with your suspicions of autism, although I feel there is something else at play here. What would have started as Asperger's Syndrome, borne out by Nick's high functioning at school in mathematics and science subjects, now seems to have been exacerbated by something, perhaps a psychotic break or early trauma, which could account for the sudden worsening of his condition. If there is anything that you are aware of that could have triggered such a reaction, it would be very helpful to know. Otherwise, I think for now careful monitoring is in order.

Nick needs a lot of support, consistent home life, and a gentle unpressured routine which should lessen his anxiety. I would suggest another assessment in a year's time, when we could also consider the use of Prozac or antipsychotic drugs, which I know you are resistant to, but I have had very good results with other patients who have similar symptoms to Nick. Let us hope that the situation improves or at least settles over the next twelve months and that we can then see where exactly on the autistic spectrum he fits.

Kind regards,
Stephen Stanniforth

I remember now, looking in the hall mirror, my head spinning, trying to see what the doctor had seen. I didn't like the letter and I remember thinking that the doctor and his chaperone nurse hadn't understood me at all.

And here I was back at the hospital and it had started again. The panic I had felt that other time was even worse now, and I was a grown-up who should use coping strategies, but I couldn't make them work. I scratched at one arm with the other, wondering whether I should go back down to the morgue; I must be late by now. I looked at my watch and it was half-past eleven. I had got to work early and so they shouldn't have shouted at me. Now they had wasted my morning and it wasn't my fault. I wanted to shout at the statue of Jesus in front of me, and ask him why he had made everyone so different and messy and demanding. I had good qualities, I was very clean, and very quiet and very neat. It was lucky for me that I didn't need to earn money; my mother had enough for both of us. I was not demanding, and I didn't need anything from anyone else.

The big problem for everyone else seems to be feelings. I know I laughed sometimes when people fell down, or when they cried. Mother was upset when I did that. Everyone has a good side and a bad side, Grandpa always says. I think he is right but I am not laughing because I am bad, I am just laughing.

At ten to twelve I went to the lift, and when the doors opened the floor was clean and dry. I went to the freezer room and put on my apron. This was better. I went to find Mark and Pete to ask them what they wanted me to do. My heart had slowed down, and I felt ready for the day ahead.

When I came into the rest area Karen was sitting there with Mark and Pete. I didn't like her being down here.

'Nick, are you alright?'

I decided to ignore her and talk to Pete instead. He is the person in charge of me. I asked him what I should do.

He didn't reply. She did.

'Nick, do you remember I told you that you would be on a trial for the first couple of weeks down here?'

My heart sped up, and I found a loose piece of thread on the arm of my jumper. I pulled it.

'Nick? This morning, when you arrived early, there was a family waiting in the room to see their daughter's body.

Do you remember, you helped get her ready yesterday? When you came in you were upset. Do you remember screaming, and kicking the bucket of water down the corridor? You were shouting, Nick, and everyone could hear you and they got quite scared and upset.'

'No one should have shouted at me. I didn't shout first, I was cleaning up the blood on the floor. Germs. I was early and now I'm late because they shouted.'

I tried to remember earlier. I couldn't remember screaming, I couldn't remember anything now. All I knew was that I didn't want to be here. I needed to go home.

I pulled my gloves off and dropped them on the floor and wanted to go and say goodbye to the bodies, but I knew that no one would understand that. I realised I was crying again and my nose was running and usually, except this week, I didn't cry. I hadn't cried for a long time. I was wailing, and no one was here to make me be quiet, not my mother, not Grandpa. I had seen the sign for stairs next to the lift, and I ran from side to side but towards it, on my tiptoes, arms waving.

Before I could get there, Pete and Mark caught me from behind, and I screamed.

'Come on, Nick, it's fine. Let's just have a cup of tea and talk about it.'

I screamed again, I remember that.

'Nick, if you can't calm down, we are going to have to call upstairs and see if a doctor can come and help. Take some deep breaths.'

I didn't want a doctor, and I knew what would happen if one came. I tried to listen to my own sounds and make them still. I needed to go home. I took the tea. Three tries to get it to my mouth, and then I took a gulp which burnt me. I nearly threw the cup across the room, but I grabbed my hand with my other hand. *Steady*.

After ten minutes, they were still talking, and I began to remember the rules. *Make eye contact* – that wasn't working. *Nod*. I could manage that. *Breathe*. I sipped and I nodded and I breathed and I blew my nose. My heart was banging in my chest, but they couldn't see that. When Karen offered to order me a taxi I nodded. When she took me upstairs and after Mark and Pete had said their goodbyes and said sorry, and what a good worker I had been, and I bit hard on my cheek to stop myself from crying again and tasted blood but I didn't shout at them, I got into the taxi and went home. Pete told me to take a couple of days at home and calm down, but I was so tired I never wanted to go out again.

I was looking forward to just being on the path leading to my own front door. It was nice not to have to smell people, and be squashed on the Tube, or in a car that smelt of curry like the one I was in now. I got out of the car and took out my wallet with my allowance in it but I didn't even have to pay, and I went towards the front door past the bins on my right. It was familiar. So much had happened and now I was just going to sleep. I had wondered if the police would come to see if it was me who had taught the couple in the park a lesson, but they hadn't. If they were going to come it would have been by now.

I went inside, and tried to breathe. It wasn't calming me down. I needed a paper bag like Grandpa brought me sometimes when I got very upset. I straightened the letters on the table. I took down my note about a job. I couldn't get the letters straight and the note was making me want to cry, again. I went up the stairs, pulling myself upwards with one hand while my feet refused to behave and my other arm waved around and my face was scrunched up so tight I could hardly get my key in the lock even though usually it was easy. I looked at my list, but it was no help. It was supposed to be work, and Grandpa was crossed out, and now I would have to cross work out. My hands were shaking too much to do it. I had a glass of water in case I was dehydrated and went past the window, covering my face with my hand so that I couldn't see the litter tray. I made it to my bed and I lay down under the covers with all my clothes still on. I had never done that before, either. I would wait for the day to be over, and tomorrow would be another day.

The house was completely quiet. My whole week had been filled with unexpected noises, but now there was nothing. The front door closed, I heard it through my pillow, but no one came in, and no children arrived. I was usually happy when the house was quiet, but even under the covers my legs were jiggling and my heart was racing. I did all my coping strategies but nothing worked. If I could go to sleep I knew I would feel better, but as I tried to think of something happy to dream about I heard banging, on the front door. Grandpa wasn't coming, and no one was supposed to be here. My neighbours have keys, the doctor's children have keys. No one should be outside, but someone was. I opened the door of my flat, and I looked down into the hall. There was a figure outside. I waited – they would go away – but they didn't, they pulled up the letterbox and shouted in, then banged again, then shouted, and the voice was a girl. I had to make it stop and make them leave me alone. I twisted and weaved my way to the door, and I opened it. This was probably what hell was like.

On the doorstep, just standing there, was the girl from the Pure Girls website, or I thought it was her. She even had the same pigtails. I stood in the doorway and closed my eyes. When I opened them again she was still there and she said hello. 'Are you Tam?'

She had an accent, but I think that is what she said. I am not Tam, I am Nick, so I said no.

'I am looking for Tam, about the cleaning job.'

Clear your head, and think about nothing. It was my most extreme way of dealing with things, but this had been a very extreme day. It didn't work. I stood still but she walked towards me, pigtails swinging back and forwards and a big smile on her face.

'Do you know Tam?'

'What is his address?

She told me, and it was the right house. I wondered if it was the policeman, but he was called Thomas, I had seen it on his envelopes when I put them in order.

'I can't help. I don't know him. You need to go away.'

'Shit, I was counting on this job. Do you need cleaner? I am very good, and very quick, and we can be friends. How old are you? We must be same age, and I just arrive in London.'

She carried on talking, but I could only hear the general tune of it now, and she didn't seem to need an answer to any of her questions, so when she followed me into the hall and up to my flat I couldn't do anything. I opened my door and quickly tried to shut it, but she was behind me.

'Come on, be nice. Let me clean your flat, only ten pounds an hour and I will be quick. Let me see.'

The energy had drained from my body. More things had happened in one day than usually happened in a month. Worse, Mother and Grandpa were coming in two days, and the flat was not up to its usual standard and I had no job, or cat.

The girl with the pigtails stuck out her hand and said, 'My name is Marta, what is your name?'

My head was buzzing, but I managed to say Nick. That was all I managed to say before she started opening and closing doors, looking into my bathroom, lifting up the toilet lid, opening the kitchen cupboards. I was unable to move.

'You relax, you want cup of coffee? Ah, I find the bucket and mop here, you very organised man. You have lots of cleaning products, I love these wipes, I can use them? I can put on radio? I clean quicker that way.'

I felt invisible, and went into the bedroom while she twiddled the knob of the Philips radio I never used, and came up with a song which seemed to be mostly a drum that was banging in unison with my head.

'You like rock? You ever hear Polish rock? You can show me nice place to go dance in London? This place won't take more than two hours, then clean.'

I sat on the edge of my bed and put on my slippers. My heart was racing, but my mind was empty now. I watched her through my bedroom door, dancing and cleaning while she sang along and the radio pounded, and every time she bent down to wring out the mop her jeans stretched over her bottom, and her jumper fell away from her breasts. She wasn't wearing a bra, and I liked her body; it was neat and she had looked after it, there was no fat and no blemishes.

She was on her knees now, scrubbing the floor and wiping over the skirting boards with my cleaning wipes, which I usually rationed to three a day. She was taking handfuls, and would have to start another packet if she carried on like this. She was sort of dancing on her hands and knees now, and her pigtails were near the bleachy water in the bucket.

'In Poland I think we say you have *zaburzenia obsesyjno-kompulsywne*. You don't know what I mean, do you? It's when you hate mess. I can see from your neat clothes, and your neat hair, and your neat cupboards. I love to clean houses for people like that.'

It was true I hated mess, but I also hated to feel taken over, and invaded. I hated being given labels, and most of all I hated being teased. I thought about the quiet of the morgue and I wanted to cry again. The girl I had liked there had been so peaceful that I could have spent all day just sitting next to her.

I sat on the sofa, but five minutes later the hoover was on, and she was bumping into the legs of my chair. 'Lift up, I have to get all the dust and then I will be out of your way.'

I didn't have strong muscles in my tummy and lifting my legs straight up was difficult for me. I swung them round and she laughed.

I stood up, and all I could think about was stopping the noise in the flat. I was so close that I could feel her breath and she stopped laughing then. Her last laugh had left a bit of spit on my cheek and I wiped it off with my handkerchief. 'You OK?'

I wasn't. The park, the night on the floor, the disruption in my house, work and now this. She walked away from me backwards and a new song came on the radio. Bang, bang, and I pushed her backwards. My hands were waving around now, I think, and I could hear the echoes of the laughter of people at school, or on the streets from behind as I walked, head down, on my toes. This was too much and I had to get things back on track. All my rules were falling away, and I tried to remember the list. *Make eye contact*. I did, and her eyes were scared, and the shape of her body under the jumper was like the girl in the park.

'Get away from me, you retarded person.'

I didn't like that word. She must have known it was a bad word and just didn't care. I walked around the sofa, the picture of the blood matted into the blonde hair of the girl in the park making me upset. I needed to make her quiet and I needed to do it with no mess. I picked up a cushion, and, as I did, she jumped up and ran towards the door.

She got to the handle, but it wasn't the simplest door to open. I had taken a long time to learn it. You have to undo the latch, then put the handle up, then down, and hold the latch with the other hand. I easily caught her, but now she was really making a lot of noise, and I was glad she was so small.

I got her on the floor easily, and then pushed her towards the sofa so her head didn't get bruised or cut. I didn't want a mess. She was against the front of the sofa now, half sitting, and I pushed the cushion towards her, covering her face, but not wanting to get any spit or germs on me.

The problem was that she didn't stop struggling, and her hands were grabbing at my wrists, then she was digging her

186

nails into my skin. I remembered the screaming into a pillow then, which my grandpa had told me to do if something hurt or when I was agitated or upset. It meant that air could go in and out of a pillow, and I realised I needed something else. The back support cushion on the sofa was harder, and I jammed it over the soft one and straddled her. It was the only way to get her to stop making a noise.

I pushed, and stretched my head back as far as I could to avoid her arms which were now groping for my face, so she could stop me I suppose, and I put all my might into the cushions, without making any sharp movements that might hurt her face. I only wanted her to be quiet and go home, but she wouldn't stop.

It took a long time, her feet were banging, the radio was banging, and the hoover had somehow come back on and it was loud in my ear. I could hear a muffled noise through the feathers and foam, and then at last her arms dropped and the noise turned into a faraway gurgle and then stopped too. I thought it might have been a trick so I only let the cushion go little by little to see if she moved, and then in the end I lifted up the edge of the soft one underneath, and I was surprised because her eyes were open.

I watched her the whole time, while I put out my hand and turned off the hoover. Then I got up, slowly, and turned off the radio, and then went back, and lifted her up. There was a wet pool underneath her, but I had seen that once at the morgue. Sometimes people came in wearing the clothes they had died in and they were wet. Peter had told me it was all the waste going out of their bodies so that they were clean like when they were born. I went and got two bin bags, a clean flannel from the bathroom, and I emptied her

187

bleachy water and filled it back up with fresh hot water and a little bit of liquid soap; I had found out at the morgue that if we used too much soap the skin got sticky.

I tried to be as gentle as I could, starting at her feet because I wanted to wash her face last of all. It was a soft flannel, and I put all my skill into making sure she was perfect and washed every inch of her. She seemed much more peaceful now, and much calmer. I cleaned the floor and put her clothes into a bin bag, all of them. I wiped the floor over with the antiseptic that kills ninety-nine per cent of all germs and I felt much better. I rolled her off the bin bags and on to a cashmere throw that my mother had bought and which was the softest thing I had ever felt. I wrapped it round her gently and put her on to the bed, where I had pulled the duvet back. I looked at her: she was totally perfect and a soft scent of lavender was coming off her skin. I bent towards her and gave her a little kiss on her mouth. She had the softest lips. Her whole body was so relaxed, and limp. No tension anywhere; she seemed much better than when she had been shouting and cleaning and singing and being insulting. The whole time in the back of my mind I thought the police might come, or my neighbour because of the noise, but it was as if I was protected. This is exactly how it was with Grandpa: no one ever came.

I got the kit I had been given at the morgue and I felt happy. I didn't need to go to the hospital to do my job. Marta looked perfect. I just needed to clean off her make-up now. Her eyes were still open and I wanted to get the blue off her eyelids. It was nine o'clock and dark now, nearly time for bed. I gently touched her left eyelid, but it wouldn't close. She was staring at me, looking at me with an accusing expression, and I tried again. Her eyes were locked open, she wouldn't close them, and I wanted her to, a lot.

I tried again with the other eye, and then both together, but she was staring at me, coldly, like Mother when I did something wrong, and I tried to pull them closed. I had turned off the radio but then pressed button number two and put it on to the classical channel and Vivaldi was spilling from the speakers, thinking maybe that would relax her, but it didn't make any difference. I left her face and tried to think what could be making her uncomfortable. I turned the radio off again, and came back to her. I bent down and undid her pigtails, and ran my fingers through her soft hair. I went and got my brush – it was soft because I hated having my hair pulled – and I brushed her hair out gently and it fanned round her head and looked like the halo of an angel.

Perhaps she wanted to be on her own for a bit. I went and stood under the scalding-hot water of the shower for twenty minutes, and my skin turned pink and clean and I came out of the bathroom. I dressed in my best pyjamas and I lay down next to Marta. I stroked her hair and then I tried to close her eyes again, gently, without looking at her, so that I wouldn't make her angry. She wouldn't let me close them, and I began to feel panicky.

'Don't worry,' I whispered. 'I'm here, it's just us, we're alone. You can relax now.'

I thought the best thing was to just go to sleep and I bent over to kiss her goodnight. Her mouth was slightly open, and I pressed my mouth on hers but her lips were stiff and her mouth didn't move. I almost screamed. 'No, stop it!' I shouted.

I half crawled, half fell off the bed, and scuttled back-wards towards the wall, where I sat, with my head banging against the base of the window. I imagined her, lying there, furious with me, her eyes angry and her jaw clenched, trying to move. I stood up, moving from foot to foot, and looked at her face, just for a moment. Her eyes were still open, and the expression had changed. She looked disgusted now, and her eyes seemed glazed over like the monster in a horror zombie film that Grandpa had once made me watch.

Why was this happening to me? I sat, too scared to move, back against the wall, in my clothes for the second time that week, and I didn't close my eyes, not once all night. I hadn't closed the curtains, and when the big harvest moon came up I got on my knees and peeped over the bottom of my bed. Her face was worse than before. Her eyes seemed to be smaller and deeper in her face. She looked grey, and I reached up into the blanket and felt her foot. It was icy. I put the heating on high; perhaps she was cold. It was autumn and the nights were getting chilly. I paced up and down my flat, trying to think of a plan. I didn't eat, and the house was quiet. It was just her and me and nothing else. Slowly I began to understand that I had done a wrong thing here, and I was being punished, but I couldn't think of a way to make it better.

It took a long, long time for the night to be over. The sun came up at quarter to seven and I didn't feel good at all but I knew I needed to assess the situation and stop being so upset.

I pulled my chair from the desk and put it by the bed. I gently pulled her arm out from under the cover and held her hand. She was still cold. I threw a sheet over her then to make her warmer, and tried to go to sleep next to her to make up for my missed night's rest. That didn't work. I could remember Grandpa telling me to take control of my life, but Marta looked so angry that I just wanted her to be gone and things to go back to normal. I wished I could take her to the fridges in the morgue, or ask Pete for advice, but I couldn't, and I got more and more panicky. I hadn't eaten since before I went to work yesterday but my appetite was gone. I felt paralysed and I had nowhere to look that didn't make me feel terrified. The litter tray was still outside one window and reminded me of the cat, and if I looked the other way I could see into the bedroom with Marta on the bed, her hair peeping out from under the sheet. I got up from my computer chair, crossed the living room, curled into a ball in the bathroom and kicked the door shut.

My neighbours came back. I couldn't remember a time when they had both been out all night, but that might have been because I didn't usually notice where they were or what they were doing. This week had changed everything. At seven o'clock I heard Dr Karen on the stairs. I knew the sound of her walk. She stopped outside my door, I could hear that too, but after a minute she carried on. I didn't want to see her, not at all. At eight o'clock, I heard the door again, and the door to the downstairs flat and the outside door both shut. Now everyone was home, and I didn't know what to do.

I opened the door of the bathroom and looked out. Marta was still on the bed, and the flat was very hot.

I had put the heating on constant and maximum and I hoped it had made her warmer. It took me a long time to get across the room, but I managed it, and her hand was still outside the blanket, and it looked warmer and a bit purple. I picked it up. It *was* warmer, but I didn't feel better. Thursday was supposed to be another work day, but now it wasn't. It would have to be a day of trying to think what to do. I didn't know where to start.

I sat thinking while people came and went. Karen stopped outside my door again and said my name quietly but I didn't say anything back. I heard banging again at ten o'clock, and wondered if it was the police. I didn't go, and I opened my door to hear but it wasn't them, it was Marta's brother, looking for her. I almost shouted out to tell him she was in my flat, he could have taken her with him, but I was too scared.

The day was long, and I picked up the phone lots of times to call the police, then stopped. Where would they put me? I knew they wouldn't understand why I had done any of the things I had done, and I didn't want to be in a prison with dirt and people all around me. I thought of getting on a train to the seaside or on to an aeroplane, but Mother had my passport and I couldn't just leave Marta here in my bed. I took off my jumper, and felt cross that she needed the flat this warm.

I decided that I couldn't sleep in the bedroom ever again, so I put on my yellow Marigold gloves that I used to clean and picked up the broom that Marta had touched the day before. I was on tiptoes again, and had to have four tries, but I got the window next to the litter tray open, and pushed it off out into the space down the side of the

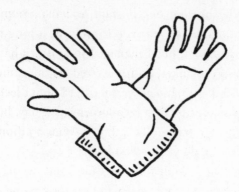

house with the broom. I didn't look at it, but even then I was a little bit sick in my mouth, and decided to throw the broom down too. I hoped the policeman downstairs didn't see, but I really didn't care any more.

I put the cushions from the sofa in a pile and took off the covers one by one. I threw the one I had used to make Marta quiet across the room, and put the others under my head under the window which was now closed tight, and the germs from the tray were gone so I could breathe without getting sick. I still had the same clothes on, but I didn't want to take them off with her in the flat and it was so hot I didn't need a blanket. I closed my eyes, back against the wall, and I went to sleep.

When I woke up it was Friday. I still had no plan but I was determined to make one. I went to the bathroom without looking at the bed at all. I had decided that I would ignore Marta and google how to dispose of bodies. When I opened the door to come out of the bathroom, I sat straight down at the computer. It took me most of the day to do my research. None of the ways they suggested seemed as if they would work now that Marta was in my flat. I couldn't cremate her without anyone noticing, or bury her, or cut her up. If I had a bath I could have dissolved her in acid, but I didn't have a bath, or acid, and I didn't know where to get any. I would have to leave if she couldn't, there was no other way. I could go to a hotel, a clean one. Before I left I would go into the bedroom and check she was still there. I thought she would be but I had remembered how often Grandpa said, *It's all in your mind, you retard. You're imagining the whole thing.*

Although I knew that Grandpa was just saying that to confuse me, I hoped that just this time I had imagined it, and it had been a dream. I put my hand on the bedroom door handle, and turned it slowly. The bedroom was even hotter than the living room, because they had the same size radiator, but the bedroom was smaller and the air hit me. I could almost taste it, a sweet smell which was like the rotten carrots that Mother had once left in the cupboard and forgotten about and which had turned into liquid before Grandpa made me throw them away. I put my hand over my mouth and ran to the bathroom. I was sick but I hadn't eaten anything so nothing came out. I splashed some water on my face. I needed to go back in there and get clothes to take with me if I was leaving. I could shower when I arrived at the Holiday Inn I had found on the internet. I covered my mouth with my flannel and sprayed aftershave in front of me as I went in. Even though I knew the smell must mean she was in there, I looked towards her now, hands waving, standing on the balls of my feet.

The bed looked different. Marta's shape looked bigger and you could see the outline of her face through the sheet as if someone had been in there with yellowish brown paint. It looked as if her mouth was sticking to the sheet and the outline was darker like lipstick even though I had washed her. I couldn't look any more, so I took three sets of clean clothes, and one pair of fresh trainers, and shut the bedroom door. Then I backed away from Marta, and the memory of the cat, and the smell, and tiptoed towards the door, trying not to make any noise. I opened it behind me, latch then handle. I was standing on the landing, with the door finally closed behind me, when I heard footsteps coming towards me and I screamed.

12 | Karen

'Everybody who is incapable of learning has taken to teaching.'

— Oscar Wilde

Thursday morning

Back to square one, that was the depressing reality that greeted Karen as she opened her eyes. Nick was gone from the morgue, and was doing his utmost not to interact with her at all now, not taking her calls or, as far as she could tell, coming out of his flat at all. She had stopped outside his door on her way to work this morning, but the flat was silent. She knew he was in there: the lights were on, and the heating was on so high you could feel it on the landing. Karen had reverted immediately to her usual pattern of overwork now that her dream case study was no longer available at the hospital or at home, and after the general humiliation of the past week, which had culminated in both her sex life and her work life crumbling to nothing. It had been enough to make her resort to a two a.m. finish and a quick sleep in the on-call room at the hospital on Wednesday night. She couldn't face Nick and she was doing her best to avoid Tam. She had only gone home to change her clothes and shower and even then hadn't been able to avoid him, coming home as she was getting ready for another pointless day at work. He had looked like a tramp, and, as he was in the same clothes he had been wearing when she had seen him on Tuesday evening, presumably he smelt like one too. She had ignored him – well, just looked at him for a minute, which was long enough to notice that he had a huge love bite on his neck that was nothing to do with her. She had dodged a bullet there. It had taken him less than twenty-four hours to soothe his wounds by finding a new sexual partner.

She had collated all the information she had gathered on Nick and it amounted to a pitiful ten pages. Even after spending the morning padding it out with observations over the last three years at Staverton Road, she had given up in the end. There was no way she had enough to present as a study.

Karen sat down and poured herself a coffee. Could she find another job for Nick? Perhaps she could employ him herself. Her life had spun full circle in the space of a few days, from a new relationship with her neighbour which had fizzled out completely, to the seeming culmination of her life's work and a fresh start with her children, to having gone not one step further forward. She wasn't prone to feeling depressed, but she certainly felt as close to futile as she ever had.

She picked up her phone: three missed calls from her ex-husband. Her finger hesitated over the call button, then she put the phone down. She couldn't take his sarcastic tone this morning. He had been almost pleasant the other evening when he had picked the kids up from her flat and would no doubt have something to say about yet another relationship coming to nothing. His words rang in her ears.

'No one could live with you; you're a work-obsessed frigid bitch with no warmth or mothering instinct in your whole body.'

For the first time, Karen thought he might have a point.

She spent the next hour googling different criteria for scientific paper submissions and tried to find something that demanded less data. Karen knew in her heart that there was no point in submitting to a less prestigious body; her ideas and research would be discredited before they were even published. All she really had left now were some nebulous ideas and a non-existent case study. She closed her computer and rubbed her eyes.

Her phone flashed green again.

'Yes, Karen speaking.'

'Karen, I'm at the kids' school. Didn't you get my message about Jamie? I asked you to come.'

'I'm at work – you know, the cupboard I go to every day to earn a living, while you make scones and daisy chains.'

Karen almost bit her lip, it had been a long week, but it never worked to go on the attack with Charlie; he just hit back harder.

'Sorry, Charlie, having a stressful day at the computer. What's the problem?'

'That makes a change. They've called me in to see the Special Educational Needs person; apparently Jamie is very withdrawn in class and not socialising. I thought that this might get you down here for a change. I know you think the rest of their education is beneath you.'

The barbed remark missed its mark; Karen was still concentrating on the first part of what Charlie had said.

'There's nothing wrong with Jamie. Where are you now?'

'I'm still waiting to go in, the appointment's in twenty minutes, which you would know if you ever listened to your voice messages.'

Karen grabbed her keys and was in her car within two minutes. She parked on the zigzag white lines outside the school and raced across the playground. She had never been inside before; parents' evenings were Charlie's territory, and she had more than enough to do already. This was something else, though, and she was furious.

The headmaster was sitting opposite her children's father when she arrived.

'Hello, I'm Jamie's mum, what have I missed?'

She had in fact completely missed Jamie, sitting on his own on the chair behind his father, hugging his knees and staring down at the floor. She had already launched into the explanation of how she knew that there was nothing wrong with her son, citing her long experience of working with children with a variety of learning difficulties from ADHD to Asperger's and every other variety of autism.

The room was quiet, and after she had finished she realised that the headmaster hadn't spoken at all since she'd come in, and Charlie was quietly shaking his head, hand on their son's shoulder.

'Hello, Jamie, shouldn't you be in a lesson?'

Jamie put his thumb in his mouth, didn't look at her, but hugged his knees tighter to him and clenched his fists. Something rang a bell deep in Karen's head, and she looked at her youngest with fresh eyes. She had left Charlie and the kids when Jamie was still a baby, and she had to admit their relationship was distant. She had been waiting for him to grow up a bit for them to grow closer – she enjoyed the company of older children, well, teenagers really, and had always thought that was when she would come into her own as a mother.

The headmaster looked at Karen.

'Thank you very much for attending today. We are all here to offer some much-needed support to Jamie, who is finding socialising and his lessons a bit of a struggle at the moment, aren't you, Jamie? I appreciate that you feel there's not a problem. Would you say that when Jamie is with you he is verbal and engaged? Sorry for being so direct, but you seem to have already come to a firm conclusion and I would appreciate your input. As you know, Jamie is by any standards gifted, despite his young age. It's been noticed by the staff who run the after-school computer club, where he is streets ahead of children several years older than him, but even his skill with computers and programming doesn't compensate Jamie for the isolation and bullying he's suffering, and we all need to decide whether this is the most appropriate place for him to further his education and maximise his potential. That's why I've asked you to come in today. Happiness is everything when you're a kid, and you aren't very happy at the moment, are you, J?'

Karen was irritated already, but the hippyish use of 'J' and the nodding from Charlie combined to bring her to the edge of losing her temper.

'I think I may have missed a few pages here. What's happened and what are you suggesting? Gifted? If Jamie is excelling in programming then this is the first I'm hearing about it. Do you understand that this is what I do for a living? Don't you think I would have recognised the signs if one of my children were in trouble? I spend my days dealing with exactly this type of presentation.'

To her left, Charlie sighed deeply then spoke.

'Karen, when I picked him up from you the other night, Sarah said he hadn't spoken all evening, and you hadn't spoken to him either. Who do you think you are, trying to tell me, or his teacher, or anyone, what he does or doesn't do in a day? Ask his sister, ask his brother, ask me – just don't pretend you have any fucking clue.'

The headmaster nodded towards Jamie, who was now rocking backwards and forwards on his chair, something Karen realised she'd seen him do before. She looked at him, then put on her professional mantle.

'Can I see the SEN assessment, please?'

Karen's voice was different now, as she thought back over the last few times she had seen Jamie. He'd been quiet, too quiet, and she suddenly got a flash of him running behind his brother the other evening in her flat. Had he been on his tiptoes or was she just projecting her own thoughts on to him? Her heart was pounding, and she turned to Charlie.

'Let me pick him up this afternoon, or take him now. I do these assessments all the time, and it would be gentler for him to have someone he knows in the room. Honestly, I know there've been huge gaps in my mothering but this is my area, Charlie, and I really want to help.'

'I'm sorry, I'm sure that you're going to be a huge support for Jamie, and we would love to draw on your expertise, but for Jamie's sake, and as his headmaster, I think we need to have him independently assessed and move towards having him statemented so that he can get the support he needs. As for not hearing about his skills with computers, we copy you in on all the children's reports every term, and you were invited to the prizegiving when Jamie received the programming cup and the technology prize. He was the only child in pre-primary ever to win either – quite an occasion!'

Karen opened her mouth to speak, then thought better of it. She looked at Charlie, who looked upset and unsure what to do next. This was her moment. She turned to Jamie.

'The most important thing to remember is that you have done nothing wrong, Jamie. We are all here to help you, and luckily Mummy helps people who feel different at her office at work every day. We will give you all the support we can, and make sure you are in the right place to get the most out of your education and your life.'

Karen asked for a word with the headmaster, and they went outside.

'Would it be alright if I took him home with me? Just today? I noticed that he's rocking backwards and forwards in his chair, and I don't think it would help anyone if he went back to class now, not the teacher and certainly not Jamie. What happened to bring this to a head? Was there an incident this morning?'

'Yes, Jamie got very upset when one of the boys in his class started making fun of him, and his teacher found him curled up in the corner of the classroom refusing to move, and screaming. We do have a strict attendance policy and Jamie's not actually physically unwell, although we take pastoral care very seriously, and mental health and bullying are at the top of our agenda.'

'Look, far be it from me to tell you your job, but there are, what, thirty-two kids in Jamie's class, with one teacher and one TA?'

'Thirty-three, last count.'

'And a lot of them don't have English as their first language?'

'No, about fifty per cent, I'd say.'

'For a child with Jamie's condition, that is tantamount to chaos, and it can't be helping. I could come in and give him some one-to-one support in the classroom until you have the budget or the personnel to help him? Surely that would be good for him and for the school. I'm more than qualified for the role. Until then, can I take him home? I'll make sure he does any work you need him to complete, and we'll be in constant touch and I can assist with the statementing process which is, as you'll know, a nightmare. If he needs to be at a more appropriate place of learning, I can help facilitate that with the help of colleagues. There are more ways of being too ill to be at school than just having a cough or cold, as you say.'

That did it. The earnest headmaster was looking concerned and Karen could almost hear him running through the seminars he had attended and remembering how important empathy and flexibility were. He took a breath.

'You make a lot of sense. OK, why don't you take him now, and we'll chat later once I've had a look at what sort of support we can offer, and you've had a chance to decide how you can help. The main issues are that day-to-day he has little or no contact with the other children and has difficulty expressing himself appropriately. He also becomes very distressed when his teacher tries to take away his headphones, which he likes to keep round his neck even when they're not turned on. In fact on one occasion his teacher had to confiscate them to try and make him concentrate a little more in class. I think your husband may have told you, we were very concerned about his reaction: he became very upset and it frightened the rest of the class.'

Karen tried to remember, and did vaguely recall Charlie telling her about a bad day at school and Jamie being in trouble. If she had realised what was going on she would have been involved before this, but work had been taking up all her time. She felt as if she was in shock: under her nose one of her own children was displaying symptoms that she was trained to look for, but she had been too busy seeking them out elsewhere to notice.

They walked back into the office; the headmaster was still speaking but Karen had tuned out. She wanted to get Jamie out of the school and assess exactly what was going on. As they went in, Karen saw that Charlie had turned his chair towards Jamie and was trying to ruffle his hair and pat his shoulder, but was being physically rebuffed and making Jamie more agitated.

'Come on, mate, cheer up.'

Karen almost laughed. If you'd written a paper on how to make a stressful situation with an autistic kid worse, this would be a blueprint. Karen ignored him, surprised by her own unexpected mental use of the word 'autistic' in relation to her youngest son.

'Jamie, we're going to go home now. You don't have to go back to class. Where's your coat?'

The little boy's face showed no reaction, but he unwound himself from the chair and walked towards the door, his eyes focused on the ground in front of him and his heels not quite touching the floor. Karen felt something close to excitement and suddenly everything made sense. Jamie was exactly the type of child that she had been researching and trying to help for so long. How had this happened? It seemed extraordinary that in a week which had seen so many highs and lows Karen now had a chance to really be involved with Jamie from diagnosis to treatment, and if all went well she could show everyone what could be done with early intervention and the proper help. Nick seemed like a distant memory and she bit down hard on her lip to stop herself welling up with a mixture of pride and relief.

Charlie trailed along behind Jamie and Karen as they headed towards the cloakroom. He was talking about the other two kids and pick-up times and Sarah having had a temperature the other evening. Karen knew that Jamie would need all her attention to make sure that there was as good an outcome as possible. She smiled at Charlie; she felt magnanimous in her new role and she nodded reassuringly.

'Don't worry, it'll be fine. I know I haven't been there as much as I could have, but I'm going to make that up to you all now. I'll take Jamie now and we can make a start on getting him back on track. I'll let you know exactly what's going on. Have you noticed anything I should be particularly aware of?'

'Just the stuff I've been telling you about for months. He doesn't talk, he won't play sport, he doesn't have any friends, he doesn't like hugs, or tickling, or even FIFA on Xbox...'

Charlie's voice trailed off and Karen ran over their conversations since the divorce. All she had been able to hear was him complaining, wanting more from her, and she hadn't heard him. She'd been stupid: if she had listened she could have been concentrating on Jamie and his symptoms all this time.

Charlie was talking again, about Sarah and Jack and their arrangements, and dealing with Jamie as a family, and Karen talking to them later, and Jack's football camp. It washed over her. She did understand that Charlie thought it was a good idea to get together with all three children and explain the implications of Jamie's problems and decide how they could all help. Karen knew that that would have to happen, but for now she wanted to get going and have some time alone with her son. Charlie clearly hadn't understood a thing about the challenges Jamie faced. Too much time had been lost already and Karen wanted to kick herself for not picking up the signs. Quiet car rides after school, watching the television with his headphones on. Then Karen had a lightbulb moment: headphones.

'Charlie, why don't you just go home and have a rest? I honestly feel awful that this is my field and I hadn't noticed a thing. Jamie and I can catch up, I'll take him somewhere quiet. Can we just try and find out where his headphones are so that he doesn't feel uncomfortable?'

Charlie disappeared into the classroom and came back a few minutes later holding them, ruffled his son's hair again, apparently oblivious that pulling away and waving hands were signs that Jamie wanted to be left alone. Her ex-husband looked lost, and for the first time since early in their marriage seemed to be looking for guidance and reassurance from Karen.

'It's OK, Charlie, I'll be in touch later, just get some rest.'

Karen bent down and turned Jamie's chin gently towards her. She held out the headphones and he took them and put them over his ears. Together they walked towards the reception, Karen filled out an absence note, the headmaster signed it, and they walked towards the car.

Karen had strapped Jamie in and was about to drive away when she saw Charlie half loping, half jogging towards them. She was running out of patience.

'Listen, Karen, he just isn't used to being on his own with you, he's very dependent on his sister, she's the only one who can get through to him really. We can come to yours later, maybe get a pizza after you two've had a chat.'

Karen thought for a moment. She needed more than a chat; she needed peace and to be able to observe Jamie over a period of time, to see what he was and was not capable of. But she didn't want another argument.

'That sounds great. I'll let you know how we get on, and we'll take it from there.'

Charlie looked relieved, and as Karen drove away all she could think of was Jamie and how finally all her theories could become something concrete. She looked across at him, lost in his own world. She wasn't going back to the house; it would be too stressful for both of them with Tam around and Nick below her. They needed somewhere peaceful and neutral with no distractions. The Travelodge near the station – they could spend the night. Sarah and Jack would be fine with their father while she worked with their brother.

Jamie wasn't fazed at all as they parked in the unfamiliar concreted forecourt of the urban hotel. Karen walked round the car, undid his safety belt and waited. Jamie slid out of the seat and walked alongside her quietly. His head moved to the rhythm of the music on his headphones, and he waited while Karen checked in and took the slim piece of plastic that passed for a key.

Their room was utilitarian: a television, a bathroom, two queen-sized beds – and Jamie happily climbed up on to the farthest bed and waved his hands until Karen turned on the television. She found a cartoon channel, and opened the bag of crisps she had bought from the machine in reception and handed them to Jamie. She needed some time, and she sat on the bed and took out her laptop, went to her documents and opened up the diagnostic questions. She filled in his name and basic information, then moved from the pages relating to toddlers and on to the questions for five-year-olds. She filled in his name, address and details at the top, then plucked up her courage, walked over to her peaceful boy, and reached down to take off his headphones.

Jamie screeched. It was as if he had only just realised that he was in a strange room alone with his mother on a school day. Karen gently steered his chin towards her again and tried to make eye contact. Whichever angle she came at him from, he avoided her gaze, and his hands were flapping frantically now. Karen pointed at the television, but Jamie wouldn't follow the pointing and lay on his front kicking and grabbing for the headphones.

Karen spent half an hour going through his responses to different questions, calming him down, showing him colours, smiling, and noting down the complete lack of engagement. No eye contact, no ability to play independently, just a desire to line up the diagnostic toys neatly over and over again. She didn't react to his distress; she had done these tests many times and knew that as soon as his comfort object was returned he would be fine.

The diagnosis was definitive. Jamie had high-functioning autism, and Karen's heart was racing. She told herself it was because she would be able to help him, but even she knew this at least was in part a lie. She walked over to him, observed the hands balled up by his sides, every muscle in his body taut, face grimacing and hands over his ears. She tapped his shoulder gently and held out his headphones. Within five minutes, his body relaxed and the tightly shut eyes opened. Karen sat down to work out an exact diagnosis and tried to suppress the feeling that somehow this was a good thing, and wondered what the protocol was on publishing papers about close family members.

There was a deep sense of purpose in her now; she felt finally as if her life had a direction as she walked over to Jamie and covered him with a blanket. She lay down on the other bed, and slept the sleep of the dead.

When she woke up, Jamie was still fast asleep, earphones on, curled up on his side. Karen needed to see him in different environments, so she decided that today it was more important for them to be together than for Jamie to be at school. She rang in and explained that he was coming down with something, then looked at her messages. Her phone was full of texts from Sarah and Charlie, asking how Jamie was, where he was, when they were coming back. She sent a text to both of them, clearing the decks for the day ahead.

Jamie fine, happy and going through everything and making lots of progress. Don't worry, will call as soon as we're home. I think he's coming down with a cold so will let him sleep and we can all have a pizza later. Sorry I didn't call yesterday, Jamie was exhausted and my phone went flat.

When Jamie finally woke up, Karen helped him get dressed and they drove together to a McDonald's drive-through and picked up breakfast. Karen had told Charlie off about his Saturday morning ritual of fast food, but there were more important considerations at play and once wouldn't hurt. Karen drove from there to a toy shop and picked up some turn-taking games, then back to the Travelodge. By mid-morning Jamie was asking for Sarah, and Karen couldn't get him to concentrate on anything, so they went to the park and as soon as she knew Sarah would be at lunch Karen called her. She was amazed how calm Jamie became as soon as he heard his sister's voice. Karen made a note of the reaction: perhaps having one person to whom these high-functioning children were securely attached was part of the solution. Sarah wanted to come and see Jamie, but Karen needed more time, and explained that it was easier to do all the tests at the same time.

'Mum, he's never been away from me for this long, can you bring him over later?'

'Of course, Sarah, I'll go back to the flat with him. It's really important that we all work together to help him, so if you can just give me a little more time we can really get on top of things and put a plan in place to make Jamie's life as fulfilling and happy as we can.'

Then Karen finally called Charlie. She needed one more day. As time had gone on, Jamie had become more and more withdrawn until Karen had given up completely, exhausted mentally and physically. She tried to explain the situation.

'Charlie, just calm down, of course I can be trusted. Look, the kind of parenting you're talking about which works so well with the other two won't work with Jamie. I know it seems harsh, but if you just let him stay one more night he can come home and we can all get back to normal.'

'Karen, I'm not leaving him with you any longer. He isn't used to being away from us all, and it won't do him any harm to come home for supper. Just tell me where you both are. Let me speak to him.'

'I know what I'm doing.'

Karen switched her phone off as Charlie carried on, shouting about custody and his rights. What about Jamie's rights? Karen wished she had never given him so much control; she should have thought ahead. What was it Charlie always said? *Stop trying to fix the world and look at what's under your nose.*

By Friday night, she was relaxed again. The weekend stretched ahead. Charlie would calm down, he always did.

Jamie was too tired to do anything else tonight, so she ordered pizza and sat next to him on the bed. She carefully cut the pizza into equal-sized pieces as Jamie watched. She offered him the box and he took a piece. Karen took the corresponding one on the other side of the box and they sat together, looking at the screen in front of them with no sound. Jamie pointed at the pictures of the deer in Richmond Park. At some point during the night Karen realised she had fallen asleep next to Jamie, covered them both with the duvet and plugged her phone in. They slept, back to back, in their own worlds.

13 | Tam

'Waste no more time arguing about what a good man should be. Be one.'

— Marcus Aurelius

Thursday morning

Banging, he could hear banging coming from somewhere, and he pulled the pillow over his head to block it out. He needed to sleep and if someone had decided to do building work today it would be the icing on the mouldy cake that was his life. It wasn't stopping, and through the fog of his hangover Tam realised that it was knocking coming from the hallway. It was the front door. He hauled himself to his feet and padded barefoot across the hall, rubbing eyes that felt as though they had glass shards in them. He was not in the mood for conversation. He pulled the door open.

'Yes, what can I do for you, mate?'

Tam tried to incorporate some menace into the enquiry, or at least convey that he was keen to be left alone, until he realised that the guy in front of him, in a wife-beater vest bearing the legend *Hutnik Warszawa*, and a tattoo on his arm of a crest involving knives and wolves, was probably not someone it was wise to be snappy with, alone on a

213

doorstep in the middle of a weekday morning. He was glaring at Tam, and his bare chest had never felt quite so inadequate, or lacking in muscle tone, as it did right now.

'Sorry, I was asleep. Can I help you?'

'I looking my sister, she come to this house address yesterday evening and she not come home.'

'Sorry, mate, I haven't seen anyone and I don't know her. Two other people live in the house – who was she visiting?'

'She cleans houses, she came about job.'

The young man took out the folded postcard from the newsagent's window and showed it to Tam. You weren't actually supposed to remove the cards, he had paid ten quid to have that there for a week, but it probably wasn't a good idea to point that out right now. Tam nodded and attempted a smile, which was not returned. He took the postcard back, on which the friendly Warsaw supporter had written *Alexsy* and then his mobile number.

'Oh, yeah. She rang me last night. I was out, and we said we'd speak later. She didn't come here. I told her I was in a pub.'

'Fucking slut girl. She always disappearing. She showed me card to let her leave. If she come here you tell me, if she come for job. Better she stay in Poland. London not good place for girls.'

Muttering to himself in Polish, the unwelcome visitor wandered off down the path and Tam rubbed his head. He plinked two Alka-Seltzers into a glass and sat down at the computer idly googling the attack in the park. Still no leads. He walked into the kitchen, opened the freezer and picked up the bin bag. Disappearing cleaners, dead cats, bags of clothes in the bin – he was either in denial and missed being a policeman, or he was overtired. He looked at his watch – ten o'clock Thursday morning. The week had disappeared again. He stripped off his lounging trousers and T-shirt. It was hot in the flat and it smelt like hell; he needed to chuck out the rubbish from the bin he'd rescued the day before. It was all too much, and the flat was like an oven. Tam lay back down and pulled the covers over his head. Things would look clearer after a bit more sleep.

When Tam woke up next he couldn't work out if he had been asleep for another twelve hours or twelve minutes. There was a sweet smell in the air mixing with the sweat and strawberries and he pulled back the curtain to look outside. It was dark.

He needed to pull himself together. Self-indulgence was fine, but enough was enough and it had all stopped feeling even close to fun. He unstuck himself from the sheets and sat naked on the edge of the bed. Looking down, he tried to assess the source of a dull pain in his cock. There seemed to be a series of burns on it, but he couldn't be sure, then he remembered the teeth. Even his ass hurt, and the pain reminded him that she had jammed some very long nails up there too. He'd been too pissed to feel much since; sobering up was not all it was cracked up to be. He walked gingerly to the bathroom and wished he had a bath to lie in. He was getting too old for this shit.

Tam sat on the loo and peeing turned out to be an act of bravery; what didn't sting ached, and he could hear himself half panting, half yelping as the different areas of damage were bathed in uric acid. Through the closed door he heard two bangs at the side of the house, and then silence. He got up, went back into the bedroom and

215

peered out into the gloom. All he could see was a broom on its side – probably the foxes after rubbish again. He sat on the edge of his bed and picked up his phone. It was seven o'clock. He clicked on to his Hungry Horse app and ordered some cheap, carb-filled dinner.

He scanned his phone looking for a message from Karen, a free pass out of the self-constructed quagmire he'd wandered into, but there was nothing from her. Tam thought he'd give it one more try. He walked up the stairs to the top floor and knocked. Nothing. He hadn't heard much movement in the house since he'd been back, just the door above him closing quietly when he had got rid of the Polish guy earlier. Now, silence. He leant against the landing wall for a few minutes. The landing was warm too, and the smell was worse up here. Maybe there were pigeons or squirrels in the roof – did that smell? He thought about investigating, then decided it was probably a job for when he was feeling stronger. All he needed was to find the maggoty body of some urban creature tonight.

The pizza arrived and Tam opened the can of ginger beer that had come with it and turned on the telly. There was a game of women's football on; he watched it, numbed out, with one hand down the front of his tracksuit trousers, gently cupping his wounds. Old-fashioned comfort. The evening passed in a haze where advert breaks allowed him to think. What was he doing with his life?

Tam woke up on Friday to the same sickly-sweet smell as the day before. It seemed to be all through the house, which was still as quiet as a tomb when he went out to get his post. He turned out of habit to the table in the hall, but it was empty and the letters were scattered all over the mat. No one had picked up their mail for a couple of days by the look of it, so maybe he had scared Karen off permanently when he had reappeared yesterday morning. He hadn't looked great, he had to admit. Fuck her, she had messed him around from the beginning, and it was up to him what he did with his days, and his nights. He tried to push down the worry that something had happened to her; he couldn't remember her ever going away before. It was time to draw a line under the whole messy relationship with Karen and move on. He stood up and headed for the shower.

Tam opened the bathroom cabinet and took out a bar of Pears coal tar soap. He unwrapped it and the smell of school nights, and his father, and cold winter mornings, hit him. He'd used it all the way through Police Academy, and this morning it felt more appropriate than shower gel. He stood under the jets of the shower and lathered his body from top to bottom. It stung the wounds from his encounter with Molly on Wednesday night, but he enjoyed the penance. He even washed his face and hair with it, and it drove the strange odour of the flat from his nostrils.

Two bowls of cornflakes later, Tam was feeling good. It was early afternoon. Fresh air was needed, and a fresh start. He tidied the bed, and gave the bathroom a once-over. The news featured another appeal by the parents of the poor guy killed in the park, and Tam instinctively picked up his phone to see if Danny had any news. There were three emails, to his new personal, non-work account. Tam had only set it up a couple of days ago, and had given that email address to Danny. He felt excited for the first time since he had parted from the commissioner the week before.

Danny had never been one to waste words, and the first one just said, *Tam, call me, it's urgent, Danny*. Then, *Tam, I am not taking the fall for this, we need to talk*, and finally, *The DNA has come back as a match, and I am not going to be responsible for some murdering bastard walking the streets while I sit on information. Get in here, you are going to have to take the rap for this*.

Tam realised that he felt better. The long hours of rest and relaxation with pizza and bad TV had left him ready to face the world, and he was excited about seeing Danny before the weekend. Tam had to think for a minute before he decided it was Friday, and called Danny's number. As usual it went to voicemail.

'Mate, it's Tam. I'm on my way in. Meet me outside the building at 4.30, and we'll sort everything out. Not sure what's happened but I'm on it.'

Tam hadn't expected to be making the journey back to work any time soon, but there was something reassuring about being on the Tube, looking clean and only slightly rough around the edges. He felt as if he was rejoining the human race.

Danny was waiting outside the building for him. 'Mate, you look rough.'

'I thought I'd pulled myself together rather well, although I'm walking a bit carefully. Two blow jobs in one night will do that. We need to find a new pub; I can't face that barmaid again.'

'You jammy bastard, my heart bleeds for you. I was up Wednesday night and last night three times with the baby.

I haven't even got tits but apparently it's more politically correct if I pick the kid up and carry it into the bedroom. Fuck it, more important things to worry about. That little favour I did you has thrown up a massive issue. The blood on that clothing's a match to the couple in the park. Not just one of them, both of them. I did it on the side for you, so what the hell do I do now? It's not like the old days: someone's going to notice. Sorry, but I have a wife and a kid depending on this job and I'm not getting any younger. I'm shitting myself. You're going to have to sort this the fuck out. As for this, get it out of here.'

Danny held a bag out to Tam, which looked like shopping, from Iceland judging by the logo. Tam opened the top and looked in. The frozen cat. This wasn't turning out to be a great day. 'Is the boss in?' he asked. 'I'll come in and give him a story. What about I made you do it? No ... I stole your access card in the pub and then put it back after I'd been in and given the clothes to forensics? I don't care, I'm happy to take the fall on this one. At least I can start again with a clean sheet.'

'Yes, he's in. He's in specially to see me; probably wants to give me the sack. Just come in, see him and yeah, good idea, say you nicked my access card. I didn't notice because you put it back in my wallet, and you tagged the bag and it flagged up a match. You might even get away with it when they find out you solved their biggest crime. Just don't throw me under the bus – I've only got eight years till I'm eligible for early retirement and a pension big enough to pay for alimony and a twenty-year-old Russian bird.'

Tam walked towards the lift. The cat was defrosting and there was a steady drip of yellowish water coming from the bottom of the bag. He dumped it in the foyer bin and pressed the lift button. He wasn't taking the stairs again, and he didn't have to warn Lucas now that Danny had buzzed him in. He swallowed hard and tried to focus. What would his dad have done? Probably had the guts to admit how much he missed the force, eaten humble pie, but kept his dignity. Tam decided to give it a try.

The lift doors opened on to the reception area of the top floor, where all his principles seemed to end up shattered on the marble tiles along with the remnants of what had once been a career. But he was here, with something to offer, even if his methods had been a bit unorthodox. Time to sort out his mess. Tam managed to negotiate Lucas and the door without tripping over his own wounded pride, and five minutes later he'd delivered his apology and waited to hear his fate.

'You did *what*? Are you seriously telling me that you stole a serving police officer's access badge, let yourself into the lab, labelled a fucking great pile of something you thought might be evidence and then let yourself out again? You've really done it this time. I'm tempted to have you arrested. It's a crime impersonating an officer, but of course you know that, you were one, or perhaps you think you still are one, except I have your resignation letter, it came in the post, very quaint. What the hell were you thinking, Tam?'

'Sir, if you'd just give me a second to explain. I had a hunch. My neighbour was acting oddly, he had blood on his clothes and dumped them in our bin, he killed a cat, he put it in the bin too, and I took the bags out and put them in the freezer. I know I went about this in completely the wrong way, but I was in a bad place and I think trying to solve this was my way of proving—'

'The only thing you've proved is what a fucking idiot you are. What am I supposed to do from here? We've known each other thirty years, Tam, and you've compromised one of my best lab techs, and a friend, by your actions. You've put me in an untenable position and presumably you realise that if I act on this I am going to be the one with egg on my face and out of a fucking job.'

Tam wiped away the sweat that was trickling down his neck from his hair. He was feeling worse by the minute but he could sense the atmosphere in the room changing. The commissioner hadn't got where he was today by being an idiot.

'Alright, mate, let's try and sort this mess out. You've struck lucky here. This match that's flagged up – is this your neighbour? Tell me about him: where he is, where he works. We need to contain this situation quickly, pick him up and try and sort the rest out once we have him in custody. You never know, we might even get a confession and then the chain of custody won't be such a bloody nightmare.'

The commissioner called in a couple of senior officers and the three of them debriefed Tam, from the day he realised that his neighbour was OCD, the letter-tidying, the bins, the clothes and right up to the present day.

'So, where is he now, have you had eyes on him?'

Tam thought back to this morning; he hadn't heard anything from above, but he hadn't heard Nick go out either. 'Sir, I think he's at work, at the hospital morgue, although I'm not sure of his days or hours and I can't say for sure. The last time I was aware of him moving around was last night, but the heating's on in his flat and…'

He paused.

'What is it, Tam?'

Tam had seen the sneaking admiration on his old friend's face as he had talked about hunches and gathering clues and observing someone he had a bad feeling about. It was textbook community policing and now Tam had another, nastier hunch. He stood up, and said, 'No, nothing, sir, just thinking.'

'Right, we'll sort this from here. Just don't do anything else to fuck it up. I'll send some uniforms down to the hospital morgue and try and catch him unawares. You just go and check into a cheap hotel and keep out of this. Don't go back to the house, that's an order. I'll be in touch once this is all wrapped up and I'll do my best to make sure you come out of it looking like a good guy. Just never do anything like this again, or I'm going to have to take action.'

Tam thought for a minute. How likely was it that his ex-boss would give him one bit of credit for this once he had Nick in custody? He needed to get something sorted now.

'Sir, don't you think this proves to some extent that old-fashioned policing has a place on the force? I really think I could be useful to you, that I fill a gap in the politically correct approach to stopping crime. I can help, sir, honestly.'

That was that, and the next few seconds were filled with handshaking, and even a clap on the back. Tam heard something about being in touch, and consultancy, and future plans, but his energy had drained away and he found himself out in the reception area again, staring straight ahead and waiting for the lift down. Danny was waiting for him in the lobby, and Tam gave him a brief summary of what had happened.

'Well done, mate – so they're going to get him? Bloody hell. Do you think I'm off the hook?'

Tam grinned, patted him on the back and said, 'I think we might both be off the hook, although you might want to get the cat out of that bin and stick it back in the freezer … they might be looking for it.'

Tam buzzed himself out, and laughed at Danny's repeated expletives as he tried to carry the leaking bag to the lift. As the door closed Tam heard him shout, 'You owe me a drink, a large one. That's a night of passion and a job back I've sorted for you in one week. Ungrateful sod.'

Tam walked as fast as he could to the Tube. The one thing that political correctness in the force had provided was time. It would take a little while for the operation to be sanctioned, and the officers put in place and mobilised. He needed to get to the house before they did. He had a horrible feeling that there was more than a pigeon rotting in the house, and he wanted to be the one to find out what was going on. By the time he walked up the path to his front door, he was formulating a plan. Perhaps he could offer Nick a cup of coffee – that had worked out brilliantly with Karen.

Just as he put his key in the door, he heard someone running on the floor above his head, and the sound of breaking glass followed by a girl's scream.

A jolt of adrenaline kicked Tam out of his exhaustion and he looked up to see Sarah's terrified face framed in the window of the middle flat. Tam took the stairs two at a time and waited for a moment on the landing outside Nick's flat. He braced himself against the doorframe and put his shoulder to the door.

The smell hit him properly now and he retched before he realised what he was looking at. Karen's daughter stood flattened against the wall with Nick in front of her, arms stretched out towards her. The bed was to their left, and a sheet covered it but did little to disguise the shape of a woman beneath. Brown stains covered the white linen and marked out her nose and mouth like a Hammer Horror remake of the Turin shroud. Tam took a deep breath and the sweetness in the air settled on his tongue and in his throat.

14 | Nick

*'Black as the devil, hot as hell, pure as an angel,
sweet as love.'*

— Charles Maurice de Talleyrand

Friday, late afternoon

I slammed my flat door behind me, stayed very still on the
landing and closed my eyes. Tight. The steps got nearer and
I could hear my heart beating in my chest. I was worried
about my blood pressure now. I could be having a heart
attack and I couldn't think clearly. It was Friday, Marta
was still here and I had no plan. I had to make a plan.
I had cancelled Grandpa on Wednesday because of my
work, but he was coming to see me with Mother because
she had missed her visit too and I would have to explain
what had happened at the morgue, and that the cat had
gone, and I couldn't stand it. I could feel the pain in my
hands where my nails were digging in and I could hear
screaming and crying and then I tried to find where they
were coming from, and then I realised they were coming
from in me, and I knew that if I opened my eyes someone
was there, and my flat had a dead cleaner in it, and I felt
like my brain might explode. It felt as if a little crack had

started, a week ago, and the drip drip drip of everything was pushing on my head and any minute now I would just break and everything would gush out like through the wall of an aquarium.

I tried to think through the panic. It could be a policeman, but they would probably have broken the door down. It could be my mother, but I could usually smell her perfume. It could be my grandpa but I knew his smell too, it made me feel sick. I began to think that it was Karen back from work, or the policeman from downstairs, but I still couldn't open my eyes. I started to breathe very fast and suddenly I heard a girl's voice that I didn't even know saying, 'Sshhhh, it's alright. Do you know that the thing you are doing with your arms, waving them around, is called stimming? My brother does it, and he twists his fingers round themselves until his knuckles hurt. Come on, it's fine, just breathe. You remind me so much of my brother. I'm going upstairs to see if he's here with my mum. Do you want to come and help me?'

There was a hand now, on my arm, and I hate being touched. It was cool and for once I didn't pull away. I stood there, slowly becoming still while someone in front of me that I still hadn't seen waited for my arms to stop waving and my face to unwind. It took a long time, and I didn't hear her move. After I had managed to get on top of my breathing and some of my muscles had untightened a tiny bit I tried a few times to open my eyes. Standing in front of me was a girl. It was Karen's daughter, I knew what she looked like from watching her through my door and seeing her on the stairs, and she was looking at me through the fringe of her hair, which had fallen out of a ponytail. I squinted through the slits of my eyes at her, and I didn't look away. Instead her eyes made me feel better and I stood, and my body unstiffened more and I felt soft and safe. She had a good, pure face and I couldn't believe that Dr Karen was even her mother. She kept talking to me and her voice sounded as if it had a smile in it.

'Do you live here? If she's there I'm going to make dinner for my mum. She works really long hours and I want to surprise her. She spent yesterday and today helping my brother and I spoke to her at lunchtime, but I'm worried because my dad is threatening to call the police because he doesn't know where Jamie is. I can let myself in, I have a key.'

I didn't say anything, but she just carried on talking anyway. 'Do you want to come? If she's there you don't have to stay, but otherwise you can keep me company. I've never been away from Jamie, my littlest brother, for this long before, and I'm missing him. He's only five. He misses me too when I'm not there.'

It seemed like a rescue. I left my door closed and walked behind her up the stairs to Karen's flat. She unlocked the door and walked over to the tap, and got me water, and put the television on. I checked the cup and without being asked she said, 'It's clean. I checked. It's been in the dishwasher.'

This was a new feeling, someone knowing what I was thinking.

'You remind me of Jamie. I look after him a lot, we're very close.'

I had never met anyone who thought I was like anyone else before, just lots of people who told me how different

I was from everybody. I wasn't sure what she meant and I carried on watching the television. She didn't even mind and just carried on chopping up carrots and talking slowly and gently. I began to think that this was a good day. If I could have just stayed there with Sarah, I think I would have stayed calm. She was exactly what I had thought the girl downstairs in my bed would be. She didn't ask me questions, and she didn't need to fill in the gaps in the conversation when it was quiet. I wished I had a sister and I wished I could stay in the room with her, listening to the sound of the knife on the wooden chopping board. It wasn't a sharp noise at all; the wood made it dull and soft.

Her mum didn't come, and Sarah decided she would cook the food and then we could eat it if no one else wanted to. She gave me a bowl and the potatoes and I peeled them. I liked them to be perfect with no grey bits and no marks so I had to throw two away but that was fine too. My mother used to tut and take them out and tell me how much I had wasted and then I couldn't eat them because they had been in the bin. Then I cut them up to be the same size. That is how you cook them properly. I looked it up on my computer.

We had mince and potatoes and peas and when we had finished I said thank you, and we didn't talk when we were eating, which was the best way to eat. Sarah ate quietly, and she asked me if I hated loud noises, and I said I did. She said her brother did too, and that I laid the table neatly just like he did. He went to the same school as her, but he was in a different part because Sarah was twelve, so she came to see him at lunchtime and break time. He didn't like many people and didn't have many friends and I felt I agreed with him. I didn't really want any, and I hadn't liked school. I hadn't even liked my brother, but I would have been able to sit with him like this if he had been quiet. He had never been quiet. He had cried all the time when he was a baby, then he had been shouty, and pushing and messy. I would line up all my toys and he would come and throw them everywhere. But I didn't want him to die, and I knew it had made my mother sad when he did. Even so, Sarah would have been a much better family member for me. I thought I would like to have her to visit me, but then I thought about my flat and my mother and my grandpa, and how I was ever going to let them in.

I didn't know, but I must have looked upset. Sometimes my face and my hands look upset to other people and I don't know. I was rocking, back and forwards in my chair, and Sarah sat quietly and watched me. It was much better than being told to be quiet, or Grandpa coming round the table, and after a while I was quiet, and Sarah waited for a bit before she said, 'Nick, you don't have to worry about anything. What's the matter? You can tell me, we're all on our own and there's no one here to make you feel sad. Tell me what's happened and I'll help.'

She did say that and I believed her and that caused a lot of problems. You shouldn't tell lies, and you shouldn't make promises that you can't keep. That is an actual rule, not made up by me, everyone says it, and she should not be upset, I should. I didn't look at her, but I did talk, and I explained that I didn't like it when my week was not in a routine, then I told her about the job and she didn't know her mother had taken me to the hospital and she stopped saying that I shouldn't worry, so I looked at her face to see what she was doing, and she looked as if she might cry. I have seen my mother look like that lots of times so I know how it looks on a face. Tight, and upset. I stopped talking about the hospital then, but I did say I liked it there. Then I told her that I had had a routine, and that it had changed, and that everyone was making me very anxious, even her mother and my mother, and I said I couldn't even go in my flat, and she said of course I could. I didn't want to tell her about the park, or the cleaner, because she is twelve and you have to keep sex a secret when you are twelve. Grandpa told me that.

I cleared the table and now it was seven in the evening and I got more and more anxious, and wanted to go and get my flat ready somehow for when Grandpa came so that he would go away quickly, but he wouldn't because he would want to see the cat. I could feel sweat coming out of my hair on to my neck and I needed to shower.

I wanted to help Sarah, because she was helping me. I needed to put the dinner things in the dishwasher but I couldn't wash the pans because there were no gloves and the dishwasher needed to be cleaned, but I just put in the plates with the tips of my fingers and closed it up, trying not to breathe in the smell of dirt. I washed my hands a lot of times with the washing-up liquid and hot water. The soap in a dish looked dirty and had black lines in the white. Sarah told me I didn't need to do anything, but it did make me feel better for a minute.

Sarah tried to ring her mother to say she had left mince in the fridge, but there was no answer, just the machine that tells you to leave a message. Sarah looked worried, and she said it was because she didn't know where her mother and her brother were and it had been two days and it was the evening and Jamie liked his routine, just like me. Sarah opened a cupboard, then another one. I didn't know what she was looking for. Then she went into the bathroom and flushed the toilet without using it.

'There's a horrible smell in this flat, I think mum must have left something in the bin. Not to worry, let's go and sort you out. I'm really good at cleaning and there is nothing so bad that I won't be able to give you a hand.'

Another lie.

I was moving a lot now, agitated my grandpa calls it, *don't get agitated*. I was on my tiptoes and my hands were flapping and I was glad it had an actual name and decided I would call it stimming in my head from now on and I told Sarah that but Sarah just smiled and I saw it from the corner of my eye. It was a nice smile. I picked up my jacket, I had folded it on the sofa. I smoothed my hair and thought I must wash my hands again. Down the stairs, down one, up one, stand still. Sarah told me not to worry. Nothing too big to sort out.

I thought I should explain so that she could be warned; what if the cleaner girl still had her eyes open? I should probably tell her how noisy she had been because she understood that I hated noise. She shouldn't go in the bedroom. I tried to remember if I had closed the door. I remembered I had, so I didn't explain.

'Come on, Nick, let's get started.'

I went in before her and she followed me, and I shut the door behind her. She gasped but I realised it was from the smell: my flat smelt like bad food and sort of sweet and not like it usually did. You could hardly smell it if you were used to the morgue, but it was there, somewhere under the top air, and it caught at the back of my throat.

'Wow, I see what you mean. Did you leave the bin full?'

Sarah put the light on to make the flat less dark. The cushion from the sofa was still on the floor and she picked it up. The flat looked messy, and Sarah was close to the door and frowning.

'I'm usually very tidy. I had a very bad week. A cleaner came, and she used too many wipes. I went to the park for my walk and there were people by the pond where I feed the ducks, and I always walk there. I have a routine but it's all messed up and I got rid of some of my exercise and replaced it with walking to the Tube and to the hospital but now that has stopped and I don't want my grandpa or my mother to visit and I don't want my flat to be messy. I am never messy.'

Sarah had stepped towards me and away from the bedroom door, and she picked up the bowl of soapy water from the floor that I had used to wash the girl in my bed. I watched her pour it into the sink, and she hummed to herself as she wiped down the surfaces. She hummed very quietly and it didn't make me upset. I tidied my papers until they were square in a pile and put them by the computer and made that straight. My grandpa and my mother didn't usually go in the bedroom; if this was all tidy then maybe they would just go home. At my mother's house he made me go into the bedroom to be corrected, but we mustn't tell anyone about that or about the sofa here or they would know we had been bad.

I realised that I was saying all this out loud. Well, not loud, but it was coming out of my mouth and Sarah was

232

just looking at me now and she wasn't humming, and then she looked like she might start crying again and I gave her some paper towel. I like it because you can tear it off really neatly. She wiped her eyes and then said to me, 'Why does your grandpa make you keep secrets, Nick?'

I closed my eyes then, because she was looking at me the same way everyone else looked at me, and I tried to remember that she had said she would help me and not to worry. But I was worried. I dug my nails into my hand hard and tried to explain what had happened and how much trouble I had been. *You are nothing but trouble.* My grandpa had told me so many times, and my mother had sat quietly in the corner crying. I don't like people touching me, or my things, and it makes me very agitated when they do. Grandpa used to scoop all my things up into a huge bag when I lived with him and Mother – all my toys, then all my clothes, just to make me cross. Sometimes he laughed, and when I was on tiptoes or waving my arms it made him laugh more.

'My grandpa makes me go into the bedroom because he loves me and he has to teach me about the nasty side of life even if I don't want to learn. He's done everything for me, and looked after me even when my mother couldn't do that. My mother told me she was sixteen when I was born. I am much more than sixteen and I don't have a baby. I didn't even like my cat.'

Sarah hadn't moved, and she was listening carefully, and didn't say anything, so I carried on talking.

'She didn't have a husband and she wasn't old enough to have a baby and I was a very difficult baby and I didn't want to have milk from her, and I was getting thin. She

233

lived with my grandparents and they helped her and helped me and gave her money and then a nice place to live and we went there together, but one day my grandpa came to get me because my mother had stress and needed a break from my nonsense. Grandpa said I had made her bloody miserable and I think I did because she was always crying. My fault because she just wanted to sit together and kiss me and cuddle me and I hate being squashed or having someone next to me or arms round me with armpits at the end, and I didn't like her food and I didn't want to talk and she got so cross she went and made another baby. He was born and he was my brother. My grandpa said he was funny and liked to cuddle and every week I went round to my mum's for my visits and Mother told Grandpa she was happy now because of her new baby but not because of me. He would sit on her lap with milk dribbling down his chin, or apple sauce all over his front, and he didn't mind the germs. I didn't like to touch him, and everyone got cross with me because I didn't like him sucking my finger, or grabbing my hair. If I screamed it made him cry, but all he had to do was stop touching me. I told him lots of times. Having me and him together was too much trouble and I had to stay nearly all the time at my grandpa's then, and my granny wasn't there any more because she died from being old and it was just us, or on Tuesdays and weekends it was me with my mother and my brother. My brother didn't like quiet, or clean. He liked wet and mud and breaking things. Once he sprayed me with a hosepipe, and once he tried to cut off my hair when I was asleep with sharp scissors. He kicked me, and even though he was only four it was painful on my leg and went blue then purple and after a long time yellow. I stopped being in the same room with him then and I didn't like watching my mother with him.

> *X marks the spot with a dash and a dot,*
> *A dot and a dash and a big red question mark,*
> *A stab in the back, blood rushes up, blood rushes down,*
> *Little spiders crawl all around.*
> *Winter's come, a cool breeze, tight squeeze,*
> *Crack an egg and let it freeze.*

'Mother would pull off his T-shirt and tickle him and he would laugh and laugh and I would stand with my face against the wall and my hands over my ears and wait for it to finish and Grandpa to come back and get me and take me to his house and a quiet place, but inside I didn't want to go. I didn't like being on my own with Grandpa and I didn't like being in the noise and dirt with my brother and mother. I couldn't even sit on the carpet at Mother's because no one ever cleaned it. I was scared at my grandpa's house, and I stopped reading books and doing maths and I didn't do my homework and I had no one to talk to because if I talked to school then they would take me away and I would have nowhere to live.'

My whole life seemed to be spilling out of my mouth and Sarah just stood there looking at me, but her eyes seemed bigger now, and I couldn't stop talking, I knew I was talking faster and faster but I couldn't make it stop.

'My brother was never in trouble. If I put my hand over his mouth to make him stop being noisy, Mother shouted at me and he would smile at me and stick out his tongue, but he was the one laughing, for nothing, all the time.

'One Saturday I went to my mother's and my brother had a temperature, and he was very quiet, just sitting on my mother's lap, sucking his thumb and rubbing a dirty blanket and being still so my mother put him down on the sofa and put cushions round him. He had very red cheeks and his eyes were opening and closing but they looked like glass and I didn't like them. He was making a funny noise like a far-away train, and my mother was on the phone to the doctor, so I went close to see what he was doing. I stayed out of reach but then his arm dropped off the cushion and he went to sleep with his eyes open. The train noise stopped but his eyes were still open and I put out my finger to close one, and behind me my mother screamed. BUT I DIDN'T HURT HIM!'

For a minute I could remember, the screaming and the shouting, and the ambulance, and the lights and the siren and the dark and the machines bleeping and the tiptoeing panic, and doctors asking me what happened and the look in my mother's eyes. Clenching fingers, nails in my skin, pushing in and blood coming, pulling my hair, the muscles in my body pulled up as hard as I could pull, teeth clenched together. My brother still and little, and quiet. Too small for his bed, and not attached to my mother at all, he was on his own in a room full of machines and plastic floor, very clean. My mother's body was going in and out in great gulps of air and she put her hand on his face and reached for my hand. I lifted my hand up away into the cool and said bye and then went and waited outside. My mother never tried to hug me again.

I had never told anyone before, not about my brother, or any of it, and I waited to see what Sarah would do, but

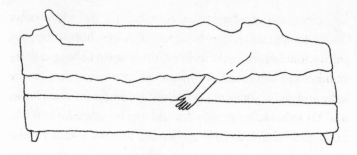

she didn't do anything, not really. She looked different, as if she was going to leave, but she took the wipes and quickly tied up the bin bag, not neatly but it didn't matter, it was an emergency. I watched her pushing tears off her face, crossly, and I went to tear some more paper towel but she did it herself and blew her nose and just put it on the side, and I wanted it in the bin and out of the flat with all the germs. She put the bin bag by the door, and ran the tap, and poured some bleach into the sink, then went into the bathroom and did the same to the toilet.

I heard her talk, I think it was to herself, but all she said was, 'Fucking retards, fucking parents.'

I had been called that before, and I wasn't sure why she was saying it now.

She asked for the hoover and went back over the carpet, all the way to where it turned into tiles by the border of the kitchen, and as she turned around to do the thin strip by the wall the hoover banged the bedroom door and it swung open, and the sweet rotten smell came out and Sarah was looking at me with a sad smile and it stopped when she smelt the smell from the bedroom, then she looked back and the bed caught her eye and she started

237

screaming, and as she started screaming I looked towards the window and saw my downstairs neighbour on the path, and then he was looking up towards the window, and my shouting mixed with Sarah screaming and Sarah banged so hard on the glass that it broke and now someone would probably tread on that and cut themselves, and my flat was filling with cold air. I tried to think what to do, but I knew it was all over. Grandpa's eyes met mine and my hands were waving in panic. Sarah didn't comfort me this time, and then her dad and one of the brothers were outside too. I heard the slamming of the front door and I backed towards the bathroom to get away from the smell and the noise, but someone was coming up the stairs now, maybe all of them were, and then there was a huge bang at my door and it mixed with my noise and Sarah's screams. I got on to the floor and against the wall and closed my eyes. I was so glad the week was over, I just wanted to go somewhere peaceful.

15 | Karen

*'Day by day, what you choose, what you say and
what you do is who you become.'*

— Heraclitus, 500 BC

Saturday morning

Karen woke up and for a moment she had no idea where
she was. The sound of the road outside the window and
slow childish breathing in the room disorientated her, until
the memories of the past couple of days came back into
focus and a sense of relief and purpose flooded through
her. She stretched, and as she did so a shaft of sunlight
landed on her arm and she lay for a moment watching the
little boy next to her, his sleeping face quiet and without
care. A lick of sandy-coloured hair lay across his forehead
and his mouth was slightly parted. Looking at him, Karen
understood why she had been led on to the path she had
taken. She was there for her son, to help him, to understand
him, and in doing so she would help so many more.

Jamie had been exhausted by the time he got into bed
last night, but Karen had all she needed now, and had
managed to get through more in thirty-six hours with
Jamie than she usually managed in months working with

a subject she didn't know. Measured intelligence, social interaction, communication, repetitive behaviours, sensory responses, motor skills – Karen had tripped through the list and felt satisfied.

She smiled to herself thinking of the many times she had inwardly laughed at exactly the same self-indulgent introspection from colleagues. She had never taken decisions based on emotions, her ex-husband would have been only too happy to testify to that. She reached over to her bedside table and looked at her phone. It was Saturday morning and she had disabled her alarm, but, as she disconnected the charger and focused, she saw she had thirty-two missed calls. She had never had thirty-two missed calls in her life, and the confidence that had started to grow in her disappeared in a popped balloon of contentment and achievement. She pressed voicemail and with an unsteady hand put the phone to her ear, thinking only death or disaster could possibly have caused this, and the fury she felt for the possible loss of her embryonic plans was almost unbearable.

Karen, where the fuck are you? Your daughter needs you, she's at the hospital.

Karen, your little protégé attacked Sarah. She's in shock, at the hospital, and your latest lame duck has been arrested. It's 10 p.m., where are you?

Listen, you bitch, you decided to put a severely autistic young guy to work in a morgue so that you could observe him like a lab rat and very nearly

*succeeded in getting our daughter killed. No one
knows where you are or where Jamie is – call me.
It's one a.m.*

The messages went on, culminating in one from a
doctor at the hospital telling her that her daughter had
been attacked and held by a man known to her, one
Nicholas Peters, and that he'd been arrested for murder.
Karen sat for a moment on the edge of the bed feeling as if
she might cry or scream. Her plans for the future were in
tatters and she walked over to the little desk, gathered up
her papers and her laptop and put them away. Jamie stirred
and she sat opposite him, handed him his headphones
and explained that they were going to see Sarah. He put
them on, then pulled on the jeans and T-shirt from the
day before, and the day before that, carefully moving the
iPod from hand to hand. He seemed more withdrawn and
refused Karen's offers of help, pushing her hands away and
repeating Sarah's name. They got into the car and drove
towards the hospital.

Jamie kept asking for breakfast, and as Karen walked
into the familiar surroundings she steered him towards the
canteen. It wouldn't help anyone to have Jamie agitated
while Sarah needed attention, so they sat quietly at the
same table where she had taken Nick for lunch only days
before. She ordered Jamie a bacon sandwich and herself a
coffee, and she carefully cut the crusts off and quartered
the sandwich before putting it in front of him. He was on
the third quarter of his breakfast when she heard her name
being yelled across the canteen.

'Karen, what the fuck?'

Her ex-husband was standing in the queue, a bottle of water and some magazines in one hand, and Jack attached to the other. He stormed towards the table, and Jack hung back, not greeting Karen, while Jamie carried on eating his bacon sandwiches, nibbling all the way round the edge then moving towards the centre.

'Stop it! I had to give Jamie some breakfast or he would have been hungry, upset and fretful and I didn't want him to be like that when we saw Sarah. Tell me what happened. Your messages were so foul that I only listened to three.'

'Your daughter apparently thought she had bonded with you the other evening and decided to surprise you by cooking supper and rescuing her brother as I was so out of my mind with worry that I'd phoned the police. Turned out she was the one who got the surprise when your little friend Nick got her into his flat then locked her in with a rotting corpse that just happened to be in his bed. What the fuck has been going on in that house and where the hell have you been since Thursday afternoon? You've been gone two whole days, Karen, with a little boy who depends on us for security. We've been out of our minds with worry. The police have been looking for you; they finally agreed to do a phone trace yesterday and they couldn't even trace you through that, because you switched the bloody thing off. What the hell were you thinking? Sarah needed you. We all needed you...'

His voice trailed off and Karen couldn't meet his eyes. She lifted one of Jamie's headphones away from his ear, turned his chin towards her, and folded his remaining bit of sandwich into a napkin. She beckoned to him and she followed Charlie. Jamie followed her, and Jack trailed behind. It was a sorry caravan of disconnected souls, a broken family, and no one said a word. Around them people in the canteen carried on, eating, serving, texting.

Sarah looked tiny on the hospital bed, white and small and young. It surprised Karen, who was so used to seeing her as a surrogate mother to the boys, or someone who could run to the shop or let herself in after school or make her own way to friends' houses. This was a child, and she lay on her side in the middle of the white sheet in a foetal position, eyes open, staring into the middle distance. Karen hesitated, then approached the bed.

'Sarah, it's Mum. What happened? Are you hurt?'

Sarah stretched out her arm towards her, but before Karen could take her hand Jamie came round from behind her and the little white limb wrapped around him. He crawled up on to the bed and lay with his back to his sister.

'Sarah.'

'Jamie, where have you been? I was so worried about you.'

The two of them lay together, and Sarah breathed in and out through her brother's hair. Karen seemed to be surplus to requirements, so she beckoned Charlie outside.

'What happened? I was trying to assess Jamie, I fell asleep, I didn't know she was coming over. Did he hurt her? Touch her?'

Karen vaguely remembered telling Sarah she would be taking Jamie back to the flat last night. She swallowed and tried to collect her thoughts, the realisation of what she had done creeping in now.

'It was fucking chaos, Karen. I got a call from the football club to say that Jack hadn't been collected. I was trying to juggle the other two kids, and you disappeared in the middle of my work conference week. I got in the car and went to get him, then all hell broke loose. The police called, and I went round to yours and found the whole place under siege: tape, police cars and lockdown. Sarah inside, Nick inside, your policeman boyfriend inside, and, as it turns out, the dead body of a girl who had come to see him about a cleaning job also inside. I stood on the pavement with Nick's parents, and our son, watching Sarah screaming through a smashed window, and you were nowhere to be found, as usual. Nick's mother and grandfather were called, they made fuck-all difference, and eventually Tam the hero policeman emerged with our daughter. I've had *enough*, Karen. You aren't a mother, you're a selfish, career-obsessed bitch. I need a coffee; I haven't slept for two nights. Go in and pretend to our daughter that you give a shit, comfort her – just keep the fuck away from me. You need to call the police and explain what happened and you need to call your lawyer when things calm down, because I want full custody of the kids. I can't let you put them through this any more.'

Karen wasn't going to explain again to Charlie that she'd been helping Jamie, or that he was better off in her hands, where he would get all the help he needed. This wasn't the time and she needed Charlie to calm down first. She put her bag down by the side of Sarah's bed and pulled a chair across the room. Jamie was awake but Sarah's eyes were closed. Only her hand, which was gently stroking Jamie's back, indicated that she was conscious.

'I need to talk to you, Sarah, I just want you to know that I'm sorry. I was trying to help Jamie, I think I know what's wrong with him, and you know my work, how important it is. I think Jamie has exactly the condition that Mum is working on, and that's why I wasn't there last night, I was helping Jamie, can you understand that?'

Karen decided that was enough of an explanation for now – just keep away from the technical stuff, there was no point in trying to explain Jamie's condition in detail while things were so fraught. Sarah's hand stopped stroking her brother and her arm tightened around him. Her eyes opened and instead of broken and sorry, the expression Karen saw was pure fury.

'Are you here to tell me about my brother, Mum? I've been telling you about him since the day he was born. You were so glad that he was quiet, and didn't need cuddling, and was happy to sit on his own. He wasn't happy. I tried to tell you, school tried to tell you, Dad tried to tell you. You were working. How can you sit down and not even ask me if I'm alright? All you're worried about is excusing yourself and getting out of here. I was in a flat with a murderer, one that you experimented on by taking him to work with you, one that you probably pushed over the edge. He isn't well, Mum – what the hell were you thinking, putting him in a morgue?'

'I was doing it for the greater good. I'm trying to collate information, to make a firm set of diagnoses and criteria for the different types of autism, and Nick was helping me with that. It's hugely important, Sarah.'

'Yes, you've been telling us that all our lives. More important than us, more important than staying with Dad. More important than remembering my music recital, or Jamie's first day at school, and more important than looking after any of us. We dragged ourselves up, Mum, with child-minders and au pairs and after-school clubs, and all the time Jamie getting more and more detached, and finally you wake up to him and how different he is, on the night when your social experiment nearly kills me. Leave us alone. You can't do anything for Jamie. You've done enough already.'

Karen was furious. She had sacrificed her personal life, her marriage and her time with her children for something more important, something that was world-changing, and she couldn't believe that her daughter thought she should have been sitting at home making fish fingers.

'Sarah, you aren't old enough to understand the decisions I've made or how difficult they were. Don't you think I would rather have just sat at home and played house? I live alone; I've given everything up for my work. It's been a tough, tough journey but I've done it because I believe my work is important. I've got the right to choose to help others, to use my brain, to share my knowledge and my resources. Surely you can see that? You're a bright girl.'

Sarah opened her hand. In it, squashed and bloody, was a small piece of tissue.

'How many teeth has Jamie lost? How many times have you forgotten his birthday? I'm the tooth fairy for the boys because she never visited me; I save my pocket money from Dad to make a cake for Jack when he wins a race at sports day. You're right, I am a bright girl, but I'll still love my children, if I'm lucky enough to have any. I'll make sure they know that they are more important than the faceless masses out there that you want to rescue so badly. You can choose anything you want, of course you can, you can give us the leftover parts of you when you can spare them, but you can't just turn up here and pretend to be my mum, or steal Jamie because you suddenly think he's interesting. You don't have that right any more.'

Karen was exhausted. She tried to think of something to say, but a doctor came in to check on Sarah and it was easier to ask if she was OK physically, and then go and get a coffee. Karen knew she'd done enough. Things would calm down; Sarah had been through a lot. Charlie was outside with Jack and hardly looked up as the mother of his children walked past.

'Charlie I know you're upset – let me take the boys. Sarah seems understandably angry and it's probably best if you can give her your undivided attention until they release her and she's calmed down.'

His face looked different now, this man she had known for years. His expression was somewhere between despair and desperation.

'I'll call my mother to come and collect them. She needs both of us, Karen, can't you see that? Have you even said sorry to Sarah? What kind of woman just checks out for two days with one of her kids and turns her phone off?'

'Me. This kind of woman. The kind who doesn't think life spent at NCT classes and in front of the television is enough, Charlie. Where's your ambition, where's your passion? You aren't a man, for fuck's sake. I checked in with you, I rang Sarah. Not everyone is attached to each other every minute of every day; some of us have things to do, and goals to achieve.'

Out of the corner of her eye, Karen saw a movement. She turned, and Jamie and Sarah were standing, hand in hand, in the open doorway of her room.

'Mum, go. Do you know that last night, when I was in that room with Nick and that poor dead girl, I thought about you? I wondered if we were in your head at all. Do you worry about us? Do you care whether we're happy? Do you think to yourself about what might make Jamie better, or what you could do to take a bit of pressure off Dad and me? Last night I decided you must love us deep down and it gave me something to hang on to, but now I think back to the nights you left us with au pairs who had just arrived and couldn't speak a word of English so that you could go back to the hospital, and then blamed them for everything when they left because they couldn't cope with your chaos and running the house, and feeding us, and being our surrogate mum. You told us every au pair we ever had stole from you, took our stuff, and every man that crossed your path from Dad to now was a bastard, or hit you, or was a psychopath. But *you're* the psychopath. You're a narcissistic, toxic person who just happens to be my mother and I want you to go and leave us alone. You've done enough now. It will take all of us the rest of our lives to get rid of the scars and you should go and write your paper on your own somewhere away from us, the idiots who happen to be your family and who you can still hurt. Just go.'

Karen looked at her daughter, and for a moment images flashed through her head. Trying to type with one hand while her baby tried to feed before she put her on a bottle at six weeks; looking at research notes while Sarah tried to tell her about the carol service, or her gold star for writing. They had even had a joke about it. Sarah used to send her emails, with a green dragon emoji and *I know you won't have time, but* attached.

The gulf between her and her daughter seemed enormous now. Karen pushed down doubt as hard as she could, despite the wave of pain washing over her. How had she got here? How had any of them got here? She felt as if she was having a panic attack, and the images of her husband as a young man flooded into her mind: images of nights they had shared, images of Jack and Sarah building a sandcastle, their father turning round and smiling at Karen. That had been the week before she left, and she could remember how much she had wanted to get off that beach. Only now, now that she knew she had lost even the possibility of a family, did she see it as it really had been. She shook her head. She could still help Jamie, and this was the last chance. Jack was crying quietly behind her in his dad's arms, and Sarah was distracted. Karen held out her arms to Jamie and tried to catch his eye.

Charlie saw what she was doing and walked, still carrying Jack, over to Sarah. They looked like a group, a family, and she didn't belong.

Charlie put his free arm on to Sarah's shoulder and looked at Karen.

'Do one decent thing if you have a heart: fuck off and leave us to try and make a life for ourselves.'

Karen walked down the corridor alone. She tried again to think what she could say to make the situation better. Jamie needed her. She would get hold of a lawyer in the morning. In the meantime, she took the lift down to the first floor, took the key to her office out of her bag and let herself in. She had all the information about Jamie from the stay in the hotel in her bag, and she wanted to get into the database. She turned the computer on, but she couldn't make her fingers work. Jamie's face and Sarah's fury were all she could think about, and she felt shaky.

She pulled her cardigan round her and stared at her screen. Something was weighing her down and she didn't recognise it. These were faint echoes of feelings, and her certainty deserted her. Karen could feel the shadows of something lost and she was profoundly tired. Sitting in the centre of her existence, her tiny office, she tried to narrow down her thoughts and identify where this terrible feeling of despair was coming from. She tried to fall back on a scientific approach; it had never failed her before, but for the first time she doubted that was true. Her heart was heavy and she sat in the room that held in its files the purpose of her life, but she was overwhelmed by the conviction that somehow she was wandering in a maze and had taken a wrong and terrible turn. She knew it, and yet she didn't get up to go to Sarah. It was just too hard.

16 | Tam

> *'Every new beginning comes from some other beginning's end.'*
>
> — Seneca

Wednesday

Tam was packing. He'd been sleeping at a hotel near the office because he needed to put this fucked-up house of murder and failed relationships behind him, and get on with his life. The hotel was out by ExCel, which was about as far as he could get from the flat and still be in London, and he'd been taking his stuff over on the train one bag at a time ever since the police let him back in. He'd been shifting stuff gradually just in case the Holiday Inn decided he was moving in, which he pretty much was until he found a storage unit and then a new place to live. Every time he walked out of his old front door he could smell the deep atavistic odour which still hung around even in the hall, in the air above the table that once held a neat pile of post, but was now covered in fingerprint powder and takeaway leaflets spilling on to the carpet beneath. Tam sifted through Karen's post and extracted his letters. One more visit and he'd be done. A shiver ran down his back, and he stepped over the faded bunches of flowers on the doorstep, put his head down and walked up the path.

Most of his life for the last few weeks seemed to have revolved around bin bags one way or another and this morning on the train he looked a pretty sight, carrying yet another black bag stuffed with clothes, while young professionals made their way to work wearing suits purchased on gap years in Hong Kong with ridiculous red linings, or pink embroidery marking out handmade buttonholes from the run of the mill. This was why the British class divide would run and run; he hadn't grown up with anyone whose dad would have told him to buy a suit in the Far East. Tam nearly laughed out loud at the absurdity of it all.

Opposite him, a tall, well-spoken guy was talking into a mobile phone. He was absentmindedly patting a bundle that was attached to the front of him and joggling a pushchair with his knee. An arm kept reaching out of the buggy to grab his trouser leg and a voice which was, from Tam's angle at least, faceless, repeated the mantra 'daddydaddydaddydaddy'. The bundle he was patting turned out to be a baby, staring glassily out in front of him, and it seemed to have no thoughts of trying to get attention. As the train pulled in, Tam saw him following a herd of other commuters all attached to babies and toddlers of various ages. What was it, bring your child to work day? Tam craned his neck to look at the sign they were all headed towards.

WE TAKE BABIES FROM SIX WEEKS, 7 A.M. TO 7 P.M.
LATE TAKE-HOME AND LET-IN SERVICE AVAILABLE.

It seemed to Tam that the Russians had tried something like this and they hadn't had a universally positive outcome. How had this happened, that it was fine for kids to be farmed out to someone probably on minimum wage rather than being at home tucked up in their cots? Tam felt old and out of step again. He wasn't a parent, thank God, but what he'd seen over the last couple of weeks made him think something in society was going wrong, and he was glad to be out of it. Thoughts of children took him back to Sarah, and a pang of sorrow, mixed with anger, flooded through him.

The events of the other night flashed into Tam's mind. Rushing back to the flat and the screaming he'd heard coming from Nick's flat. Sarah's frantic cries for her father as Tam had burst in were still ringing in his ears. He needed to close that door for the last time, and sit by himself with some IPA and ten takeaways in a row. He leant back against the cool of the glass behind him and tried to still the images and the rising panic which kept taking him by surprise. Nick's face, the sheet covering the bed, it just kept playing like some demonic Faustian play. So many bleeding hearts and no one to fix them.

It had been chaos. First through the door, he had been in the flat within thirty seconds of hearing a scream. Nick had been standing between him and Sarah, and the flat was gloomy with that sweet smell of rot that still seemed to be living in his mouth and nose.

It had taken him about twenty seconds to push down the rising bile in his throat, adjust to the gloom and decide what to say. Police training – old-fashioned police training.

'Sshhh, Sarah, calm down, I'm here, stop screaming, let's try and talk to Nick and explain that we aren't here to hurt him, then we can sort everything else out.'

While he talked, Tam had been looking round the flat. There was only one door in and out, obviously, and it was behind him. Nick was on the floor, sitting, back against the wall, below the window which looked out over the garden of the house and Staverton Road. His eyes were closed and he was wailing like a banshee, his hands moving in a frantic pattern and his whole body twisted like a ball of wire. Sarah was behind Tam in the doorway of the bedroom, by the smashed window that looked over the path and bins, standing in a pile of broken glass, her eyes fixed on the bed and her hands clamped over her mouth and nose.

'Nick, come on, we know each other, mate, don't do anything silly. Sarah's your neighbour, you don't want to hurt her. Just let her go past you and find her dad and then we can talk and sort all this out.'

'It can't be sorted out now. I want to go somewhere peaceful and have a routine. I don't want to go to my mother's house; I don't want to go there. I don't want to go in the bedroom. I don't want to be here.'

'I can see that, Nick. Come on, let Sarah go past you and we can sort this out.'

'She said she would help. It's a lie. I don't like it here and she said she would help. I don't feel good here.'

'Nick, I can see you've had a rough time; what I find is that something goes wrong, then one thing after another makes it worse. Let's sit down and try and work out what happened and make a plan.'

Tam remembered the next few seconds clearly, Nick starting to calm and the rocking and twisted arms seeming to relax for a moment and him standing up, as if he was ready to go with Tam. Then suddenly he caught sight of a movement outside and Nick looked down at his mother and grandfather on the pavement. Tam had never heard keening, that strangest of human noises, but Nick started it then. A high-pitched wail of agony, and then another layer, an echo of Nick's pain in Sarah's sobs and cries mixed with the wailing, until amidst the frantic repetition Tam could suddenly make out words.

'Don't make me, don't tell.'

'Nick, no one is trying to make you do anything, it's OK.'

'Sit down, sit here.' Nick beckoned to the floor, and soon Tam and Sarah and Nick were huddled together while outside the sounds of cars arriving, and teams with loudspeakers, made Nick rock ever more frantically back and forth while Sarah looked more and more terrified.

Tam dug deep and tried to remember what he'd been told on the ridiculous hostage seminars he'd been forced to go on. He knew that eye contact was recommended, but that wasn't an option here. He tried putting a reassuring hand on Nick's shoulder, which was also less than helpful as it was met with a jerk and a shout. He looked at Sarah, and then spoke to them both.

'Listen, we're all in this together. We need to get this sorted and get out of here so that we can all get back to our lives and our routines.'

He remembered that: repeat words back that the perpetrator finds comforting. He had learned that on a course.

'Nick, just let me go to the window and let them all know we're OK, and that we need some peace and quiet to talk. Is that alright with you?'

Nick scrunched up his face; his hands were over his eyes. Sarah put a hand gently on his arm, as she had earlier, and his eyes sprang open. Tam noted that he didn't jerk away when Sarah touched him.

'You lied to me, you said you would help me.'

Sarah was frozen, unable to talk, and Tam took over.

'I will, I'll do that, I'll help you sort this out and get somewhere quiet; let's just get the noise to go away and we can see what the problem is. Look, we're all here, and we're all safe. Now we can deal with the rest of the problems.'

'I am the problem. I am the problem. My mother doesn't want me and I don't have anyone else. Just because someone dies, it doesn't mean it's your fault. I had a brother and my mother doesn't love me and I am the problem. Grandpa told me that.'

Tam had got gently to his feet and headed for the bay window at the front of the house. He waved down and gave a thumbs-up and then put his finger to his mouth in a shush sign. He remembered making eye contact with Sarah's father, he recognised him from Karen's flat, and he tried to convey that everything was alright but that they needed everyone to back off for a bit.

Things quietened down. Tam sat back down on the floor and Nick slowly became less frantic. Sarah had pulled herself together and now she started talking gently to Nick, in an almost singsong voice. It was gentle, and even made Tam feel better.

'Do you remember I told you that my brother and you were so similar, Nick? He's my best friend and I would never let anyone hurt him. If someone's hurt you, or you've hurt someone, we can make it better, I'm sure. Just talk to me.'

The silence seemed endless and Tam waited to see what Nick would do. His arms slowly stilled, he stopped moving and eventually he locked eyes with Sarah and just started talking. It was a different voice and a different Nick, as if he was digging deep, shocked out of his carefully created world by the chaos around him.

'It's always been the same. I'm different. I know I am. I can remember the first time I knew. I came into a room and I tried to join in, and the expressions on the faces made no sense. I didn't have any of that information. I just knew that nothing made sense to me that made sense to everyone else. Everyone was playing, but I didn't know the game, so I sat down and put all the toys into lines, green, blue, big, small. I tried to see the patterns and the more I tried to make it neat, the more I was different. Then someone came along and kicked them all over the floor, and it was my fault for scaring everyone and shouting and I wanted to go home.

'My mother would look at me, and try and pick me up, and I hated that feeling and then she stopped. After a while she didn't take me to see other people and soon it was just me and her and then we were a unit. *We are a unit, Nick,* she told me that. I woke up, and put on my clothes and made a neat parting, and washed my face, everything. Then I concentrated on being good; I could do it really well.'

Tam remembered the desperation rising in the room, the sounds of movement on the staircase. Nick was dragging the recollections from some part of himself which he had long ago discarded. Tam needed to move things along, God only knew what would happen if they scared Nick now.

'Nick, everyone is different. What happened to make you so unhappy?'

'I didn't hurt anyone. I just got more and more scared, and the more scared I got, the more I could only see the straight lines, and that's why my grandpa had to come and take me away from my mother and teach me how to be a man. I didn't have a dad, and I didn't need one, but Grandpa wanted to set an example. He said I needed to learn to listen, and that no one could get through to me. *No one can get through to you, Nick, you little freak. You're so fucking sensitive, crybaby.* I didn't like the lessons, but I wanted to be good so badly that soon I stopped fighting and I was quiet. *Keep your mouth shut, Nick, open your mouth, Nick, you little retard.* I took the bits of me that could feel and I stuffed them down below my ribs, where no one could hurt me any more. Now I can't get them back. The last time I tried was when I put my hand on my little brother to see if he was alright, but he died. Grandpa thinks he died because of me. *You're pathetic, Nick, who'd feel sorry for you? You're a fuck-up and we're all sick of making allowances for you. You don't like it here? Your brother's gone, your mother's a wreck, and you whine every time I come near you even when it's for your own good. Move out, then, see how that goes. Wash your face twenty times a day, get a routine, you love those. Just don't come snivelling back here, and don't fuck up, because you have one chance, Nick, one chance. Then it's back to learning about real life.'*

Tam felt as if all the air in his body had been knocked out at once. Sarah's hand had been resting on Nick's arm as he talked. She had a way with him; for a young kid it was extraordinary. Nick seemed to have used up all the energy in his body, mental and physical, and he curled in on himself and wound into a tight foetal position on the floor. His eyes closed and Tam watched as he silently withdrew back to wherever he felt safe, alone within himself.

Tam tried to pick Sarah up from the floor but she wanted to stay next to Nick. He was quiet now, and, getting carefully to his feet with Sarah's help, Tam went to the window to beckon Sarah's dad into the house. The evening was sticky, one of those Indian summers that often arrived in London in September, and the smell in the flat wasn't getting any better. The front door crashed open, and, instead of Sarah's dad appearing, the room had filled with armed police. The terrified wailing from Nick as he was pulled to his feet, bent forward and handcuffed, would haunt Tam for many years to come whenever he drifted in that strange land somewhere between reality and dreams. It was the sound of injustice, and pain, and a life never lived.

The 'raid', which was completely unnecessary and that even ten years earlier would have been achieved with two coppers and a truncheon, now involved a massive amount of shouting and strange arm signalling. Anonymous faces shouted GET DOWN FLAT ON THE FLOOR at Tam and Sarah followed by PUT YOUR HANDS ABOVE YOUR HEADS while the room was made safe and 'cleared' in an echo of a television terrorist cell discovery. When each kitchen cabinet had been thrown open, and the fridge and freezer doors left hanging open, Nick was half pulled, half pushed towards the door as he tried to get away and restore order to his flat.

The Met scene-of-crime officers arrived and Nick's hysteria mounted to a crescendo. Tam had looked up at one of his colleagues and said, 'Just get him out of here – he's a neat freak; he'll totally lose it in a minute. You need to get on to the Vulnerable Persons Unit. He needs help.'

Sarah meanwhile was softly talking to Nick, constant and gentle-toned. She must have been aware that he couldn't hear her any more in the anguish of his carefully constructed life being destroyed in front of his eyes, and she was silently crying. She didn't stop, though, and perhaps she knew that her voice was enough to offer some comfort. Tam couldn't help wondering where she'd learned that.

Then Nick was gone, but as he was pulled past them his eyes met Sarah's and he shouted, 'You said you would help me. Everyone lies to me.'

Tam lay still, patting Sarah occasionally, and wondered to himself how the level of fucked-up had got this extreme in a couple of weeks. Total fucking bedlam in his own house – you couldn't make it up. At this point the level of hysteria had lowered slightly even with a dead body in the bedroom and a group of armoured police that looked like *Star Wars* battletroopers patting them down on the floor without any word of comfort for the girl, even though she was now shaking like a leaf and obviously in shock.

'What happened here, Tam?'

He recognised the voice, and tried to see through the mask. 'Can we do this downstairs or at the station? She needs to be with her dad; he's outside. She's a kid.'

'Yeah, of course, sorry – procedure.'

He gestured to his partner and they pulled off their masks: human faces, Tam wondered what the point of the macho display was. Maybe they were channelling the SAS.

Tam gently helped Sarah to her feet, slowly, and when he put his arm round her shoulders she leant almost all her child's tiny weight into him for support. Together they walked down the stairs, where a female officer was holding out foil insulation blankets for the pair of them. Tam put one round her and walked past his – load of bollocks, but it made the police look as though they were doing something useful to help.

He led Sarah to her dad and looked around for Karen. Nothing – just Jack, the middle son. Totally fucked-up family, he thought to himself. He could certainly pick them. Sarah squeezed his hand as he turned away, and said thank you. It was the first time since he had lost his job that Tam thought he might cry.

It had been natural then to walk over to his colleagues. After twenty-five years on the force there were a few faces he knew but more he didn't. Young, enthusiastic kids from the new intake that thrived on paperwork, targets and initiatives. Two of them were patting Nick down while he struggled and resisted, and a few feet back, behind a cordon of yellow police tape, a young woman – well, young to him, mid-thirties, Tam guessed – was sobbing, standing awkwardly and separately next to a much older man who must have been her father. That had to be the grandfather who'd been such a bastard to Nick; Tam was determined not to let him out of his sight. He might not be the most PC guy around, but he knew a wrong 'un when he saw one.

Nick was trying to turn in the direction of the weeping woman, and was now as taut and as agitated as Tam had ever seen him. His hands were twisting, he was on his toes, and from his contorted mouth came a stream of appeals. 'Stop, don't touch me, no, stop, no!'

Tam walked towards them, and Nick met his eyes.

'Let me help here. He's my neighbour, I was in there with him. We have a relationship of sorts.'

They hesitated; it was obvious that everyone had a good idea who he was, and his reputation had gone before him. The officer in charge spoke.

'The gaffer said that if we saw you in or anywhere near the house we were to arrest you.'

Tam shrugged. The scene spoke for itself: they needed him. They hesitated, not sure what the consequences would be of taking help from a non-conformist ex-copper, but by this point even the guys with the least EQ had worked out that, whether or not he was a killer, Nick had some serious issues, and they were beginning to panic about the level of visible distress, and were on their radios to the Vulnerable Persons Unit. The officer in charge, who was trying to shield Nick from the mobile phone cameras of passers-by, called Tam over. 'What a fucking mess. Are you off the force or on leave?'

'On leave officially ... I think.'

Why he had done it baffled Tam now, sitting as he was trying to write up his witness statement and wondering what he'd done to deserve the last couple of days, but at the time he'd felt it was important, to see this through, and to somehow be a familiar face for the two kids involved. Both of them seemed to be lost souls, and being looked after by another bunch of lost souls didn't seem as though it would help anyone.

He'd talked to Nick then, trying to calm him down and making the guys searching him let him turn round so that he was facing the sobbing brunette. The grandfather did not have a kind face; his body was wiry, and something in his manner was aggressive. Tam was already mentally making a case against him, through listening to Nick earlier and witnessing his distress; Tam now noticed that the grandfather was staring at Nick with a menace Tam had only seen a few times in his life, a look of threat and contempt with a bit of hatred in there for good measure.

Tam turned to his boss. 'Sir, I was in that apartment with the perpetrator and he was talking a bit. The grandfather featured in Nick's story, and it seemed to me like he sexually and emotionally abused him as a kid. We should take him in. He's over there on the pavement.'

'You sure? That boy doesn't exactly look like a reliable witness.'

'Take the grandfather, and maybe the mum too, down to the station. There's something rotten here. Trust me: old-fashioned instincts.'

Dan, the on-scene commanding officer, lifted up the cordon and walked over to the couple. Tam watched him talk to them for a minute and was struck again by the dynamic: the pale face of the woman painted with insecurity and angst and a shadow of real fear, referring always with a nervous glance to her father, and then following behind him as he walked towards the police tape and Nick. As his mother disappeared behind his grandfather, Nick's agitation heightened, and the screams of 'No!' got louder and more desperate. As the old man walked past his grandson, he seemed to dominate the space, and turned at the closest point to look Nick full in the face. He smiled at him then, a smile of triumph.

'I always said you'd fuck up your life, you pathetic little piece of shit.'

Tam was between them before he knew he was going to move. He pushed the older man on to the bonnet of the nearest car and shouted for handcuffs.

'Um, we don't really do the whole *Sweeney* thing any more for people we've only asked to assist with enquiries, but here are the cuffs.'

It was some smartass twenty-five-year-old, a female one at that, and Tam let her put the cuffs on and make the arrest, hand on his head as he was put into the back of the car to make sure he didn't hurt himself. Nick was in cuffs behind them, and they were about to place him into the back of the same vehicle, until Tam stepped in and beckoned another car. A few moments of peace followed after Nick and his grandfather were driven off and Tam took a breath. What to do now? He knew he was in too deep to drop it, and he shrugged and resigned himself to a long night at the station. He just hoped the Powers That Be would see it the way he did.

He needed his keys to get to the station. Ignoring the guy on the door, he walked back into the house, which was forever changed after the past few days, and let himself into his flat. He sat for a minute on his still unmade bed, and picked his keys up off the floor. He was tired.

When he got back outside, everything was over, and reporters were arriving now that there was nothing left to see. Tam was walking to his car, feeling vaguely as if the day was never going to end, when he realised that Nick's mother was still standing on the pavement, alone, staring back at the house. In the confusion earlier no one had taken her to the station. She oozed vulnerability and she was very attractive – Tam's Kryptonite. Enough crazy, complicated women; he needed to get his life straight and get back to work. He put his head down and fixed his car in his sights, but just as he was about to pass her he heard himself say, 'Are you alright?'

Then, into the silence which met his question, he poured unasked-for information.

'Hi, my name's Tam, I'm Nick's downstairs neighbour. I'm a policeman. D'you want to come with me down to the station? I'd offer you a cup of tea but the house is a crime scene, I'm afraid, and it might be days before I get back in.'

He was getting no response, so he held his hand out, and said again, 'Tam.'

No response, no hand. She was obviously even more of a fruitcake than he'd thought.

'Are you alright? Anything I can do for you?'

'I'm Emma, Nick's mum. They've arrested him, and my father. I don't have anyone else.'

'Come on, Emma, let me give you a lift, then. You can't just wait here on the pavement; the place is heaving with reporters. Let me get you down to the station so you can check on Nick.'

Tam walked towards the car, slowly, but Emma remained where she was, looking completely dumbstruck and unable to move. Tam felt bad but he had to get out of there. He sat in the driver's seat for a few moments and was just about to pull out and drive off when an over-enthusiastic young man in a Marks and Spencer suit stuck a microphone under Emma's nose and began asking her questions. She was being pushed backwards towards the bins. Tam hadn't been behind the wheel of his car for months – he didn't know why he hadn't sold it – but now that he was driving he felt he could offer some protection, and she couldn't use public transport or drive herself in the state she was in. He got out of the car, walked back towards Emma and put his arm round her shoulders as the panic rose in her face. He sheltered her with his body as questions were fired at her. They got to the car and he opened her door. She got into the passenger seat and he told her to get her head down. She looked like a beautiful frightened deer, and he suddenly felt like a hunter or a voyeur. As they sped off he wished they had met under different circumstances and was already regretting his intervention.

When he managed to get safely round the corner and on to a quiet road, he stopped and turned to her. 'Police station or home?'

'What do you think I should do?'

Tam hesitated then, he felt himself standing on the edge of a familiar, mossy field. One that looked beautiful but which, once you took a step into it, might pull you down into a bog you couldn't see and never let you up. It was a path he'd walked before, and he tried with all his might to resist answering. He waited, sighed, and focused on Emma's face. The pleading look, and the sadness made his mind up. He took over, but made a decision there and then not to get sucked in any more than was professional. He didn't have another emotional rollercoaster ride in him.

He looked straight ahead as he talked to her.

'Come with me to the police station, and if you feel up to it we can talk about how things have got to this point. I think you might feel better if you were close to Nick, and then, if you're strong enough later, you can tell me what you know about what might have driven him to this.'

They rode in silence to the station, although he could feel her eyes on him, and when they arrived she waited for him to come round and open her door. He didn't have any ID and Tam found it unnerving to have to approach the window like a member of the public, and ask for the officer in charge of the murder – or was it double murder now, or even triple? He had obviously been more use earlier than he'd realised, though: they were expecting him, and the officer in charge was there in a matter of minutes. Tam had known the guy for years, and he'd obviously taken instructions from on high before coming to meet him. He took Tam to one side and in hushed tones began to fill him in.

'Jesus, these fucking idiots – you have no idea what I'm dealing with. We all got back here, and when I asked for you no one had any idea where you were. Apologies, Tam, here's a temporary warrant card. Can we count on you for help on this case, and hopefully beyond? I think we've all learned a lot of lessons. Can you spare the time, mate? We really need you on this one, then we can talk about consultancy, or make this work one way or another. The gaffer wants to have a round-table once he gets through the press conference and briefings. We've all missed you, mate.'

Even if Tam could have stuck to his guns at the beginning of the week, taken his pension and started down a new path, the events of the last few days had made him feel chaotic, unsafe and in need of the familiar, a routine. Being back in a nick, and being needed, was making him feel a whole lot better, about himself and his life. He made up his mind: he would do what he could from the inside and stop dreaming about changing the world.

He took a deep breath and beckoned to Emma.

'Sir, this is Nick's mother, Emma. We have her son in custody in connection with the murder and the kidnapping in the flat earlier and, as you know, he's a person of interest in the park murder and GBH last week. I think it would be helpful for us to sit down and have a chat about Nick's background and try to find out as much as we can about him. Nick said some pretty disturbing things while we were in the flat together and I would like to try and get some insight into the background while we're here.'

Tam's senior colleague stuck out his hand towards Emma.

'Charles Metcalfe, excuse my manners. Would you mind accompanying Tam to an interview room? You aren't in any sort of trouble; we just want to understand Nick and what's happened to bring him to this point. We could also do with some medical history. We want to make sure we're meeting all his needs.'

Tam led her through the locked door into the back of the station and towards an anonymous lino-floored room. They sat quietly while Tam waited for an officer and a fresh tape to record the interview. He wanted all this on record, and he wanted Emma to be able to unwind a little.

'Where is Nick? I really need to see him.'

Tam glanced down at the table. He imagined that Nick was having his clothes removed for forensics, had been seen by a doctor and probably sedated. He was more than likely on his way to the Vulnerable Persons Unit in an ambulance if they'd managed to find a place for him with all the budget cuts. He was probably also in restraints and handcuffed.

He didn't say that.

'Nick will be being processed, don't worry. They'll make sure that a doctor is looking after him, and they'll take him somewhere to be observed and kept safe. The best thing you and I can do for him is to get as much background as possible, so that we can help him and then we can try and arrange a visit.'

Emma stared ahead, not being unhelpful, but apparently having nothing to say. Tam noticed how unlined her face was. 'You must have been very young when you had Nick?'

A young female constable came in and loaded the tape recorder. Tam recorded her name, his own and Emma's and they began.

'Yes, I was young. I was sixteen. I'd never had much attention from the boys at school, and then a teacher saw something in me, and began to help me after lessons were over. He was so kind, and things at home were very difficult.' She paused. 'Where's my father?'

Tam watched her as he replied. 'He's helping us with our enquiries, Emma.'

It was pitch dark outside now, and the atmosphere in the bare room was heavy. It was a moment that seemed charged with something important, some anticipation or difficulty. Tam felt himself overcome with the desire to lean in and help her, and had to look away from her face to break the spell.

Emma seemed to breathe out now that she knew her father wasn't suddenly going to appear, and she began to open up.

'He's not a good man, my father, I know that. It's been very difficult with Nick and me and him. I was terrified of him the whole time I was growing up, and then the first time someone showed me kindness I just soaked it up. I thought my teacher was such a good man; he seemed to really care about me. But as soon as I turned sixteen he slept with me, and I think it hurt even more than what my dad had done.'

'Sorry Emma, who are we talking about here?'

'The teacher, Nick's dad. He gave me after-school lessons then slept with me. He got me pregnant. He didn't want anything to do with me or Nick once he found out, and my dad was furious. Dad locked me in my room and called me a slut and a whore. I cried my eyes out. He even hit me across the face when I told him, and when he'd had a whisky he would come into my room and scream at me about how I had let them down, Mum and Dad, and what an embarrassment I was. I wouldn't tell him who the father was. I protected him.'

'So, then what happened when Nick came along? Did you both live with your parents?'

'My mum was alive and she kept Dad under some sort of control in the beginning, I suppose, although my dad was quite involved. He thought Nick shouldn't be growing up in a female environment, and made it his job to teach him manners, and do the discipline side of things. I was working part-time by then, and I tried to keep going, but my dad had Nick on the days I worked even though it used to make me feel sick with worry leaving him with Dad. I didn't have any choice; I couldn't afford to move out, I couldn't cope. From the time he was a baby I knew that Nick was different; he didn't need to be cuddled, didn't respond to his name. By the time he was three it was obvious that something wasn't right, and when he started school he'd missed a lot of developmental milestones and that's when the SEN got involved, but Nick just got more and more withdrawn. He was statemented and diagnosed with mid-range autism when he was five and that was the year I got pregnant with Billy.'

Tam watched her face; the ghosts of her lost child and the lost dreams for Nick were walking across it. Her eyes filled with tears.

'My mum died when Billy was six months old and my dad never really got over it. It just seemed to make him meaner. We carried on living together, the three of us, but he picked on Nick day after day, calling him names, hitting him. I'd left my job when Billy was born, and tried never to leave Nick, but it was hard to take him with me everywhere; he didn't like shops, or mums and babies groups, and it was just easier to take Billy. One day I got home from work and Nick had locked himself in the bathroom. I could hear him screaming from inside and my dad had already kicked out a panel in the door. I went to the council with Billy and they found me a two-bed flat. I moved in with both boys but my father was furious. He would come and visit when Nick was at school. He never gave me a chance to get free. He hated Nick, and the more I tried to sort him out, the more involved Dad got. In the end Nick started staying at my Dad's most of the time; I was too exhausted to argue. I know how terrible a mother I sound, but he wore me down, and Nick was such a handful.

'One Saturday, Dad came over with Nick. Billy had a really high temperature and had been ill for a couple of days. I rang the doctor, who told me to give him Calpol and keep him cool, but when I was in the hall arguing with Dad Billy had a convulsion and died. Nick was in the room with him. It was meningitis and I'd missed it. I should have taken him to the hospital; I should have spotted the rash. I've never forgiven myself, and nor has my dad. I never had the strength to fight him again. When he was a teenager I got Nick to a psychiatrist for a full evaluation because I thought it might make Dad stop, but he insisted on taking him instead of me, and it made Nick even worse and didn't change my dad's behaviour at all. All I could do was use the money my mum had left to put down a deposit on a flat for Nick as soon as I could, and he moved in when he was twenty. I failed both my boys. I loved Nick so much, but I couldn't protect him. I thought he was safe. I'm so sorry; I thought he was fine. He's never hurt anyone in his life.'

Tam listened to the story and his focus shifted from Nick to Emma's father. What kind of man drove a vulnerable child with autism to the brink? Who treated his own daughter like that?

Emma looked up at Tam.

'Nick was the sweetest boy. I used to tell him that we were a unit. We understood each other. I could have got the best there was out of him. I know he had his problems, but Dad wouldn't let him be, and I didn't keep him safe.

Without my dad Nick would still have been autistic, of course he would, but my dad made him worse, not better. All children need encouragement, help, guidance, but children like Nick need it most of all, and my dad broke what was already cracked instead of trying to mend it. I'm so sorry.'

Tam had tried to think of a way of protecting her from what he had to say next. There wasn't one. He took a deep breath.

'Emma, I listened carefully to what Nick was saying today when we were in his flat. I need to ask you something and I want you to think carefully before you answer. Do you think it's possible that your father was sexually abusing your son?'

One year later …

17 | Tam

'Permanence, perseverance and persistence in spite of all obstacles, discouragements and impossibilities. It is this, that in all things distinguishes the strong soul from the weak.'

— Thomas Carlyle

Tam was not familiar with Notting Hill. He had never realised that within the grubby, multicultural vastness of London there existed sunlit pockets where everyone drove Teslas and Bentleys and shopped for collapsible Lumo plastic bowls to carry in case your Boston terrier got thirsty outside a trendy restaurant. There was even a gritty side to it, with the street market and the demographic, millionaires' mansions side by side with tower blocks and, not far away, the burned-out corpse of Grenfell Tower. Tam hadn't wanted to work here, but he was loving it.

Before this, Tam had only understood rubbish on pavements and discarded Chicken Cottage containers, not shared platters for breakfast served on Italian olive wood, or a choice of five different varieties of freshly squeezed orange juice. It was the relaxation of affluence and Tam did his best to kick against it, but the exhaustion of the past year had slowly overcome his reservations, and he had started to find community work, as well as the fact of actually seeing results with kids he was helping, personally rewarding in a way he had never expected. He had even toyed with taking up running, and the other morning had wondered what wheatgrass tasted like. Any desire he had once had to challenge the world, or put society right as a whole, had fallen away, and Tam spent his days on his pet work project: Nick.

It had been a long few months, and he had succeeded, despite his past form, in resisting his attraction to Emma, and keeping his relationship with her purely professional while offering support and comfort. She had been distraught about the damage that the arrest and assessments were doing to her boy, and Tam, seconded to the case, had tried to give her as much news as he could on a daily basis without compromising the investigation in any way. Months had passed of limited visitation, meetings with lawyers, hearings and the presenting of medical information, until finally the decision had been taken that Nick was unfit to stand trial and he'd been committed to Broadmoor. Tam had seen him through those first few weeks, the trials of getting his meds right, and getting his room the way he needed it. It was helping Nick that had finally persuaded Tam that perhaps he could be of real use helping one person at a time.

It had been Tam who had broken the news about Nick's detainment under the Mental Health Act, but Emma had been so terrified of him going into the prison system alone and vulnerable that it had actually come as a relief. Tam had explained to her that Broadmoor was a hospital, an NHS hospital, and that people ended up there for many reasons. It wasn't *One Flew Over the Cuckoo's Nest*, and the help that Nick would get there was second to none. Tam had seen plenty of cases over the years where criminals had gone to jail and been unable to deal with the chaos, the overcrowding, the noise and the people with whom they had to spend their days. Many of them had suffered breakdowns or resorted to self-harm, and it had been Broadmoor that had glued them back together.

It hadn't been an easy decision to accept for the families of the victims, and it hadn't been easy for Emma. Nick was oblivious in his sedated state in his isolation cell, albeit with a professional to talk to every day. Emma was still at her original address and the phalanx of reporters were there day and night; sniffing for scandal, their numbers had increased, when her father was charged with incest and paedophilia. Tam had used everything he had to get her into a safe house until the trial. He'd succeeded.

The Met had decided to set up a 'Troubled Person Community Action Group' and had asked Tam to head it, which was a feather in his cap, and in some ways he felt it was what he'd always needed. He could decide who needed his help and how he was going to provide it. Work had always been his love and, once he had changed the name to something which was less of a mouthful, he really felt his life was turning a corner. He just needed to get to the end of Nick's grandfather's trial and he could really put the past behind him.

He still had to concentrate every time he met Emma for a briefing or just a catch-up, so that lines didn't get blurred between them. She was like a child in many ways, and hung on his every word. It was hard to resist her, but he did.

Friends rang, asked him to the pub, and Tam went. He didn't feel like it, but soon the Met camaraderie kicked back in, and he accepted the claps on the back and congratulations for solving the case, and the thanks for putting the policing back into the police. He had often wondered what had happened to Sarah, and her mother, and had been really happy to receive a letter out of the blue from her five months later. She had thanked him for his help on that dreadful day, and it had given Tam some closure to know that things were much better for her now. She didn't mention her mother, just her father, and Tam drew his own conclusions.

Meanwhile, the hospital had got Nick stabilised, and Tam had been quietly preparing him to give evidence by camera link so that he didn't have to confront his grandfather in Court. It was still a difficult task, keeping Nick on subject and getting him to tell the story clearly, but Tam really wanted that bastard behind bars. He couldn't believe he was pleading not guilty – who treated their family that way and then put them through a trial as well? Often, Tam thought of his own grandfather, and the evenings when he would sit with him in his two-up, two-down, by the coal burner, and pick questions from his puzzle book. He had been a bookkeeper, the best man Tam had ever met, and the happiness of the times he had spent with him seemed to make Nick's experiences with a man he should have been able to trust even more horrific. Tam thought of his grandfather as a man without a blemish on his character, and you only needed one of those to guide you through life. Nick hadn't had anyone, and God knew he had needed someone now. Tam was trying to be there for him.

Tam picked up his phone and dialled Emma's number. It was Friday and the trial began on Monday. He wanted to see her one last time and go over what was going to happen. He met her at a pub near the safe house, and, as usual, when she came round the corner she took his breath away.

'Hi, Emma. I really appreciate you coming. I know Monday's going to be tough for you and for Nick, but I've tried to put everything in place to make it go as smoothly as it can. Your father will be in the dock, and you'll be best sitting on the left-hand side of the court. I'm really hoping that Nick will be able to tell his story clearly and we'll get a conviction.'

Even he could hear that he sounded doubtful.

Emma looked at him now, and put her hand on his arm. 'I know you've done everything you can for us, Tam, and I just want to thank you so much. I don't know how I would have got through it without you. I'm scared about the trial, I'm scared about seeing my father. I don't know what I'm going to do afterwards without you to lean on. I won't be able to do it.'

Tam looked into her eyes, which were full of tears, and for a moment he tried to think what to say.

'Emma, listen. You're strong. You've overcome things that would break most people and you're still here. You think you failed your boys, as a mother? You didn't. You got Nick out of that house as soon as you could. Billy's death was not your fault: meningitis is hard to spot, and you called the doctor. All you need to think about going forward now is yourself. You've never been on your own, you've never found out who you really are or what you're capable of. Get the trial over with, go back to school, travel, enjoy yourself. I'll always be here, but the last thing you need in your life is a cynical old copper with the best part of his life behind him, not ahead. I'll always be your friend, but you don't need me. You don't *need* anyone but yourself.'

Tam felt proud, and watched her face as she battled to believe him. He hoped she would find someone out there who would treasure her and let her grow, and he felt like a grown-up for hoping it.

Monday morning came around and Tam put on his only suit. He had left it in a bag taken from the Staverton Road flat just a bit too long, and it looked sorry for itself. When he arrived, Emma was standing on the pavement outside looking terrified. He gave her a smile, told her it was going to be fine, and they walked into the Court together.

When Emma's father came up into the dock, his eyes darted round the courtroom until he found Emma. His eyes fixed on her, then he took in Tam, and then looked again at his daughter. Fury, menace and something else that was hard to read were written on his face. Later on Tam would decide that it was disgust, but as the jury was sworn in he was more intent on breaking the lock between the old man's eyes and Emma's.

He talked to her about Nick, and where she might go on holiday. Anything that would distract her for a few minutes until it was time for the camera link and Nick's story. The evidence from Nick was tough to watch; Emma clamped her hand over her mouth, and Tam sat bolt upright, listening to the litany of cruelties that the man in front of him had visited on Nick and, by default, on Emma. Nick began to get very agitated when he explained about his grandfather correcting him, and mocking him, and when Emma's eyes turned to her father the flicker of a smile played around his lips.

'Emma, don't listen to this,' urged Tam. 'Nick can't see you; come outside. It's not good to get upset like this, it's really not.'

'I have to know, Tam. I feel like it's my fault.'

As hard as he tried, Nick did not make a good witness. The cross-examination of someone who'd already been deemed unfit to stand trial was over before it began. Dates, times, specifics... Nick had been too young to remember, and he became increasingly frantic trying to explain just how painful his life had been, and the torment he'd been through. Emma was crying, and when Nick couldn't go on any more she shouted out, 'Nick, don't worry, it will all be alright.'

The summing-up was quick and brutal.

'In the light of the lack of evidence, and the medical condition of the main witness...'

Before the judge could finish, Emma was on her feet. 'I'm a witness too. Let me speak.'

The prosecution barrister asked for a recess, and Emma was led into Chambers to talk to him and the judge. It wasn't until she was on the stand that Tam knew what she was going to say. Tam tried to meet her eye as she was sworn in, but she seemed to have moved to a place where he couldn't reach her. She asked for permission to sit down, and some water. Then the questions began and Tam held his breath.

'Ms Peters, could you tell me how old you were when your father first started sexually abusing you?'

Emma's eyes turned towards her father and for a moment she looked scared, like a small child again, and Tam saw a flash of menace cross her father's face. Emma hesitated, then pulled her face round to face the Court.

'About eight years old. I would say eight years old.'

'Thank you, and how long would you say the abuse went on?'

'It started with my father coming to kiss me goodnight, and giving me massages, and back scratches, and it turned into sex when I was ten. That I remember. I was ten. It was on my birthday. My mother went out to pick up my birthday cake and my father raped me.'

Tam sat rigid in his seat while she tried her best to speak calmly and clearly.

'If you were so terrified of your father, and presumably of sex, can you explain how you ended up pregnant at sixteen by a teacher at your school, and again five years later?'

Tam watched Emma take a breath and steady herself.

'I wanted to get away from him, away from home. I got pregnant by my English teacher. He was the first person who had ever been kind to me. He thought I was clever, and lent me books, but in the end he did the same to me as my dad. It was as if men could tell...there was something about me, a "young girl who knows about sex" aura that seemed to surround me. I just wanted someone to love me, to rescue me. He told me he would marry me, we would live together, and I believed him. I even believed him when he told me he was so in love with me and that he hadn't told me he was married in case it hurt me. I protected him. I hid the baby under baggy jumpers, learned how to be sick silently, until one day my father came into my bedroom and realised. He slapped me across the face and called me a whore, and from that day on he used my baby to control me.'

Tam listened to her, and as she talked she seemed to grow stronger, putting down this burden that she had carried all her life. More than anything Tam wanted to catch Emma's eye, to reassure her somehow, but she was staring into a place far from here, reliving a horror from a time long ago.

'Why didn't you realise that your father was also abusing Nick? You were living in the same house for much of the time; surely you must have been aware that he was upset?'

'I didn't realise because by then I knew that Nick was different from other children and I thought his behaviour was because of that, not because of my dad. I thought because Dad had abused me, he liked girls... it never occurred to me that he would touch Nick. Nick had been like that since he was tiny. He didn't smile, he didn't respond to his name... he was different. Even at mother-and-baby groups I could see it. But he was so clever. He could do things no other kids of his age could do. His reading – he used to get a subject in his head and he could tell you anything about it. Ancient Egypt, dinosaurs – there wasn't a statistic he didn't know. He and I would sit by ourselves for hours, me asking him questions and him sitting apart from me on the sofa; we'd be in our own little world. The one thing he couldn't talk about was emotions. If he was upset he screamed, and there was no comforting him, but if you weren't there you would never have known ten minutes later that anything had happened. We had rules. No cuddling, but we would touch hands; dinner at the same time every night, same foods in a pattern on the same plate. He was my world, and if I had known that my dad had touched him ... '

Emma's voice broke. She had done it. She had stood up and told the world that her father had betrayed her in the most profound way, and had abused both her and the child she loved when he was at his most vulnerable.

Tam sat and listened as she then told the Court about Billy, and his sad, short life. She told them about using her mother's money to help Nick move into his own place, just so that she could make sure that he was away from her father and not bullied any more. It was the story of someone who was used to putting herself to one side to try and keep the people she loved safe. Tam had never been prouder. He waited until she had finished, and watched her look straight at her father for one final time. He didn't look arrogant any more, and there was no smile on his lips.

Emma sat back down, and the verdict was delivered. Guilty. She had found her courage, and Tam felt the pride of a job well done. Outside the court they said goodbye. Tam looked down at her and could see a strength that was growing with every passing day.

'You see?' he said. 'I told you all you needed was your-self. Life is going to start from here. Look after yourself, Emma. You know where I am if you need me.'

Emma smiled and walked off into the crowd of reporters. She only looked back once, and Tam saw that her smile was even broader and her eyes were full of tears. Happy tears.

18 | Karen

'*How sharper than a serpent's tooth it is to have a thankless child.*'

— William Shakespeare

'Fuck it!'

Karen screamed the words at her computer. Another email from the Prison Authorities explaining to her why visiting Nick was 'completely inappropriate' and how it would be 'detrimental to his recovery'.

Karen sat surrounded by the latest studies on the increase in autism rates. No sooner did she include one in her monolithic paper than it was discredited by a different scientific body. All she had now was her work. Charlie had stuck to his word and ignored all help she had offered. Jamie was in a school in south London which was exclusively for children on the autistic spectrum, which almost made her cry on a daily basis. A child whose mother had made a life's work out of demonstrating how well children with Asperger's could contribute in all arenas of life had a son who'd been taken out of mainstream society and segregated. The irony wasn't lost on Karen, and she'd long ago decided it was a revenge strike, however happy

Charlie told her Jamie was. Sarah hadn't spoken to her since that visit at the hospital, and Jack seemed happy going to football matches with Charlie and his new girlfriend.

'Fifty per cent of all babies born in the US will be autistic by 2025.' It seemed an extraordinary claim, but it wasn't just a headline in the *Daily Mail*, it was a study by an MIT scientist, and Karen set about extrapolating the data and checking the maths. Frustrated in her attempts to research ways to integrate autistic people into society, she had changed the focus of her work and had been collating all she could on the causes of autism. A few weeks after Nick had been arrested, feeling lost and blocked, she had stumbled across a graph which showed the rise in the use of a weedkiller containing glyphosates and the rise in autism in two parallel lines. They ran almost exactly concurrently, and the night that Karen had first looked at it had been the defining moment of her life.

The main problem was that no one had put all the many theories, hypotheses and facts together. Karen lay awake at night running through the history of the autistic spectrum since it had first been given a name in 1908. The stock phrases from those early days, 'a powerful desire for aloneness' and 'an obsessive insistence for persistent sameness' remained true today, and for a moment Jamie's face popped into her head, looking through the car window into the middle distance as his father drove him away.

She went downstairs to put the bin bag out. The word 'aloneness' resonated with her. Every time she went onto the landing, the aloneness of being the only person left in the house tried to catch her; but she would turn her thoughts back to her work, and her eyes front. She never looked towards Tam's door, or hesitated at Nick's any more, but it sometimes felt as if they were still there, when she was drifting off to sleep, and the echoes of a slamming door, or footsteps on the stairs outside her flat comforted her. She even longed for the noise that had accompanied her children's visits, although those thoughts never lasted long.

Karen sat back down at her desk. She took down the sub-file on abuse and violent behaviour in autistic adults. Children with autism were forty-five per cent more likely to be abused than children without it. Eighty per cent of adults in prison for violent crimes were on the spectrum. The figures flashed round in her head. These things really mattered. Certain children had a particular vulnerability, that was obvious, but what that susceptibility was she hadn't yet discovered. She did her nightly search for new articles that might contribute to her body of empirical evidence and an article jumped out at her. If you drove from Aberdeen to London in your car, you could now do the whole journey without washing your windscreen once – the air was no longer filled with insects. This might be the connection she needed. Perhaps she could find a link between weedkillers, declining insect populations and autism. She took down an empty box file, and printed the article to add to it. Weedkiller was present in the urine of pregnant women, in breast milk, in the glucose syrup in your bread, in the meat you ate, in chips, in cereal. It was in rivers, ditches, water treatment plants. She had now gathered so much circumstantial evidence that it gave an urgency to her work, and even when one article seemed to contradict another she filed them, feeling that she was

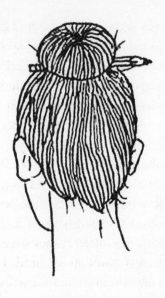

working towards a conclusion. She hoped to offer herself as an expert on all things autistic to the evening news programmes or breakfast television. The time was coming, she was sure when everyone would listen.

Television, though... She had looked in the mirror the day before and had to admit a little work would be needed before she was suitable for public viewing. Five inches of white hair led into frizzy orange ends that had been broken by old elastic bands. Then there were the unplucked eyebrows, sallow skin and a frayed cardigan wrapped round her in place of a coat or heating. Days passed when she didn't know what time it was and she slept when the words on her screen no longer made any sense. She had taken to ordering a takeaway on a Friday, which she ate with a spoon from the fridge for most of the rest of the week whenever she was too hungry to think clearly.

Karen re-read an article she had found in the *Huffington Post*. In ten years the cost of treatment in the United States alone would reach 400 billion dollars annually, and there wouldn't be enough undiagnosed adults to man the Armed Forces. Her dreams jumped from theories on absent parenting causing disconnection, to statistics on weedkillers, vaccines, fields of corn waving in the wind bereft of poppies, bunches of rape growing alongside motorways – it was all linked, and Karen wanted to be the one to put the whole picture together. She added Prince Charles to her list of influential figures who were anti-GM foods, along with the World Health Organisation.

Karen stretched and showered. She longed for her little office, or her car, both gone now. She'd lost her job in the whole fallout from Nick's job placement, and she missed having somewhere to go, and the prestige that went with it. Dressing in the same clothes she had taken off earlier, she sat back down and looked at her list. She needed to concentrate. She checked over a paragraph she had written about Einstein explaining how he would have been diagnosed as on the spectrum today. He would have been joined by Lewis Carroll, Mozart, Andy Warhol; she had a list.

An hour later, Karen picked up her mug. The tea she sipped was cold, made before her shower, and the mug was misshapen. She remembered that Sarah had made it for her years before at a Christmas pottery club. It had a green dragon painted on it, which had once been a private joke when they emailed each other. The roughness of it touched something inside Karen and she pushed it away. She checked her emails again. One from the BBC telling her that they weren't looking for a science correspondent, and she had received a similar one last week from Channel 4. Before she knew what she was doing, she had picked up the biggest file and thrown it across the room.

She was on her knees picking up papers with tears running down her face, a tumbler of whisky in her free hand, when she heard the front doorbell. Reluctantly, she got up. It was a cold night. She hesitated and pulled her cardigan tighter around her. She heard a car start directly outside and got up to look out of the window. Her stomach growled and she realised it had been a while since she'd last eaten. For a minute she tried to remember whether she'd ordered a takeaway, but she was nearly sure she hadn't. Instead, two small figures were walking up her driveway and for a moment Karen raised her hand, ready to knock on the window, but at the last minute she pulled back and turned away.

And there was one moment, only caught in her peripheral vision, that would stay with her always, as hard as she tried to expunge it. It was the image of the turn of heads towards her as she got to the window, a collective excited intake of breath, and the looks of tremulous hope on the faces of her children, Jack and Sarah. As Karen stood in the shadows she watched the car reverse up the path, past the bins, past the spot where she had last seen Tam and Nick, and they drove off into the night.

Karen told herself she would call. As soon as the paper was finished, she would take them all away on holiday. Perhaps they would see her on Sky News and she could explain to them that it had all been worth it. She could get Sarah some work experience. The thoughts calmed her, and she reassured herself that there was time. No good dwelling on it: she needed to get this file sorted, and then everything would fall into place.

It would be years later when Karen realised that this particular evening had been the last time her children had come to see her. By then, a carapace had grown over her soul and she reminded herself often that while she had been doing vital research that would ultimately benefit her children and their children, they had not cared enough to stay in touch, and had for their own selfish reasons rejected her. The shadows that ran past her front door in the middle of the night eventually became familiar, and they muddled along together. Just occasionally that three a.m. shiver would run down her spine while the sweet smell that had filled the air for weeks after Nick was arrested ghosted round her nostrils and she would turn for a moment over her shoulder, and look back quickly at her monitor before she could see what was there.

19 | Nick

'Whosoever is delighted in solitude is either a wild beast or a god.'

— Aristotle

I'm twenty-five. I've never really felt still enough to think about my age before, but now I talk to someone every day, and I have antipsychotic medication and I feel much less scared and much less in a hurry as if my dread has been pushed down and can't find the way out. Twenty-five is young. I didn't know I was young.

In my screaming, crying weeks of rooms and needles and germs and strangers after the park and after the job in the morgue and after Sarah came to my flat and after the cleaner was in my bed, I wanted to die. I can't remember a time when I felt so twisted up and tight and curled and attacked. I wanted to run away so much, more even than when I was in the bedroom with my grandpa.

The police came into my flat, and broke my door, and opened all my cupboards. They pulled out my clothes and put germs everywhere, waving guns, and wearing masks. I wanted to curl up and I clenched my hands over my ears. I had so much to sort out, I couldn't think how I would get my flat tidy, or the cleaning girl out of my bed, or get a new bed, or get my routine going again. I felt like my head inside was going to snap. So much fear and so much panic and so much wanting to scream and not stop, but I couldn't even do that, and, just when I thought it couldn't get any worse, policemen hurting my arms and pulling me down my stairs, and I couldn't even put my coat on to be warm.

Then taking my things from my pockets and not giving them back, and in front of everyone patting me when I hate being touched, and reading me the rights about going to court when I didn't want to go, then shouting again when I got upset. My mother was on the pavement and crying and I thought she had come for me and I calmed down a little bit when I saw her, but then I saw him. My grandpa. He was with her, just behind, and I really started to scream inside then and then out loud. He spoke to me, but I couldn't hear the words over my own crying and the hands on my ears. I was pushing tight to keep him out.

The police station was even worse, bright lights, and they took all my clothes and put me in other ones that weren't mine, made of paper, and I didn't have proper shoes because they took those too so how would I get home? Scraping my nails, cutting them when they were already the length I like them, combing my hair when I was in handcuffs...there was not an inch of me they didn't look at, and I had to shower in front of a stranger, and I just sat down on the floor of the shower and cried. I had a dirty bar of soap, no antibacterial shower wash, and then I was in a dirty room with rings of germs on the table. I asked to go home, and no one answered. I wouldn't sit on the chair; it was stained.

Then Tam my neighbour came and he is a policeman, and he came to help me even after I kept him in the flat and kept Sarah there. He even came as a witness when I was being interviewed and he brought a doctor and the doctor waited with me in the corner and got me a new chair, and wiped it with wipes which kill germs and I sat on it. I didn't want to talk to anyone, I wanted to go home, but Tam told me that you have to tell when you hurt someone and explain what happened and why you did it. They had a tape recorder so I would only have to tell it once, and I had someone with me who was a responsible adult and when I got upset I could stop. I had to stop a lot.

The hardest bit was when I had to explain about being scared. I don't like being scared and I was scared all the time. My grandpa was the hardest thing to say out loud, and I had to do it with my hands over my ears. Don't hear what you are saying, but you still can when it is you speaking even when you block out all the noise outside.

I told them, though, and everyone even said I was brave. Very brave. He hurt me, and I knew then that it wasn't my fault, because everyone told me so even though my grandpa had said it was. My mother even started crying when she came to see me, and she said that all the lessons from my grandpa were wrong, and she wished he was dead. I had so many horrible pictures in my head, of my grandpa pulling my hair, and shouting at me, and telling me to bend over, get up, be more careful, touch this, stroke this, fucking suck it up. He told me how stupid I was and how everything was my fault. Over and over. Every time we were on our own. It didn't make me better like he said it would, it made me scream inside.

Ed who talks to me every day now because he is my doctor always tells me I am doing well and I have my pills and feel like I can look at myself from a bit further away. I have Asperger's syndrome and OCD and depression and psychosis and these are actual illnesses and conditions, and in the beginning when I was good at school and Mother and me were a unit, then I only had Asperger's and the rest came because of my grandpa and my brother dying and my mother being young, and because I started off different. Tam says that even if we are different we must feel sorry about hurting people, that the man and the woman in the park were good people just enjoying themselves in the sun, they weren't disgusting, they weren't doing what my grandpa did to me. The cleaner didn't mean to be noisy, she was just young, and she didn't realise that it would make me upset.

It is nearly a year since I came here and the screaming months at the beginning seem like another person to me now. The panic and the fear are still there, but now that my room is square, and I know what is happening every single hour of every single day, I don't let it rise up in me. My mother comes and sometimes I lie on my bed and she reads to me and they are the stories from a long time ago that she used to read to Billy and me, and then I could never be still and now I can. I can listen to a whole story without moving too much and I laugh at the funny bits but I know when to stop.

This is a life. I understand who I am. I am on the autistic spectrum. It is a condition. It is not evil – that is what my grandpa did – that is evil. I have done terrible things that I didn't have the tools to understand were terrible. My mother says I am a victim, and Ed my doctor says I am a casualty of my upbringing, and that comforts me. I think that is right and I wish that my grandpa had known good from bad, and had a Jiminy Cricket on his shoulder like in the cartoon of *Pinocchio*.

My room is white, everywhere, and everyone knows my routine, and it got painted specially for me to make me feel calm with lead-free paint, and I have my own bedding and my mother takes it and washes it and I trust her, and she brings it back and it has no germs. I have a place for my clothes and a shower and a lavatory and a bed and everything is brand new because I couldn't stop the panic about the germs, and I do art as a hobby. Every week when I finish a new painting I put it up on my wall and I take down the one that was there before and my mother takes that one to her house because my grandfather is locked up in a prison and now she can choose everything in her life because he is not in charge. He is having a trial and I am going to tell everyone what he did to me and Ed will come and won't have to see my grandpa in real life. My mother comes on visiting days and I am glad she comes and then I am glad she goes because I don't like crying and questions.

Sometimes I do pictures of Billy, sometimes of my mother, and sometimes of things I dream about. My mother had a pond when I was very little. It was full of tadpoles and every day I went outside and lay on the stones next to it. Mum says I was three or four, but she doesn't remember which because she was very busy then. In the beginning they were dots living in jelly, then they got bigger and started to wriggle inside it and it was see-through and then they were like jerky black lines. Soon they got little bumps of heads and tails and got bigger and I lay and caught them on my hands and kept them in jars. I watched them get back legs, then front legs, and then their tails dropped off and they were tiny tiny frogs and then they could jump and I put them back in the pond, then they hopped on to lily pads and I draw them a lot, with all their different bodies, and different ways of being. I draw the stones round the pond, and the long green lawn, and my mother on the step calling me, and the long line of lavender, and the smell is in my head when I draw it and my mother bought me a lavender pillow and it helps me go to sleep, and I have a lavender beanbag and I can put it on my shoulders when I get panicky. I can draw with my eyes closed. Sometimes I can remember it so clearly, being by the pond. It's the last memory I have which has no panic in it, just me every day with tadpoles, sometimes on warm stones, sometimes on cold.

I never draw my grandpa. I never draw him dragging me up by the hand and knocking my jars of tadpoles over and the dark room where I was crying as I thought of them, wriggling trying to find the water then crying from the pain, or the panic will just come back and the shouting will be in my head.

There isn't a good conclusion, my mother says, and I know what a conclusion is because Ed told me. It is an ending. You could say I have a story that ended before it started, but that is just what people say. I have a story. I have Asperger's syndrome, and that is nearly the same as high-functioning autism, and everyone says that in a low voice because it is a bad thing. I don't know what it's like to not have it, but I do know that I don't have the sadness and I don't have the guilt and I don't have the questions that everyone else has. I just have an understanding of what has happened to me now. If I can stay peaceful and have my routine, then I am where I want to be.

I have focus, and now that I am here for a long time and now that I know that, I can plan, and I have things I want to study. I have my room, and people to make my meals, and people to explain things to me, and exercise outside, and I don't have my grandpa. I have my mother, and people to help me, and I understand that what I have done has made a lot of people unhappy. I try not to do the list of them when I am going off to sleep – the parents of the man and the lady in the park, their friends, the people they worked with, they are all sad. The people in Poland who loved the cleaner who came to the flat, her brother. The list could go on but who would it help? I don't have a prison sentence, I wasn't well enough, and that made a lot of people cross, but you can't help it if you are ill, or you can't talk, or if you are a victim even though you have hurt other people. My mother wants me to come home one day, and we can have a life together like we did when I was little, but I tell her it's better for me to be here, and she should get a new Billy and a new life and I will still be here, with everything I need, and she can visit me then go home.

I drew a picture of the girl in the morgue when I was in art therapy, and she was still and calm and cool like the things are in my head after my medicine in the mornings now. Sometimes I still wish that I could have a friend like that, a girl who is beautiful and just wants to stay with me and be quiet. Ed says that one day if I work very hard then I can leave but I think that in life some things never end. I will study interesting things, while the world outside talks about nothing and people upset each other.

There is a big wall outside my wing and it wraps round the garden where we get fresh air. I like the wall because it keeps me safe and everyone else safe. I like my weeks because on Wednesday the pat dog comes in and I love him. He isn't my dog, but he is a Labrador retriever and he belongs to Joyce and she brings him in and he loves me. He comes straight to me and puts his head on my leg and I can sit next to him on the floor, and looking in his eyes doesn't make me upset. He even licks me and Ed told me that a dog's mouth is cleaner than my mouth but I still wash my hands afterwards. When he licks me it makes me laugh and I put my head back and laugh properly like when my mother tells me stories of when I was little and we were on our own and she wasn't sad at all.

So Mother is right and there is no conclusion, and perhaps there is no normal. I know when I am at social time that lots of people in here are the same as me. I know that this is a ward for people who have autism, because a lot of people have it now, but when I get my laptop after I have been stable for six months then I can look to see who has made the rules for normal. In here I feel happy because everyone understands that there really is no normal. There is lots of pretending in the world, and there is love which makes a lot of things better, but in here we don't worry about that. We don't talk back and forwards about nothing, and we don't want to make friends with each other. I still always try and check if someone is telling me the truth. I don't like it when Ed says, 'That is the biggest dog I have ever seen.' It isn't the biggest dog he has ever seen and I don't know why he wants to say that if he is a doctor – probably because he thinks it makes me feel better. It doesn't. I think you should check your facts, and find a subject that interests you and research it, even if you only have books like I do. I am reading about comas. The lady in the park got better after a long time but her boyfriend died because I hit him so hard with the wooden branch. I was glad they didn't turn off the machine keeping the lady from the park alive. They could have, and she would be dead, but then she woke up. It's been worrying me, how they decide whether to turn you off, but I need my laptop to do a proper study.

I don't need to worry about that now, Ed says. The worst is over, and I am safe. My mother tells me that too when she visits and says she loves me and she is sorry. I don't know why she should be sorry; she wasn't bad. I have a room that is square, and clean. I have people around me who make me feel I am not alone, and I understand them. I don't stand at the edge of a conversation with the panic any more, trying to find the right answer, trying to understand the people talking.

There is a film library and I chose a film with Ed helping and my mother came and we watched it with Ed because he has to be in my room when my mother comes, and it says, 'It will be alright in the end; if it's not alright it's not the end.' My mother was crying then, and tried to squeeze my hand, and I didn't want her to.

I don't want their alright. I am alright. Why is your alright better than ours? Do you think that you are happy with your tears and your failed loves that you write about, and your pubs and your talk and your dreams? Too many emotions, too much pain.

Some things in life never end.

Acknowledgements

I am so grateful to all the people who got me to this point. I have had a wonderful team next to me helping every step of the way. I have always wanted to write a book, but it was only after I took time out to do the Faber Academy Write a Novel course that I actually applied myself seriously and finished *The Man on the Middle Floor*. Gillian Slovo was a benevolent taskmaster who treated us like writers and really produced results. On that course I met Rebecca de Ruvo-Akerlund, who became a great friend, and who came up with so many ideas for *The Man on the Middle Floor* for which I will always be very grateful. She has been a writing companion and a friend, and her books have spurred me on. The others on the course, Hina Belitz, Barry Florin and my soon-to-be-son-in-law Dave Atherton, all contributed in different ways and I love them all.

Thank you to my family, who have had my back and put up with endless hours of having to be quiet while I wrote, bringing me cups of tea and encouraging me to keep going. In this I include the polymath who is Andrew Staples, creator of my website, taker of pictures and headshots, and singer of beautiful opera music to keep me calm. A massive thank you also to Debbie Elliot from HarperCollins who generously pointed me in all kinds of helpful directions and was a fount of wisdom, and to Mopsy Wass, who put us together again and offered encouragement at my lowest points. Massive thanks to Louise Gillespie from Pillar Box PR, who listened to my frustrations with the publishing process, helped with every aspect from editing and angst about covers without complaint at breakfasts at Colbert and lunches at Trinity and never ignored a WhatsApp, and to my friends who read the book and gave me feedback: Katherine Robertson, Wendy Ryan, Emma Norris, Caroline Craig, Katie Martin and my South African touchstone Michelle Mundell. You should all write books.

To the team at RedDoor, who are changing publishing one book at a time, Clare Christian, Anna Burtt and Heather Boisseau – you guided me through the stressful post-writing phase of *The Man on the Middle Floor* – and a special thank you to Anna for showing me how to 'do' social media and remain sane. I am also eternally grateful to Linda McQueen for her editing skills, which were invaluable. Thank you also to Patrick Knowles for the cover design.

Thank you to Mrs H., my English teacher at Rowan Hill, to my parents for giving me a life full of stories, and to my grandparents and Jeff John who taught me kindness and who loved me.

Above all, to my people, all of you, who have had faith in me and confidence in my abilities. Finally, and most importantly, thank you to my three daughters, to Tommy for his beautiful illustrations, for having to listen to me read out endless pages and never doubting me for a second, and to my gorgeous South African husband, Gerry, for breaking his rule never to read a book in case it ruins his eye for a ball, and who has spent twenty-three years loving me better.

Why I wrote *The Man on the Middle Floor*

I have four children. My first, Philippa, was born when I was still twenty-one, and by the time I was twenty-five I had three daughters under the age of three. I absolutely love motherhood, nurturing and babies. This book was never supposed to be the first book I wrote; instead I was going to write a thriller that was part memoir and part fiction based around my childhood.

Then I had my fourth child, who is now nineteen, and I realised as he grew up what a massive shift had taken place in the twelve years since my last daughter was born. Political correctness had invaded every corner of parenting and childhood. Academic exams started almost as soon as the toddler stage was over. There was homework and no time for play, children were much more likely to have been in nurseries very early and not at home.

These are all sudden and rapid changes, and I have asked myself often how schools can have our children for such long periods and then let them emerge with no social skills not knowing the difference between an oak tree and a willow tree, or how to manage money, or how to change a car wheel, while the government changes targets and literacy levels compulsively.

All these are subjects for discussion, but, distilled down, are the questions that were most pertinent and which informed *The Man on the Middle Floor*, gleaned from the hundreds of children and young people I have had in my home and got to know. Why are they so much unhappier, and why is there such a huge increase in disconnection? This generation has the highest suicide rates, the highest depression rates, and the number of children on the autistic spectrum has increased dramatically.

Society, attachment, love and kindness are in my opinion what define us as human beings. Compassion and intelligence, using our judgement and being able to express opinions without being shouted down, are vital. *The Man on the Middle Floor* asks why we are so lost when we have so many tools for social interaction these days? Why the increase in solitude? Where are we going, and should we turn back before it's too late?

Book Club Questions

1. Do you think that the number of single-person households has increased the breakdown in relationships?
2. Do you think that Nick's actions are as a result of his Asperger's or brought about by society's inability to deal with people on the autistic spectrum adequately? Nature or nurture?
3. Do you think that political correctness in government or in the police is positive or negative?
4. Bearing in mind that even in the Natural Kingdom animals still have a need to bond with a primary carer, should we be thinking again about how we treat our children during infancy and childhood?
5. While writing *The Man on the Middle Floor* I was encouraged at several stages to remove characters that were controversial but exist within society. Do you enjoy reading controversial characters in books? Why?
6. Karen puts her work before her children in a very extreme way. Do you believe that there is always a choice for women ... it is possible to have it all?
7. Karen's daughter fulfils an adult role of carer at a very young age. Do you think there should be provisions to help children in this position, and, if so, what?
8. Do you think that the breakdown of face-to-face interactions such as going to church, going to the shops,

Women's Institutes, Working Men's Clubs and so on has contributed to the general feeling of solitude?

9. Do you think that the rapid increase in the rate of autism can be attributed to the following: the food chain, changes in society, social media and television, lack of face-to-face interaction. If none of these, then what do you think?

10. Do you think that we are moving towards a new kind of societal structure and should forget about old-fashioned ways of doing things and look forward?

About the Author

Elizabeth Moore lives in South London with her South African husband, son Tommy, two Labradors, and daughters who come and go when they are not singing, diving or travelling. Her friends call her Lizzy and she spends her time with her family, eating out with friends and writing about it, and plotting out novels. She loves politics, is fascinated by people's motivation in acts good and wicked, and is always about to turn into a domestic goddess who bakes and is mindful. She has two more novels and a Young Adult novella in the pipeline, and writes for a wide range of magazines and national newspapers. She loves hearing if you have enjoyed her writing... or not. Reach her at elizabethsmoore. com, and keep up with appearances and thoughts in her newsletter.